Firebird

Firebird

JANICE GRAHAM

LITTLE, BROWN AND COMPANY

A *Little, Brown* Book

First published in Great Britain in 1998
by Little, Brown and Company
Reprinted 1998

Published by arrangement with G P Putnam's Sons, a member
of Penguin Putnam Inc.

The moral right of the author has been asserted.

The author gratefully acknowledges permission to quote
8 lines from *When You Are Old* by WB Yeats, taken from
'The Collected Poems of WB Yeats'. Reprinted by permission of
A P Watt Ltd on behalf of Michael Yeats.

A CIP catalogue record for this book
is available from the British Library.

ISBN 0 316 64524 9 HB
ISBN 0 316 64751 9 CF

Printed and bound in Great Britain by
Clays Ltd, St Ives plc

Little, Brown and Company (UK)
Brettenham House
Lancaster Place
London WC2E 7EN

Acknowledgements

 Poet Jimmy Santiago Bacia has alluded to writing as 'a sparkling fountain of energy that fills your spirit'. Without the encouragement of the following persons, I might never have known that ecstatic state which is my only true home. To each of you, wherever you are, I owe a debt of profound gratitude, for helping me to find my way home:

David Karr, entrepreneur, enigmatic wonderman, father figure and friend, who first planted the seed in my mind all those years ago in Paris when he said to Cecilia, after reading my *lettre de démission*, 'You tell that girl she oughta be a writer.'

Jim Boyle, USC screenwriting instructor, who unwittingly started me on my way.

Mort Zarcoff, USC Film Department chair, who first 'named' me, as Doris Lessing calls it.

Herta Galton, painter, Anglo-Austrian exile in Los Angeles, my creative mentor; her mere presence sends the muses into ecstasies of dance and song.

Karen Custer Holthaus, old and true friend, enthusiast, my first reader.

ACKNOWLEDGEMENTS

I would also like to express my sincere appreciation to the following people who contributed, each in their own way, to the publication of this book:

Drew Bogner, friend, soccer dad, academic dean of Kansas Newman, closet editor and writer.

Jane Koger, Flint Hills cattle rancher, whose Prairie Women's Retreat opened their doors to me.

Julie Grau, my editor at Putnam, whose gracious beauty, brains, and style on the page as well as in person make business a true delight.

Leslie Gelbman, Berkeley publisher and editor-in-chief, who, through her many excellent suggestions and contributions, has nudged this winged creature from its nest.

Cathy Fox, Putnam's brilliant subsidiary rights director, who has spread the fire around the world.

Phyllis Grann, Penguin Putnam's CEO, a truly grand lady, whose enthusiasm gave *Firebird* its wings.

And lastly my literary agent, Bob Tabian, who gets it all, every bit of it. The man who made the difference. Bob, hardly a day goes by when I don't thank God for you.

FOR MY PARENTS.

Jack and Madeline

One

So far as we know, no modern poet has
written of the Flint Hills, which is surprising
since they are perfectly attuned to his lyre.
In their physical characteristics they reflect
want and despair. A line of low-flung hills
stretching from the Osage Nation on the
south to the Kaw River on the north, they
present a pinched and frowning face to those
who gaze on them. Their verbiage is scant.
Jagged rocks rise everywhere to their surface.
The Flint Hills never laugh. In the early
spring when the sparse grass first turns to
green upon them, they smile saltily and
sardonically. But, as spring turns to summer,
they grow sullen again and hopeless. Death is
no stranger to them.

— JAY E. HOUSE

PHILADELPHIA PUBLIC LEDGER (1931)

Ethan Brown was in love with the Flint Hills. His father had been a railroad man, not a rancher, but you would have thought he had been born into a dynasty of men connected to this land, the way he loved it. He loved it the way certain peoples love their homeland, with a spiritual dimension, like the Jews love Jerusalem, and the Irish their Emerald Isle. He had never loved a woman quite like this, but that was about to change.

He was, at this very moment, ruminating on the idea of marriage as he sat in the passenger seat of the sheriff's car, staring gloomily at the bloodied, mangled carcass of a calf lying in the headlights in the middle of the road. Ethan's long, muscular legs were thrust under the dashboard and his hat brushed the roof every time he turned his head, but Clay's car was a lot warmer than Ethan's truck, which took forever to heat up. Ethan poured a cup of coffee from a scratched metal Thermos his father had carried on the Santa Fe line on cold October nights like this, and passed it to the sheriff.

'Thanks.'

'You bet.'

They looked over the dashboard at the calf; there was nowhere else to look.

'I had to shoot her. She was still breathin',' said Clay apologetically.

'You did the right thing.'

2

'I don't like to put down other men's animals, but she was sufferin'.'

Ethan tried to shake his head, but his hat caught. 'Nobody's gonna blame you. Tom'll be grateful to you.'

'I sure appreciate your comin' out here in the middle of the night. I can't leave this mess out here. Just beggin' for another accident.'

'The guy wasn't hurt?'

'Naw. He was a little shook up, but he had a big four wheeler, comin' back from a huntin' trip. Just a little fender damage.'

She was a small calf, but it took the two men some mighty effort to heave her stiff carcass into the back of Ethan's truck. Then Clay picked up his markers and flares, and the two men headed home along the county road that wound through the prairie.

As Ethan drove along, his eyes fell on the bright pink hair clip on the dashboard. He had taken it out of Katie Anne's hair the night before, when she had climbed on top of him. He remembered the way her hair had looked when it fell around her face, the way it smelled, the way it curled softly over her naked shoulders. He began thinking about her again and forgot about the dead animal in the bed of the truck behind him.

As he turned off on the road toward the Mackey ranch, Ethan noticed the sky was beginning to lighten. He had hoped he would be able to go back to bed, to draw his long, tired body up next to Katie Anne's, but there wouldn't be time now. He might as well stir up some eggs and make another pot of coffee, because as soon as day broke he would have to be out on the range, looking for the downed fence. There was no way of telling where the calf had gotten loose; there were thousands of miles of fence. Thousands of miles.

Ethan Brown had met Katherine Anne Mackey when his father was dying of cancer, which was also the year he turned forty. Katie Anne was twenty-seven – old enough to keep him interested, and young enough to keep him entertained. She was the kind of girl Ethan had always avoided when he was younger; she was certainly nothing like Paula, his first wife. Katie Anne got rowdy, told dirty jokes, and wore sexy underwear. She lived in the guest house on her father's ranch, a beautiful limestone structure with wood-burning fireplaces built against the south slope of one of the highest hills in western Chase County. Tom Mackey, her father, was a fifth-generation rancher whose ancestors had been among the first to raise cattle in the Flint Hills. Tom owned about half the Flint Hills, give or take a few hundred thousand acres, and, rumor had it, about half the state of Oklahoma, and he knew everything there was to know about cattle ranching.

Ethan had found himself drawn to Katie Anne's place; it was like a smaller version of the home he had always dreamed of building in the hills, and he would tear over there in his truck from his law office, his heart full and aching, and then Katie Anne would entertain him with her quick wit and her stock of cold beer and her soft, sexy body, and he would leave in the morning, thinking how marvelous she was, with his heart still full and aching.

All that year, Ethan had felt a terrible cloud over his head, a psychic weight that at times seemed tangible; he even quit wearing the cross and Saint Christopher's medal his mother had given him when he went away to college his freshman year, as though shedding the gold around his neck might lessen his spiritual burden. If Ethan had dared to examine his conscience honestly, he might have eventually come to understand the nature of his malaise, but Katie Anne had come along, and the relief she brought enabled him to skim over the top of those painful months. Once every two weeks he would visit his father in Abilene; always, on the drive back home, he felt that troubling sensation grow like the cancer that was consuming his father. On several occasions he tried to speak about it to Katie Anne; he ventured very tentatively into these intimate waters with her, for she seemed to dislike all talk about things

5

sad and depressing. He yearned to confess his despair, to understand it and define it, and maybe ease a little the terrible anguish in his heart. But when he would broach the subject, when he would finally begin to say the things that meant something to him, Katie Anne would grow terribly distracted. In the middle of his sentence she would stand up and ask him if he wanted another beer. 'I'm still listening,' she would toss at him sweetly. Or she would decide to clear the table at that moment. Or set the alarm clock. Mostly, it was her eyes. Ethan was very good at reading eyes. He often wished he weren't. He noticed an immediate change in her eyes, the way they glazed over, pulled her just out of range of hearing as soon as he brought up the subject of his father.

Occasionally, when Ethan would come over straight from a visit to Abilene, she would politely ask about the old man, and Ethan would respond with a terse comment such as, 'Well, he's pretty grumpy,' or 'He's feeling a little better.' But she didn't want to hear any more than that, so after a while he quit trying to talk about it. Ethan didn't like Katie Anne very much when her eyes began to dance away from him, when she fidgeted and thought about other things and pretended to be listening, although her eyes didn't pretend very well. And Ethan wanted very much to like Katie Anne. There was so much about her he did like.

Katie Anne, like her father, was devoted to the

animals and the prairie lands that sustained them. Her knowledge of ranching almost equaled his. The Mackeys were an intelligent, educated family, and occasionally, on a quiet evening in her parents' company when the talk turned to more controversial issues such as public access to the Flint Hills or environmentalism, she would surprise Ethan with her perspicacity. These occasional glimpses of a critical edge to her mind, albeit all too infrequent, led him to believe there was another side to her nature that could, with time and the right influence, be brought out and nurtured. Right away Ethan recognized her remarkable gift for remaining touchingly feminine and yet very much at ease around the crude, coarse men who populated her world. She was the first ranch hand wearing pale pink nail polish he had ever watched castrate a young bull.

So that summer, while his father lay dying, Ethan and Katie Anne talked about ranching, about the cattle, about the land; they talked about country music, about the new truck Ethan was going to buy. They drank a lot of beer and barbecued a lot of steaks with their friends, and Ethan even got used to watching her dance with other guys at the South Forty, where they spent a lot of time on weekends. Ethan hated to dance, but Katie Anne danced with a sexual energy that he had never seen in a woman. She loved to be watched. And she was good. There wasn't a step she didn't know or a partner she couldn't keep up with. So Ethan would sit drink and with his buddies while Katie Anne danced, and the guys would talk about what a goddamn lucky son of a bitch he was.

Then his father died, and although Ethan was with him in those final hours, even though he'd held the old man's hand and cradled his mother's head against his strong chest while she grieved, there nevertheless lingered in Ethan's mind a sense of things unresolved, and Katie Anne, guilty by association, somehow figured into it all.

Three years had passed since then, and everyone just assumed they would be married. Several times Katie Anne had casually proposed dates to him, none of which Ethan had taken seriously. As of yet there was no formal engagement, but Ethan was making his plans. Assiduously, carefully, very cautiously, the way he proceeded in law, he was building the life he had always dreamed of. He had never moved from the rather inconvenient third-floor attic office in the old Salmon P. Chase House that he had leased upon his arrival in Cottonwood Falls, fresh on the heels of his divorce, but this was no indication of his success. His had grown to a shamefully lucrative practice. Chase Countians loved Ethan Brown, not only for his impressive academic credentials and his faultless knowledge of the law, but because he was a man of conscience. He was also a man's man, a strong man, with callused hands and strong legs that gripped the flanks of a horse with authority.

Now, at last, his dreams were coming true. From the earnings of his law practice he had purchased his land and was building his house. In a few years he would be able to buy a small herd. It was time to get married.

Two

Ethan pulled the string of barbed wire tight and looped it around the stake he had just pounded back into the ground. It was a windy day and the loose end of wire whipped wildly in his hand. It caught him across the cheek near his eye and he flinched. He caught the loose end with a gloved hand and finished nailing it down, then he removed his glove and wiped away the warm blood that trickled down his face.

As he untied his horse and swung up into the saddle he thought he caught a whiff of fire. He lifted his head into the wind and sniffed the air, his nostrils twitching like sensitive radar seeking out an intruder. But he couldn't find the smell again. It was gone as quickly as it had come. Perhaps he had only imagined it.

He dug his heels into the horse's ribs and

took off at a trot, following the fence as it curved over the hills. This was not the burning season, and yet the hills seemed to be aflame in their burnished October garb. The copper-colored grasses, short after a long summer's grazing, stood out sharply against the fiercely blue sky. They reminded Ethan of the short-cropped head of a red-haired boy on his first day back at school, all trim and clean and embarrassed.

From the other side of the fence, down the hill toward the highway, came a bleating sound. *Not another one,* he thought. It was past two in the afternoon, and he had a desk piled with work waiting for him in town, but he turned his horse around and rode her up to the top of the hill, where he could see down into the valley below.

He had forgotten all about Emma Fergusen's funeral until that moment when he looked down on the Old Cemetery, an outcropping of modest tombstones circumscribed by a rusty chain-link fence. It stood out in the middle of nowhere; the only access was a narrow blacktop county road. But this afternoon the side of the road was lined with trucks and cars, and the old graves were obscured by mourners of the newly dead. The service was over. As he watched, the cemetery emptied, and within a few minutes there were only the black limousine from the mortuary and a little girl holding the hand of a woman in black who stood looking down into the open grave. Ethan had meant to attend the funeral. He was handling Emma Fergusen's estate and her will was sitting on top of a pile of folders in his office. But the dead calf had seized his attention. The loss, about $500, was Tom Mackey's, but it was all the same to Ethan. Tom Mackey was like a father to him.

Ethan shifted his gaze from the mourners and scanned the narrow stretch of bottomland. He saw the heifer standing in a little tree-shaded gully just below the cemetery. To reach her he would have to jump the fence or ride two miles to the next gate. He guided the mare back down the hill and stopped to study the ground to determine the best place to jump. The fence wasn't high, but the ground was treacherous. Hidden underneath the smooth russet-colored bed of grass lay rock outcroppings and potholes: burrows, dens, things that could splinter a horse's leg like a matchstick, all of them obscured by the deceptive harmony of waving grasses. Ethan found a spot that looked safe, but he got down off his horse and walked the approach, just to make sure. He spread apart the barbed wire and slipped through to check out the other side. When he got back up on his horse he glanced down at the cemetery again. He had hoped the woman and child would be gone, but they were still standing by the grave. *That would be Emma's daughter,* he thought in passing. *And her granddaughter.* Ethan's heartbeat quickened but he didn't give himself time to fret. He settled his mind and whispered to his horse, then he kicked her flanks hard, and within a few seconds he felt her pull her forelegs underneath and with a mighty surge of strength from her powerful hind legs sail into the air.

The woman looked up just as the horse appeared in the sky, and she gasped. It seemed frozen there in space for the longest time, a black, deep-chested horse outlined against the blue sky, and then hooves hit the ground with a thud, and the horse and rider thundered down the slope of the hill.

'*Maman!*' cried the child in awe. '*Tu as vu ça?*'

The woman was still staring, speechless, when she heard her father call from the limousine.

'Annette!'

She turned round.

'You can come back another time,' her father called in a pinched voice.

Annette took one last look at her mother's grave and knew she would never come back. She held out her hand to her daughter and they walked together to the limousine.

Three

Often father Colt would say when we urged
him to leave Kansas with us, 'I had as lief
lay my bones in Kansas as in any other
place'; and so it has come to pass. But to
think of a death in Kansas, in that wild
though beautiful country – to be laid away
in a rough box, in a grave marked only while
the mound looks newly made, away from all
kindred and friends who would drop on it a
tear or plant on it a flower, seems to me
horrible in the extreme.

MIRIAM DAVIS COLT

*WENT TO KANSAS, BEING A THRILLING ACCOUNT
OF AN ILL-FATED EXPEDITION TO THAT
FAIRYLAND AND ITS SAD RESULTS (1862)*

Eliana Zeldin got up on her knees and turned to
look out the limousine's back window at the horse and

rider pursuing the fleeing calf. She had a zealot's love of horses, and she could ride well, but this was another world, a world she knew only from the pages of picture books and old television movies. When the rider tried to rope the calf and missed, and then threw again and missed again, she bounced with excitement and gripped her mother's shoulder.

'Maman! Il faut que tu regardes ça!'

'Sit back down and fasten your seat belt,' thundered her grandfather.

The little girl turned sad eyes to her mother, eyes suddenly extinguished of all joy, and with painful remembrance Annette recognized herself in those eyes. She had a sudden urge to cry out, 'Damn the seat belt!' but instead gently resettled the little girl and tightened the belt, pinning her to the dark, dreary boredom of the limousine's interior, cutting her off from the marvelous excitement outdoors.

Annette did not like being alone with her father. She feared him. She had never really wished to examine these fears; instead, all her life she had focused on fear itself. When she saw it on a face in a painting, she felt akin to it, and when she read it in the notes of a concerto, she played it with shivering intensity. Fear was not the only thing she played well. She played rapture and confusion, triumph and loss, shyness, sorrow and serenity all with equal beauty. The strings of her instrument examined these hidden depths for her and brought her some measure of peace. It was the peace she yearned for; fame and glamour had been her ambition.

Riding in the backseat of the limousine with her father, her daughter between them, Annette felt anxiety rising in her chest. She was acutely uncomfortable. She hadn't seen him in five years, not since her parents had moved away from Wichita, which had been her father's last parish, and retired to the town of Cottonwood Falls, where her mother had been born and raised. Her mother had always been there, protecting her from his rages and rigid severity, and now Annette instinctively drew her daughter away from the man, a gesture that immediately made her feel guilty because he look so profoundly sad and isolated on the other end of the wide backseat.

She need only endure it a few weeks, she thought, the time to help her father get through the first stages of his mourning, then they would be back on a plane to Paris, where Eliana could play in little square parks with tall old trees and dense flowering shrubs surrounded by high black wrought-iron fences that gave a strongly defined feeling of security, far away from this terrifying space, where there was nothing but prairie for ever and ever. She would never come back to Kansas again.

The thought brought a sudden wave of relief over her. Always drawn to this place, always obliged, indebted, because her family was here. Apart from her parents, she never wrote to any of them. When her first recordings had been released, she had received all kinds of congratulatory notes from cousins and the like. Later, when her life had been shattered, when her fame had receded and she had withdrawn from public view, no longer receiving the international accolades that had been flung at her during her performing years, her warm well-wishing cousins no longer clambered to see her and lunch with her when she was in town, and her family ties narrowed. Only her mother and father bound her to this Wonder bread land. And now her mother was dead. There was only her father. This was not how she had wanted it to be. She had always wanted him to go first, so she could have her mother back again.

The limousine followed a narrow blacktop that curved back through the Flint Hills, and Annette gazed at the smooth undulating lines. On the way to the cemetery they had driven by a few ranch houses built out of white limestone rock quarried near by; these alone had withstood the violent elements throughout the past century. Everywhere else were signs of men and women who had struggled and failed, who had gone on, or back, or just died. Abandoned houses with their plaster walls caved in, their wooden beams splintered and decayed. Abandoned machinery and cars. Abandoned graves.

They reached the crest of a high hill and met with a glorious panorama of the hills to the east. The swiftly scudding clouds cast moving shadows on the land below and a string of cattle snaked through the copper red valleys, guided by a handful of cowhands and herding dogs. Annette turned to her daughter.

'*Regarde*,' she whispered, tapping the window, and Eliana leaned over her mother's lap and peered out the window.

'I wish you'd teach that child some English,' grumbled the old man. 'It's just plain rude, always talking in French like that.'

'She does know a little English, Dad.'

'Then why doesn't she speak it?'

Annette stared silently out the window, her mind retreating deep into the quiet recesses of her mind, as it always did when her father spoke to her like this.

'I asked you a question, Annette,' he said with an irritated tone in his voice.

'I don't have an answer,' she replied, and squeezed Eliana's hand. They rode in silence the rest of the way until the limousine arrived in Cottonwood Falls and deposited Charlie Fergusen, his daughter, Annette Zeldin, and his granddaughter, Eliana, in front of the modest home of Nell Harshaw, who was hosting a reception for the family of her beloved friend, Emma Reilly Fergusen, deceased.

Four

The reception was a strain on Charlie Fergusen. He had never dealt particularly well with death, and the death of his wife was no exception. As a minister, the calls he was obliged to make to families of the deceased were always brief and terse, like Charlie, and buffered with scripture. Charlie would leave outdated little booklets about dealing with death, promise his prayers, then hurry away. As a child, Annette assumed this was just the way it was done. But when she grew older and moved out of the dark shadow of her father's influence into a world where men of God at times showed true compassion and mercy, she began to wonder why her father had ever chosen such a profession. If Charlie was appreciated as a man of the cloth, it was not for his sermons, which , like his house calls, were dry and short, or for his sense of humor (he was a sadly humorless man), or for his spiritual guidance (if he had spiritual depth, he hid it well), but for his ability to raise and invest money for his church. Charlie liked to think of himself as God's business manager. When it came to the material world, Charlie worked miracles. He turned water into wine and made loaves multiply. He was a dedicated fund-raiser, an ingenious entrepreneur, and a shrewd investor; he refurbished sanctuaries and expanded properties, and still the church coffers grew. The city leaders recognized this genius in him and so forgave him his inadequacies in the more traditional roles expected of him; they came to hear his dull sermons and prided themselves on how their church was financially sound.

But the people who surrounded him this afternoon were not his parishioners. The people of Cottonwood Falls had known and loved Emma Reilly as a girl, and had welcomed Emma Fergusen back to their fold when she returned at the age of sixty-five with her husband. But they knew of Charlie only what they had seen for the past five years, and so his genius escaped them, and Charlie Fergusen felt very, very alone.

Annette recognized this as she watched him try to mingle with the townsfolk. She alone knew how he struggled to hold together his shattered composure, how he fought back the tears that were so foreign to his eyes, how the muslces in his face were so contorted from the effort that he looked quite unlike himself. Even more disturbing to her was the way he looked when Nell Harshaw took Eliana in tow and walked her around the house, introducing her to everyone. They had never seen Emma Fergusen's one and only grandchild. Nell and the others fawned over her, and their eyes followed her around the room. Charlie was ignored, thrown over in his crotchety old age by a little French girl who spoke English with a British accent and who did not at all worship him the way he had always expected his grandchildren would. Indeed, the child virtually ignored him and always deferred to her mother. Charlie particularly disliked the twinkle in their eyes when they talked to each other. He suspected they were talking about him.

The entire town of Cottonwood Falls flowed through Nell Harshaw's modest home that afternoon, and long before they had all departed Eliana crawled up on her mother's lap and went to sleep. Annette carried her daughter home and laid her down on the spare bed in the back room of her father's house. The room was poorly heated, and Annette took off her long sable coat and covered the child. The little girl shivered and pulled the black fur up around her face.

'It smells like you,' she murmured.

'Go to sleep, precious,' Annette said, and kissed the child. Eliana opened her eyes.

'Everybody kept staring at it.'

'Did they?'

'I heard a man in the kitchen at Nell's. He was saying something mean about you, because of your coat. But then I walked in and he shut up.'

Annette smiled gently and smoothed back her daughter's hair. 'I suppose I shouldn't have worn it here.'

'Why?'

'It's a bit too fancy for this place, don't you think?'

'I'm glad you wore it. I love it.'

'So do I. It's very old, you know. And when I wear it I feel very safe and warm.'

'That's the way it makes me feel, too.' The little girl snuggled down under the coat. '*Tu es si belle, Maman*,' she sighed. She had dark circles under her eyes, and as Annette ran her finger across her soft, downy cheek, her eyelids closed, and within a few breaths she was asleep.

Annette took a shower and washed her hair, and she cried in the shower, where no one could hear her. When she came out, her father was sitting at the yellow Formica table in the kitchen, counting out his pills for the week into a long slotted plastic box. More than once he dropped a pill into the wrong slot, and then, with trembling fingers, he would clumsily try to retrieve it. She noticed how his hands had aged since she had last seen him. As she pulled up a chair to sit down with him, she accidentally jostled the table and two red pills rolled onto the floor. The lines around Charlie's mouth tightened.

'I'm sorry,' muttered Annette as she leaned down, but Charlie impatiently pushed her arm aside and picked up the pills, meticulously dusting off each one with a napkin.

'Floor's dirty,' he mumbled.

'Let me help you, Dad.'

'Are your hands clean?'

'Yes, Dad, my hands are clean.'

He told her how many to put in each compartment, how many blue ones and brown ones and red ones.

'Your mother always got the coffee ready before she went to bed. It's on a timer,' he said when they had finished.

Annette prepared the coffee and kissed him good night on his whiskered cheek.

She sat on the edge of her bed in her nightgown, listening to her father open and close the drawers in his room next door. Suddenly, she didn't want to be alone. She got up and went into the room where Eliana was sleeping. Upon their arrival, her father had shown them to the guest room where they were to sleep, but while Annette was unpacking, Eliana had found this room and had insisted on sleeping here. In a vaguely dismissive tone of voice, her father had referred to it as her mother's sewing room, although the sewing machine was closed and looked as though it had not been touched in a long time. Annette had been too preoccupied to give it much thought, but now, looking around the room, she understood what her daughter had sensed immediately. This was her mother's room, and she suspected her father never came in here. He must surely have disliked it. It spoke too eloquently of all the things he had tried to crush in her, things he had assumed were gone and dead, but that somehow, in later years, had reemerged with sudden vigor.

Annette looked around the room at the things that had belonged to her mother. The walls were covered with photographs of Annette and Eliana, framed press clippings from Annette's concerts, photographs of Annette shaking hands with the Queen of England and the Israeli prime minister. Even more noticeable were the photographs that were not there, the years and the faces that were absent from the walls, the things she had lost, the things they had all lost.

There was a sewing machine in the corner, and against the far wall stood her mother's piano, the keyboard open and music on the stand as though she might walk in and sit down to play at any moment. There were postcards Annette had sent from cities around the world, and her mother had framed them in inexpensive but elegant little gilded wooden frames. There was an old movie poster of Rita Hayworth in *Trouble in Trinidad* that Annette had found in London and sent to her, although at the time she wondered where her mother would be able to hang it without a prolonged battle with her father, and another she had found in Munich, an equally obscure film of Humphrey Bogart's entitled *Morocco.* Then there were photographs of her mother's true idols, the divas, Maria Callas and Joan Sutherland, and the younger Kiri Te Kanawa whose voice sounded so much like her mother's had once.

She stood shivering in the middle of the room, listening to the wind, and thought of her mother's sweetly scented body lying alone in the cold ground in those lonely hills. Suddenly she had a frightening thought, that spirits might have fetters just as bodies did. She kneeled at the side of her daughter's bed and hastily crossed herself, then, in a muffled voice, half-aloud, she offered up a single prayer: that her mother's spirit would not be bound to this land; that it would come away with her, away from this place, and be free. Then she crawled into bed next to the child. She groped for her daughter's hand and found it, soft and warm under the blankets, and held it in her own.

She lay quite still, listening to the wind. Annette had always hated the Kansas wind. When she was a child it had terrified her at night, screeching and moaning around the house like a devil from hell, a faceless, deadly black wind that came on dark wings to level the land, and yet the white people who settled here had never given it a name. The naming of winds had disappeared with the Indians. She remembered a story she had once read about an aboriginal people shooting at the wind with their guns, and beating at it with their brooms, and in the quiet of her mind she screamed at the wind and swung at it with her fists.

She tried to sleep, but every time she closed her eyes she saw her mother's grave. She wanted to see her alive, coming toward her with her arms open wide, the way she did in later years, when her father had finally lost control over her and she was free to turn her love elsewhere. Annette began to cry softly, and outdoors the wind rose to a piercing whistle. She rolled over and placed her hands over the child's ears so she would not be awakened, so that she too would not be summoned by the wailing land and called to die here.

After a while she thought she heard music. She listened carefully, trying to identify the tune, for it immediately struck her as something familiar, but it was masked by the wind that seemed annoyed at the appearance of a rival on this cold autumn night, for it became even more raucous and rattled the window. The music sounded faintly like a Schubert lied, one of her mother's favorites, but she could follow it only intermittently. She turned her head, thinking perhaps her father had turned on the radio in his room, but she could not locate the source.

The music intrigued her and for a moment her grief was forgotten. From time to time the wind would halt to catch its breath, and the music would fill the silence; it was the most piercingly beautiful sound she had ever heard, and as she descended into sleep she wondered what this was, and from where it came. As she drifted off she had the feeling that something within the room was protecting her and her child from the world beyond, and at last she fell into a deep, dreamless slumber.

Outside, the wind dropped, quite suddenly, as though throttled by an unseen hand grown weary of its irascible ways, and the night was filled with the music of the spheres.

Five

Jerry Meeker could pound in a fence stake with his bare hands and bring a wild horse to his knees with a single jerk on the lead, but he was having serious trouble getting a big leather club chair up the narrow stairs of the Salmon P. Chase house to Ethan's office. Ethan was at the top and Jer was holding up the bottom, straining so hard his face had gone red and his bright blue eyes were swimming in tears.

'Set the damn thing down,' gasped Ethan.

'Can't,' whispered Jer through clenched teeth.

'Just set it down.'

'Keep goin',' grunted Jer.

Ethan took another step, and then another, and finally his heel touched the flat landing at the top of the stairs.

'Okay, buddy, we're here.'

'Damn, this's heavy,' said Jer as he wrangled his end up to the landing and then collapsed into the chair. 'Nice, though.' He fingered the brass studs. The leather was very smooth. 'Why didn't Tom want it?'

'Didn't have room for it.' Ethan wiped his brow with his sleeve. 'Come on, let's get it in my office.'

'I ain't movin' yet, pal,' said Jer.

'You're gonna have to. I'm expectin' that French lady any minute now.'

'You mean Emma's daughter?'

'That's right.'

Jer rested his head on the chair back and his eyes fell on the plaque that hung next to Ethan's door. Nothing identified the place as a law office; there was only one word on the plaque - *Wordsworth* - and below that, a framed quotation by the poet that read:

Where are your books? - that light bequeathed
To Beings else forlorn and blind!
Up! Up! and drink the spirit breathed
From dead men to their kind.

Jer didn't read much, just an occasional magazine, and he had always found Ethan's office a little strange for an attorney. Inside the spacious attic office were walls of books, many of them having nothing to do with law. It was Ethan's sacred domain, and although Jer didn't understand it, he honored it, and held his tongue.

Jer looked down at his stomach. There was a dark blue patch in the middle of his shirt where the sweat had soaked through the denim.

'Well, I guess this won't make much of an impression on her, will it,' he said, slowly getting up. 'So I'll move. Just for her sake. Not yours.'

'So, I'm supposed to be makin' an impression on Madame, am I?'

'Why didn't you go to the funeral?'

'Actually, I did go. Sort of.'

'What d'ya mean?'

'I'll bore you with it some other time, pal. Come on, we gotta move this thing. You ready?'

'Yeah.' Jer squatted and positioned his hands underneath the chair. 'She's a mighty pretty lady. You'd probably like her.'

'I doubt it,' Ethan said as they lifted the chair together. 'She probably has one of those little yappy poodles with bows in his hair.'

The office door, which was never locked, swung open as Ethan backed into it. 'You doin' okay there, friend?' he asked.

'Yeah. Just take it easy,' answered Jer.

'Beats me how any relation of Emma Fergusen's can

have anything in common with a bunch of little Nazis with no balls,' said Ethan as they slowly inched the wide chair through the doorway. He rambled on, 'You remember the time they tried to put French crêpes on the menu down at Hannah's? It was on a Saturday night. Old Burt walked in, all spruced up in his good overalls, all clean and pressed, and then he sat down and picked up the menu. He took one look at the Saturday Nite Special and said, "That goddamn cook's full of crap." And then he slapped down the menu and walked out. Burt's never been back to Hannah's since.'

It was perhaps the physical exertion, or just Ethan's remembrance of the look on old Burt's face, but mirth got the better of him, and his voice rose in a high-pitched, boisterous laugh that came straight from the heart. He laughed so hard his breath came in little snorts and tears swam down his face. It was not a mean laugh, for there was not a mean bone in Ethan Brown's body, but he was a Kansan and his prejudices were deeply rooted in a proud conservatism and a cowardly lack of imagination.

'Better put this down before I drop it,' said Ethan, his shoulders heaving in the throes of laughter. He swept his hat from his head and wiped the tears from his cheeks. When he looked up he saw Jer had turned livid. He was gaping at something over Ethan's shoulder. Ethan spun around.

In the middle of his office stood Annette Zeldin. Her

soft brown eyes mirrored utter disbelief. She was holding one of his books which she had taken from the shelf.

'Excuse me,' she said quietly. 'I'm looking for Mr Brown. The attorney.'

'I'm Ethan Brown.'

The look in her eyes froze into a hardened stare. 'I'm Annette Zeldin. Emma Fergusen's daughter. We had an appointment this morning.'

'Yes, yes, come in,' boomed Ethan. With a frantic gesture he smoothed back his hair and put his hat back on. Then he remembered his manners and took it off again.

'I'll see ya around, Ethan. Good day, ma'am,' said Jer and disappeared out the door. When Ethan looked around he was already gone.

'Yeah, thanks, Jer,' called Ethan after him. He turned back to Annette Zeldin and stepped forward, extending his broad hand to her, mustering an amiable smile. 'Ethan Brown, attorney at law.' It was the greeting he always used with folks out here and they loved it. It was the greeting of a man strong and sure of himself. But Annette Zeldin ignored his outstretched hand, and Ethan felt embarrassingly fake.

'Please, have a seat.' He gestured to a chair in front of his desk. 'Sorry to keep you waiting. I didn't see a car outside.'

'I walked.' She was still clutching the book. She had

evidently taken it from his shelf, and Ethan recognized it immediately: *The Collected Poems of W. B. Yeats.* He started to comment on the book, but she spoke first. 'You should put a sign up, Mr Brown. Or do you only practice law as a hobby?'

Ethan's smile faded, and the gentle spirit that usually animated his eyes retreated under his dark eyebrows.

'I apologize for that, ma'am. Should have told you. Everyone around here knows me by Wordsworth. Please, sit down.' Again he gestured to the chair and Annette sat down.

Ethan sifted through the jumble of files on his desk.

'I'm very sorry about your mama. She was a lovely lady.'

Annette was unmoved. 'My mother left me some land. I'd like to sell it,' she replied coolly.

Ethan studied her for a moment.

'You might want to reconsider. It's a real choice piece of property. Matter of fact, I just bought the property adjacent to it on the south. The old Norton ranch. Some of the best grazing land in the hills. Nice place to raise a kid, too. And believe me, this kind of land just doesn't come up for sale –'

'Mr Brown,' she cut in, 'I have a home. In Paris.'

Annette spoke deliberately and gently, as though explaining this to a child, and it swept over her how she had tried so hard to explain this to her father for years, using these same words, this same tone of voice. 'I've lived there for seventeen years now. I have no desire to move here.' She wanted to go on. She wanted to tell him that if she had a choice between hell and here she would choose hell. But she only looked him firmly in the eye and held her tongue.

The absolute opposition of their lives was clear to both of them at that instant. It ballooned upon them both like an epiphany, and had the remarkable effect of making them instantly aware, however painful and unwelcome it might be, that they were staring at another human whose very identity was built upon a construct that was hostile to their own self.

In short, Annette believed herself to be a superior being of a superior culture. Ethan, to whom the sight of manure was a daily thing, thought she was full of shit.

'Have you ever seen this land?' he asked.

'No.'

'It's beautiful.'

She started to speak, halted, then, pronouncing the words carefully, 'In these matters, beauty is very much in the eye of the beholder, is it not?'

Ethan smiled, a kind of respectful acknowledgment of the subtle antagonism that sat rigid between them.

'I'll be glad to take care of it for you,' he said quietly.

'Thank you,' she replied.

Ethan quickly scanned through Emma Fergusen's will.

'We'll need to get your father's written consent before you sell.'

'Why? My mother left it to me.'

'Under Kansas law the surviving spouse has a claim to half the property. But don't you worry about it. I don't anticipate any problems. Your mother went over all this with him.'

Ethan closed the file and tapped it on his knee. 'I'll get the consent forms drawn up and send them over to your house tomorrow morning. And we won't have any trouble finding a buyer for your land, I promise you.'

Annette stood and Ethan rose quickly to his feet. For a brief moment they stood only a few inches apart, Ethan towering over her, and she noticed the clean smell of his starched shirt and judged him married, although he wore no wedding ring.

She started for the door, then noticed she still had the book of poetry in her hand. She looked back, glancing at the shelves of books. 'At first I thought I'd walked into the city library,' she said.

'It is,' nodded Ethan. 'Best darn library in the county,' he replied proudly.

'Does anyone around here ever read Yeats?' she asked as she set the book of poetry on the table.

She said it pleasantly enough, but Ethan wondered if she had misunderstood him on purpose. 'Oh, a few of us starved souls do,' he answered. Then, finally, his ego got the better of him. From memory, in a gentle and expressive voice, he recited:

> 'When you are old and grey and full of sleep,
> And nodding by the fire, take down this book,
> And slowly read, and dream of the soft look
> Your eyes had once, and of their shadows deep;
>
> 'How many loved your moments of glad grace,
> And loved your beauty with love false or true,
> But one man loved the pilgrim soul in you,
> And loved the sorrows of your changing face ...'

He picked up the book and held it out to her. 'You keep hold of that 'til you go,' he said. 'I don't charge for the poetry, just the prose.'

When she said good-bye, her eyes left him thinking he had, for a brief moment, impressed her.

After she left, Ethan dictated some notes to his secretary, Bonnie, then quickly closed up his office and headed for the Mackey place. Annette Zeldin had made him feel extremely uncomfortable. He felt if he could just get out to the stable and saddle up his horse, he just might well shake it off before it really got under his skin.

* * *

That evening at the South Forty, Ethan sat alone in the booth, watching Katie Anne dance. He had avoided his buddies at the bar and chose to sit quietly with his beer and reflect upon the events of the last few days. The idea of getting his hands on Emma Fergusen's property was a dream come true. Indeed, *all* his dreams were coming true. He should feel as though all was right with the world. Happy. Contented. He felt none of these things. What really annoyed him was that Mrs Zeldin kept intruding upon his thoughts. He was relieved when Jer slid into the booth next to him.

'So, what'd you think of her?' asked Jer.

'Who?'

'Mrs Zeldin.'

'It was like sittin' on barbed wire.'

'Serves you right.'

'One stuffy broad.'

'I didn't think so. I talked to her at the reception at Nell's house. I liked her,' said Jer quietly.

'You can't be real.'

'What d'ya have against her?'

'Vichy and De Gaulle, for starters.'

'She just lives there.'

'Yeah, by choice. That's my very point. I mean if you're born there, okay, I can make some allowances. But to make it your home?'

'Why're you gettin' all worked up about this?'

'I'm not all worked up.'

Jer shrugged. 'Okay. So you're not all worked up.'

Ethan took a long draw on his beer. 'I was thinkin' about asking Katie Anne to marry me.'

Jer burst out in a broad and long laugh. 'I knew there was somethin' naggin' at you.'

Ethan looked up to see Katie Anne approaching him, her soft brown hair curling in damp ringlets around her face the way it always did after she had worked up a sweat on the dance floor. She was always very appetizing then, her face flushed, her own scent mingling with the light floral perfume she wore.

Jer saw her coming. 'I'm outta here,' he whispered, and slipped away.

Katie Anne slid in next to Ethan on the booth and ran her hand up the inside of his leg, and Ethan forgot all about Mrs Zeldin.

'Hi, handsome.' She grinned. 'Will you go get me a beer?'

'I can't,' he answered gruffly. 'Not unless you want me to embarrass myself.'

She took a sip of Ethan's beer with her free hand. 'I'll just drink yours,' she said, her eyes dancing.

'How about April?' he asked.

'April who?'

'For our wedding.'

Katie Anne grew still, but Ethan didn't notice; he was

trying to catch the attention of their waitress.

'If we have the light winter we're expecting, the house should be finished by then,' he continued.

She removed her hand from his leg.

'What's wrong?' he asked.

She shook her head and began to play with one of the damp tendrils of hair at the back of her neck. 'Are you really serious about it this time?'

'What do you mean?'

Katie Anne hesitated before replying. 'Well, you keep finding reasons to put it off.'

'No, I don't.'

There was an edge of exasperation in her voice. 'Ethan, this is precisely the third time this year we've talked about setting a date.'

'We just discussed it. But we never set a date and we haven't put it off.'

She heaved a sigh of frustration and turned away from him. 'Oh, whatever,' she mumbled.

Ethan hated that expression. It made her sound juvenile and not very intelligent.

'I just want us to have a house of our own.'

'We've been living together for over a year. Why do we need to wait until your house is built before we can get married?' she asked.

'I want things to be right.'

'Things can never be right enough for you, Ethan,' she

answered. She turned her back to him and watched the dancers.

Ethan was silent for a long time.

'I sure didn't think this would turn so unpleasant,' he replied after a while.

'Is it unpleasant?' she said, her back still to him. Her voice sounded odd and he wondered if she was crying.

'It is for me.'

The waitress brought their beers. Ethan took a long swig of his. Katie Anne's sat untouched. Finally, he put his arm around her and pulled her close to him. She laid her head on his shoulder and whispered, 'April's fine.'

As soon as she said it, Ethan felt a faint nausea sweep through him, but he attributed it to the unusually heavy cigarette smoke in the club that evening.

Six

∾ Mealtime had never been an enjoyable part of the day in the Fergusen household, and the misery of those childhood moments crept over Annette as she picked away at her dinner. Charlie lifted his eyes from his plate and cast a severe glance at Eliana. Annette unconsciously stiffened. *What is she doing wrong,* Annette wondered. *What could she possibly be doing to annoy him?* After all these years it seemed as if nothing had changed. All he had to do was turn his gaze on you and you squirmed, she thought. He was doing it now to Eliana. But Eliana had no fear of the man. Though she hardly knew him, the little six-year-old was an excellent judge of personality. She quickly sensed her grandfather's pall of disapproval and she disliked him for it, but she did not fear him.

'Annette, tell Eliana to put the salt back in

the center of the table, where everyone can reach it.'

Ah, that's it, thought Annette as she took the salt and set it in front of her father's plate. Charlie, silently vindicated, went back to his dinner.

Eliana carefully wiped her mouth and looked up at her mother. '*Est-ce que je peux aller jouer au dehors maintenant?*' she asked.

'Yes. But first take your plate to the sink.'

Once Eliana was outside, playing with the neighbor's dog through the chain-link fence, Annette relaxed. She was constantly trying to protect her daughter from her father's wrath, the wrath she had known all too well as a child. She was not expecting Charlie's next words.

'I don't want you to sell that land.'

Annette spun around from the window to face him. 'Why not?'

'I'll agree to sell it only if the money's put into a trust account for Eliana. Something she could use for her college education.'

'Universities are free in France.'

'Maybe she won't want to go to college in France.'

'Dad, I need that money. The cost of living is very high in Paris and it just keeps getting higher.'

'Then why don't you move back here?'

'Because this isn't my home.'

Charlie got up from the table and rinsed his dishes, then carefully stacked them in the dishwasher. 'You can move back here and live in the place, but if you sell it, you put the money into a trust. It's your choice.'

'Dad, I'm not moving back here.'

'Then I'll tell the attorney to set up the trust,' he said as he dried his hands on the dish towel and went into the living room. He sank into his recliner and clicked on the television. She rose, went to the sink, and emptied her uneaten dinner into the garbage disposal.

Seven

Annette sat in Ethan Brown's office with her hands quietly folded in her lap, listening to him apologize. If she had ranted and raved, Ethan would have been able to retrieve some of his self-respect. But her haughty silence only provoked him to more effusive and transparent verbosity. Finally, disgusted with himself, he fell silent.

When at last she spoke, her voice was cool and controlled. 'Mr Brown, I'm very disappointed in the way this has been handled. I was told you were one of the best civil-law attorneys in the state.'

'I don't know about that, ma'am. But I know I care a lot about the folks around here.'

'I'm sure of that.' Her voice softened suddenly, and the change arrested his attention.

'You don't like me, do you?' she said. It took

Ethan a moment to recover, and she went on. 'But no matter. The point is, if you cared about my mother's final wishes you would have handled this differently. My mother had nothing to leave me except this land. She was not rich . . .' Her voice caught in her throat. She stopped to regain her composure. 'She left me great wealth, of course, but not in material things, I mean.'

Ethan nodded.

'My father has said he will allow me to keep the proceeds from the sale of the land only after his death, and only on condition that I live here until he dies.' She looked away and was quiet for a moment. 'My mother never intended for me to come back and be tied down to this place.'

'Mrs Zeldin, I want you to know I did try to persuade her to get his written consent when the will was drawn up. But she didn't want to do it. She assured me there wouldn't be a problem.' He paused. 'She was afraid it would hurt him.'

She stared blankly at Ethan for a moment, then looked down at her hands. 'Yes,' she said quietly. 'Yes, I see.'

Ethan felt very uncomfortable with Mrs Zeldin riding in his truck. He thought it was because she was wearing that damn fur coat and the same black dress she wore every time he saw her.

'Don't you have any jeans, ma'am?' he asked as he swerved around a pot hole and Eliana, sitting between them, clutched the dashboard and grinned.

'No.'

'Don't women wear jeans in France?'

'The young ones do.'

He wondered if she was inviting a compliment, but the serious, far-off look in her face told him her mind was far removed from such trivial games. For the first time he was aware of her beauty, the way she held her hands and her shoulders, the way her breasts moved when she sighed, the way she always sat with her legs gracefully intertwined at the ankles the way little girls had been taught to sit in etiquette classes when he was a kid. Her dark hair was very short and very feminine, and her face bore only the faintest touch of makeup. He knew how old she was, he had all the relevant statistics in her file, but only her hands betrayed her forty years. And her eyes.

Eliana twisted around to check on Traveler, Ethan's border collie that rode in the back of the truck, then she said something to her mother in French. Her mother shook her head. Eliana looked wistfully out the back again. Ethan caught Annette's eye.

'She can ride in the back if that's what she wants. Perfectly okay.'

'I'd rather she didn't.'

'I'd slow down.'

Annette was caught off guard by his concern. He had read her mind.

'Maybe on the way back.'

Eliana understood, and she smiled at them both and bubbled over with enthusiastic French. Ethan understood not a word, but he was surprised at how it sounded. The only French he had ever heard was the guttural and sputtering sounds spoken occasionally by his old high school German teacher.

'Eliana, you have a dog at home?' Ethan asked.

Eliana shook her head and replied that their dog had died when she was little and her mother didn't want to get another one. Ethan was surprised to hear her speak with a British accent.

'Maman doesn't like little yappy dogs,' Eliana said. 'And she says we won't get a big dog until we can get a place in the country.'

Ethan shot a quick look at Annette. She was looking out the window, trying to suppress a smile.

They reached the top of a hill, and Annette leaned forward. She had never imagined country this lovely in Kansas. She had been raised in the west, the flattest part of the state, but this land was nothing like what she had known as a girl. The low-flung Flint Hills were grasslands stretching as far as the eye could see. There was not even a telephone cable in sight. The nearer hills were a lush emerald green, and the farther ones were muted, softer, fading into a purple-blue haze that shrouded the most distant hills. A few cottonwoods and oaks struck bright dots of orange and gold.

Ethan turned off the dirt road onto a gravel entrance, but the gravel quickly disappeared. After a few hundred feet there was nothing left except tire tracks overgrown with grass. The truck climbed a steep hill, and as they pulled to a stop underneath a cluster of cottonwoods Annette saw the old farmhouse. Although battered by the elements and overgrown with tall grasses, it was clearly once a noble house.

'I didn't know the house was still here,' whispered Annette. Eliana threw an uneasy glance at her mother and quietly reached out and took her hand. It was a gesture Ethan would remember.

'All that land out there, to the west. That's yours,' said Ethan.

Eliana nudged her mother out of the truck. '*Allez, Maman. Sors.*'

Ethan whistled to Traveler, and the dog sailed from the back of the truck and raced with Eliana down the gently sloping hillside.

'You've got over one thousand acres of this,' said Ethan.

Annette was quiet for a long time as she gazed at the

hills. Ethan had never known a woman who was comfortable with stillness. Katie Anne always seemed to be filling it up with words or gestures.

After a while Annette turned and walked toward the house. Ethan unlocked the front door and she stepped inside. As her eyes passed over the rotted window frames and the uneven wood floor thick with years of dust, her mind saw another house, the one in the little village near Aix-en-Provence. It was only a three-acre plot, but the land was overrun by centuries-old olive trees. She and David were going to buy it; she had convinced him it would be a balm to their tortured souls. It was at a time in their lives when they were in desperate need of a refuge, a place with no memories, where they would not be haunted by murmurs and cries. But other things had happened, and the property was sold to someone else. In her mind, she had seen her mother's land as a means to rebuild that dream; she had planned to sell this property and find something like that again, in Provence, where she and Eliana could go for the summers. It would have thick rock walls, cool even in the summer heat, and high ceilings buttressed with dark, smoky beams. The smooth red brick floors would be worn by centuries of foot traffic. The grounds behind the house would be full of creeping thyme and olive and lemon trees, and they would eat there on summer evenings, on a patio flagged by brilliant red geraniums, at a long table where friends would sit elbow to elbow, their bare brown arms still radiating the heat of sharp Provençal light, their faces wrinkled from laughter and too much sun, their voices giddy with well-being, their eyes sultry with contentment, their lips flushed with wine and a longing to make love.

The screen door banged in the wind and Annette looked around to find Ethan Brown's eyes on her.

'It's still livable,' he said. 'And there's plenty of room for a big dog.'

Annette laughed. She could see why he was so well liked. His thoughtfulness was sincere, and he was earnest in his desire to please. She had a sudden urge to explain her dream to him, and why it was vital to her sanity. But she checked herself. His vision was so different from her own.

She mustered a pleasant smile and turned to him. 'Where's your land, Mr Brown? Show it to me.'

Ethan took her outside and pointed to the south.

'See that tallest hill over there? That's Jacob's Mound. That's the boundary. This time next year I hope to have a little herd of my own grazin' out there.' He turned back to the north. 'Up there, all that land to the north, that belongs to the Mackeys. Tom Mackey.'

'They own a lot of land around here, don't they?'

'That they do.'

'Aren't you engaged to his daughter?'

'Now, how'd you hear that?'

'Nell Harshaw.'

Ethan laughed pleasantly. 'Doesn't take long for word to get around.'

'Your life isn't your own in a place like this.'

'I don't have anything to hide.'

'I'm sure you don't.'

They stood in the blustery wind, succumbing to the silence between them. Tall billowing thunderheads darkened the northern edge of the horizon, and the temperature was falling steadily.

'Rain's movin' this way. Where's your little girl?' asked Ethan.

Annette pointed to a gully below, where Eliana and Traveler were ambling along the dry creek bed. Ethan whistled and Traveler came trotting with Eliana close behind.

'I tell you what, Mr Brown. It looks like I'm just a thorn in your side. Why don't you buy me up and then you can be one big happy family?'

Ethan was silent, watching the girl and dog reluctantly make their way up the side of the hill.

'Don't you want this land?' she asked when he failed to reply.

'Of course I do. If that's your decision. To sell.'

'That's my decision. The money will go to my daughter.'

'I guess I just hate to see anybody give up something like this if they have a chance to keep it.'

'That's exactly the way I feel about my home in Paris. About my life there.'

Ethan looked at her face, the silhouette earnest and attentive as she watched her daughter approach. She felt his gaze and turned to meet it.

'Forgive me, ma'am. I guess I forget that anybody can love anyplace else as much as I love this.'

'They can. They do.'

The wind blew at them, disrupting that subtle and wordless thing that made Annette's heart quicken and Ethan shuffle his feet and caused them both to look away, fixing their attention on the approaching rain clouds.

That night Annette dreamed of the house. But it was not her house in Provence; it was the one in the Flint Hills, all dust and decay. Her mother was there, mingling with all the guests from her funeral, and she looked so lovely and everyone was so happy to see her. She was welcoming them to this old house, built by her grandfather, inhabited by three generations of Reillys. All of them were to take a look around, stay as long as they liked. There were plenty of bedrooms, they could spend the night if they wished. So enraptured was she to see her mother again, risen from the grave, that Annette gave no more thought to the subject of houses.

Eight

It was Ethan who made the arrangements for Eliana to ride later that week. Jer had only one horse that was trained for dressage, but he was a beauty. A big Arabian named Mike. Jer knew next to nothing about what the horse could do, and when he saw Eliana working him, his respect for the horse, and the child, mushroomed into instant awe. He was already a little awestruck around Annette, which may have had something to do with the fact that he occasionally listened to classical music and had seen her picture on the cover of a CD when he was looking for a Mozart violin concerto at a music store up in Kansas City. Only there, in a labyrinthine suburban mall, protected by an army of anonymous faces, did he allow himself these guilty pleasures. He had never made it known to his friends in Cottonwood Falls that he had such taste in music, not wishing to expose himself to Ethan's – or anyone else's – ridicule and scorn.

'I got that horse for next to nothin',' said Jer as he leaned against the corral next to Annette.

'Is she okay out there?' asked Annette. 'I thought maybe you might keep the lunge line on him until she got used to him.'

'Ma'am, Mike's in love with that little girl. I can tell you that right now. I ain't never seen him so damn mellow, excuse my French.' It came out without thinking, and he was genuinely embarrassed. Annette smiled and let it pass.

'He does seem responsive,' she said.

'He was trained to do all that dressage stuff, but he got passed along to me and I've just used him as a stud. To be quite honest with you, I've never seen him do this. He's eatin' it up. He loves it.'

'I suppose it seems silly to you, doesn't it? Out here horses have a practical function.'

'Well, yes, they do. But to get these animals to obey you, whatever you ask 'em to do, sure ain't silly.'

'I doubt if Mr Brown would agree with you on that.'

'Ethan and I don't always see eye to eye.'

'I find that reassuring,' she said with a smile.

* * *

The week went by, and Charlie Fergusen would not be swayed, so Annette instructed Ethan to proceed with the sale of the property. To make matters worse, Charlie, who had little confidence in women when it came to managing financial and business matters, named Ethan as co-trustee of the estate with Annette after his death. Wishing to leave as quickly as possible, Annette left the entire matter to Ethan to handle in her absence. He would purchase the land himself and promised her a very advantageous deal. To soothe his own conscience, he offered to handle the sale and set up the trust with no charge to her or the estate. Annette gladly agreed; she may have found him stubborn, bigoted, and lacking in imagination but she never questioned his integrity.

The night before they were to leave, Nell Harshaw invited them all to dinner. Knowing how miserable meals with her father could be and needing a break from his humorless oppression, Annette begged off and stayed at home with Eliana to pack. As soon as Charlie's car pulled out of the driveway, Eliana, who had been watching through the curtains, streaked through the house to the back room where her mother was packing.

'Maman, il es parti!'

Annette threw back her head and swelled with relief. 'Put on some music, precious.'

◯ They ate dinner that evening in the sewing room. They spread a tablecloth on the floor and made a picnic with fried eggs and bacon and biscuits that Annette had whipped up from some Bisquick in the cupboard. They drank 7-Up out of crystal glasses Annette had sent her parents for their fortieth wedding anniversary and pretended it was champagne. They set a place and filled a third glass for Emma, and Annette sneaked sips from it, pretending it was her mother's spirit who was dining with them. They played all her mother's old LPs, all the great divas, recordings of Joan Sutherland and Maria Callas, and they played games. In short, they had their own little wake.

After dinner they worked on the puppet figures Eliana was making from cutouts in a coloring book, and so intent were they on their play and their singing (Annette was listening to Violette's heart-wrenching plea in *La Traviata* for the third time, much to Eliana's annoyance), they didn't hear Charlie come back until the door opened.

'I'm going to bed now. Keep it down, will you?' he said. His voice was tight.

'I'm sorry, Dad. I didn't know you were home.'
Annette quickly rose and turned off the record player.
'How was your dinner?'

'Okay. Nell isn't the best cook in the world.'

'I know, but she's a good friend.'

He started to shut the door.

'Dad?'

'Yes?'

'I'd like to take some of these recordings with me.
Would you mind?'

'Don't ask me to make those kind of decisions now.
That's not being fair.'

'But you never listen to this music.'

Charlie's bloodshot eyes bulged with a tired rage.
'They're still her things, and she left all her worldly
possessions to me. After I'm dead you can do as you damn
well please with them.'

He turned and slammed the door.

They sat still for a moment, hearing nothing but the
pinched timbre of his voice echoing in the air. Then,
their gaiety wilted, they wordlessly picked up their
clutter and got ready for bed.

Annette sat on the edge of the daybed and leaned
down to kiss her daughter good night.

'Maman, I'm going to miss Mike.'

'Mike?'

'Mike! Big Mike!'

Big Mike, the horse. Of course. Annette smoothed back her child's soft hair.

'What about the horses you ride back home?'

'Oh, Maman, they're nothing like Big Mike. I've never ridden a horse like him before. He's fantastic! He does everything I ask him to do and if I make a mistake he doesn't get upset with me. He's so much fun to ride . . .'

'Honey, you can tell me all about Big Mike in the morning. It's time to go to sleep now.'

'Okay.'

Annette kissed her again and stood. Her eyes took in the room as they had the first night. 'So you don't think it would be so awful to live here?' she asked her daughter.

'Not if we didn't have to live with Grandpa.'

'Your grandfather wouldn't want us here. We'd have to live in your grandma's old house.'

'Oh! Could we? I'd love that! Then we could have a dog, or two dogs, and I could ride Big Mike every day. Maybe Jer would let . . .'

'Honey, we're not going to live here. It's out of the question. I'm sorry. I don't know why I even brought it up.'

'I think it'd be fun.'

'Wouldn't you miss your friends?'

After a pause she answered, 'My real friends are you and the horses.' She thought again for a moment.

'Besides, my friends in Paris could come here to visit in the summer. They'd love it. They think cowboys are neat.'

'That's because they only see them in the movies.'

Nine

The storm that had announced itself earlier as Annette Zeldin stood beside Ethan Brown on the hilltop was quite different from the gentle rains that wash down the gray stone facades of Paris each winter. Fury after fury was unleashed upon the plains when the storm arrived that evening. The rain, carried by fierce winds, slashed at the flesh like cold knives; it whipped under umbrellas (which were of no goodly use; most Chase Countians never carried them) and climbed inside windbreakers and jackets, circulating with such ingenious mobility that one might think the powers of gravity momentarily suspended. Just after nightfall the temperature dropped below freezing, and on came a sudden rush of hail, pummeling the earth with dull thuds, clattering against glass and metal with a ferocity that sent all living creatures flinching and cowering into shelter. After the hail the wind returned, and lightning and thunder rocked the hills late into the night.

Annette crawled into bed with Eliana, but the child slept through it all. As Annette lay there listening to the storm, her eyes remained fixed on the piano, and sometime, very late, well after midnight, she heard once again that achingly beautiful music she had heard her first night here. This time the strange harmonies elicited no surprise and little curiosity, for deep in her subconscious where intimations of immortality reside, that place from which she drew those nameless forces that lent genius to her work, she knew what she was hearing. Nearing the mysterious oblivion of sleep, her powers of critical thought at a low ebb, angels ushered the music into her soul. As she slept, it brought her the message it had been sent to bear.

Annette awoke full of enthusiasm. In less than twenty-four hours she would be stepping off the plane in Paris, and already she longed for the gentle, dreary gloom of its gray skies. The winters she had often bemoaned, with relentless clouds hanging low, penetrated only by a soft chilled light from dawn to dusk, now appealed to her with all the charm of a flawed but great lover.

She found her father in the dimly lit kitchen preparing his breakfast. He had slept poorly because of the storm, and was ill humored and not to be tampered with this morning. Annette bathed and dressed, then awoke Eliana and herded her through her morning routine. Charlie sat in his lounge chair reading his newspaper until Annette tactfully reminded him that they needed to leave shortly. As Charlie folded up his papers and neatly rearranged them in a pile next to his chair, Annette noticed how slight his shoulders seemed. He had always been sensitive about his shoulders. She touched him gently on the arm.

'Dad?' she asked softly.

He looked up. His eyes were rimmed in red.

'I won't be long,' he said. He patted her hand, then shuffled off to his room.

Despite all her efforts they were late getting out of the house. Eliana went out back to say good-bye to the neighbor's dog and got her shoes caked in mud. The shoes had to be removed and washed, and Annette had to bring the suitcase back inside and dig through it for clean tights for the girl. Meanwhile, Charlie had to take an important long-distance call from a member of the board of the Kansas Conference of Methodist Churches. All this made Annette so nervous she went outside and smoked a cigarette. As she leaned against the hood of Charlie's old Buick, shivering in the cold, she looked around. Now that she was leaving she could see the place with a more benevolent eye. It was a very picturesque town. Much prettier than the towns she had grown up in.

There was a slight air of distinction about the place, owing in part to the fact that it had been the county seat back when that meant something to the growing population of immigrants. An imposing slate-roofed Victorian courthouse made from huge limestone blocks towered over the little town. It looked over Main Street, which consisted of two blocks of the functional and the whimsical, notably a hardware store, a coffee shop, a single-pump corner gas station, a small independent grocery store (Cottonwood Falls boasted no fast-food restaurants or chain franchises), an ice cream parlor with a gazebo in its courtyard (they had just installed an espresso maker that summer), an art gallery owned by a local landscape artist (her daughter owned the ice cream parlor), and a 1930s movie house that opened only during the summer and school holidays. The street dead-ended at a park looking out over the Cottonwood River and the falls from which the town took its name. Behind the courthouse spread the residential properties. Though none of the houses was grandiose, many were authentic turn-of-the-century Victorian and maintained proudly by their families. The people who lived in Cottonwood Falls manifested a particular fondness for the town; unlike Strong City just opposite them on the river, which had stolen the county seat when it won the battle for the railway line, the town was not loaded with conveniences. What it did have, although the Chase Countians never called it that because it sounded much too pretentious, was charm.

Annette saw its charm, however, the word not being anathema to her, and as she carefully doused her cigarette in a puddle of water and tossed it into the trash, she thought perhaps she might return for a visit again one day. Finally, Charlie emerged from the house, effusive with apologies, and as Annette went off to look for Eliana once again, he rearranged the suitcases in the trunk to his liking and started up the car.

They were all the way past Strong City when Annette remembered the book.

'Dad, stop. I've got to go back.'

'Back? What for?'

'That book.'

'What book?'

'That book the attorney lent me.'

'Ethan?'

'Yes.'

'Forget it. He won't care.'

'He will.'

'I'll take it back to him.'

'Dad, go back, please.'

'Annette, you'll miss the plane.'

'No, we won't.'

Charlie made a U-turn in a driveway and they drove back to the house.

As Annette scoured the house for the book, in the back of her mind she was wondering from where this bizarre compulsion came. She turned over pillows on the sofa, got down on her hands and knees to check under beds, looked on top of the refrigerator, pulled furniture out from the wall to check behind it, and as she rushed frantically about she began to grow alarmed. She knew she should stop and get back on the road, but she couldn't. She could send him a book of Yeats's poetry from Paris. She could write him a profusely apologetic note. She could call him long distance and explain. But none of these alternatives, once contemplated, could alter her momentum. The longer she searched, the more obsessive she became. She returned to the same places she had looked before; she dug through Charlie's piles of newspapers and magazines that had not been touched for weeks; she looked in places where she knew the book was not to be found. She seemed no longer capable of rational thought or action.

Charlie honked his horn a few times, then he sent Eliana in to get her mother.

Eliana found her mother sitting quietly in the sewing room.

'Maman! What are you doing?'

Annette looked up and at the sight of her daughter a great peace washed over her. She smiled.

'Go. Go play outside in the mud.'

A sly grin crept over Eliana's face.

'Do you mean it?'

'Yes. Tomorrow we'll go find you some jeans.'

Annette heard her shouting the glorious news to Charlie before she sprang off through the backyard. Then she heard the car door slam, the screen door slam, and the slow purposeful steps as her father approached. She looked up at the old man in the doorway. He wore a peculiar expression of fear mixed with hope; Annette had never seen him look quite like that.

'I'll stay until spring. We'll go back then.'

Charlie looked at her and nodded. 'You don't want to miss the spring. Prettiest time of the year.'

'I won't stay any longer.'

'I know.'

'And I'm not doing this so you'll change your mind about the trust.'

'That's good, because I'm not going to change my mind.'

'Frankly, Dad, I don't give a damn about the money anymore.'

He nodded and gave her a rare smile. 'I'll put the car in the garage.'

Annette found Ethan Brown's book in her suitcase, where she had packed it by mistake.

Ten

That afternoon, Annette enrolled Eliana in school and the following morning she walked her daughter four short blocks to the two-storey brown brick building where the child would attend class that winter.

In Paris, Annette and Eliana's morning walk to school had always been one of their favorite moments of the day. The smell of freshly baked bread, the swishing sound of straw brooms on the wet pavement, the sight of venison and rabbit and quail hanging in the window of the butcher's at the end of the street as Christmas approached – all these things delighted their senses. Eliana never failed to notice the Indian woman working in the kitchen below the pizzeria, steam billowing out from the ground-level basement window onto the sidewalk, her dark arms moving ghostlike through the white vaporous clouds through which Eliana would sometimes catch a glimpse of her dark face and the bright red tikka on her forehead, just between her eyes. Eliana was a little afraid of the woman who never looked up and never smiled, who seemed to live in a hot, slaving world where there was never any rest and never any joy. Farther down the street was the small pastry shop that made Annette's favorite prune turnovers. A bell on the door would tinkle as they entered, and from the back would emerge an immaculately dressed lady who'd greet them with a civil 'Bonjour, mesdames.' They rarely ran into other customers in the shop, but the refined, delicate pastries carefully arranged under the glass were always gone by the end of the day. Appearance, or 'presentation' as the French called it, was a virtue in France. In the hierarchy of virtues, it came much closer to God than hygiene. Eliana preferred the simple tastes of a pain au chocolat, which they generally bought at the bakery on the next block. There was always a line at the bakery, morning and afternoon, and the three women who worked the counter, the mother as cashier and the daughters to package up bread and pastries, flew from task to task with the precision and efficiency of a finely crafted engine, slicing baguettes, wrapping loaves, whipping together little pastry boxes, and securing them with bright ribbon in a flurry of skilled motion that seemed bred into their hands. Annette had noticed how different the American and French notions of service were. Americans would tolerate considerable bungling if it was done quickly and with a smile. The French, on the other hand, never confused civility with friendliness. The bakers, the greengrocers, the waiters were all proud professionals, not disgruntled students or artists, and they looked upon their clients with an eye of equality if not condescension.

This particular morning, however, on the way to school in Cottonwood Falls, held none of their accustomed pleasures. The raw wind cut through them as they walked in silence, their heads lowered, and Annette noticed more than one car or truck pulling out of garages to drive a few short blocks to school, with sleepy children staring at them bug-eyed through the dirty windows. She left Eliana in front of the school and watched as the little girl marched down the walk to the entrance, ponytail swinging gaily from side to side, betraying none of her nervousness.

Annette was waiting in the same place that afternoon when the dismissal bell rang. She spotted Eliana in the onslaught of children and waved. As the child approached, Annette saw she was on the verge of tears.

'Precious! What's wrong?' asked Annette in French as she dropped to her knees and looked into her face.

'Pas maintenant,' mumbled Eliana and pushed her mother away. Annette took the child's hand and they

walked together through the crowd of children stream-
ing toward the waiting cars and trucks in the street.
Annette squeezed the little hand, and Eliana responded
with squeezes of her own, that simple way they had of
communicating, in silence, in secret, their compassion
for one another.

'How about some ice cream on this smoldering hot
day?' asked Annette.

Eliana looked up at her mother, a smile eclipsing the
gloom in her eyes. 'In the ice cream parlor?'

'I thought we'd give it a try.'

'Thanks, Maman,' she said, and she pressed her
mother's gloved hand against her tearstained cheek.

They found the ice cream parlor closed with a sign on
the door saying Gone to Lunch: Back at 1:00, but since it
was already three o'clock, they decided to walk back up
the street to Hannah's Cafe. They opened the door to a
noisy, smoke-filled place that smelled of unidentifiable
fried things. As they stepped inside, the noise momentarily subsided and heads turned toward them. All were
men, and Annette immediately wished they had not
come. Unwilling to be intimidated, however, she ushered
Eliana into the warm room and shut the door behind
them. There were several seats at the counter, but
Annette was not willing to perch like a sitting duck
before these strangers. She crossed the room under the
onslaught of their scrutinizing stares, gripping Eliana

firmly by the hand, and maneuvered them into an empty booth at the back of the cafe. A waitress with arms that sagged like taffy barreled out of the service door loaded with orders, and as she passed their table she paused, thrust her right hip at them where a menu projected from her pocket, and said with a wink and a nod, 'Take a menu, girls. Be with you in a sec.' Annette pulled the menu from her pocket, and the waitress moved away to her tables.

'Now,' said Annette. 'What happened?' She reached across the table and stroked her daughter's cheek. The cold wind had erased the puffy red splotches from her face, but her eyes still burned with unhappiness.

Eliana's reply was interrupted by the arrival of a second waitress who burst into the room with her long bleached hair swinging recklessly as she tied an apron around the waist of her snug, short uniform.

'Sorry I'm late, Bea.'

'Yeah, sure,' answered the taffy-armed waitress. 'Get those ladies in the corner, will ya? I'm swamped.'

Annette turned her attention back to Eliana. They spoke quietly in French.

'Tell me.'

'They called me a frog.'

'They what?'

'They said it was because we ate frog's legs. And at recess they got down and hopped. All the kids did. No one was nice to me. One little girl came up to me at first, but then the others made fun of her too and called her a frog lover, so she wouldn't play with me, either.'

'They're very ignorant, Eliana. They know nothing about the world outside these hills.' Gently, rationally, all the while holding her daughter's hand, Annette tried to explain how ignorance bred fear, and fear bred hate. Although she spoke calmly, her heart pounded, and she felt as though someone were leveling a shotgun at their heads. Their conversation drew stares. The two old men in the booth opposite watched them with the unguarded curiosity of spectators watching animals in the zoo.

The blond waitress had stopped to chat with some young men at the counter.

'Patti,' scolded Bea as she charged across the cafe carrying stacks of dirty dishes. 'The ladies. Get those ladies!' Bea shook her head and sighed as she disappeared behind the swinging doors.

Patti shuffled to their table, counting on her fingers. 'Six months. Six months 'til my birthday.' She seemed to be talking to her order book as she pulled it out of her apron pocket. 'I was supposed to get married on June first. But that's off.' Bea reappeared and Patti turned, calling across the floor to her. 'I don't know what to do with the band. I've already paid for them. I guess I could have a party. My mother's birthday is May thirty-first.'

Bea walked up to her and whispered emphatically in

her ear. 'Patti, take the goddamn order.'

'What can I get for you?' asked Patti finally.

'Two chocolate milk shakes, please,' said Annette.

'Sorry, don't make 'em.'

Annette's heart was still pounding.

'Do you have ice cream?'

'Sure. Vanilla, chocolate and strawberry.'

'Do you have milk?'

'Yeah.'

'Then please put some milk and chocolate ice cream in a glass and mix it up.'

'We don't have a mixer.'

Annette consulted the menu for a moment. Eliana, keen to her mother's sensibilities, touched her arm gently.

'It's okay, Maman, I'll just have a Coke.'

Annette felt the anger rise within her. She glanced at Eliana, who was watching with pleading eyes.

'Come on, lady. We're pretty busy right now. You want more time?' said Patti.

'No,' said Annette, slowly folding the menu and handing it back to her. 'No, I don't want more time. I just want a chocolate milk shake.'

'Well, lady, I can't make it for you.'

'Okay, then give us some frog legs.'

'What?'

'*Maman, arrête!*' pleaded Eliana.

'*Frog legs!*' shouted Annette. All conversation stopped and heads turned. Annette glared at the waitress, at her black roots, her fake nails, the safety pin that fastened her dress where the second button should have been. She stood, grabbed Eliana's hand, and pronounced contemptuously, '*Vous êtes tous de pauvres cons!*'

Eliana gasped.

Annette threw her black sable coat over her arm and stormed out with her child in tow.

The ice cream parlor next door was now open, but Eliana was so humiliated she refused to go in. They walked home, took Charlie's car, and drove into Strong City to the supermarket, where they bought two half gallons of ice cream, chocolate syrup, and milk, and Annette rode the grocery cart down the sloped parking lot with Eliana in the basket. Annette laughed so hard she nearly peed in her pants and Eliana forgave her completely for the scene in Hannah's Cafe.

Others, however, were not so forgiving. Patti Boswell was Katie Anne Mackey's best friend, and by the end of the day Ethan Brown had been told the entire episode, slightly exaggerated. Ethan, however, who thought Patti a dolt, silently laughed while pretending righteous indignation to his fiancée. He made a mental note to ask Annette Zeldin what she had said to them in French.

Eleven

⟲ Katie Anne wanted to be married in white leather pants, a white fringed shirt, and a white cowboy hat, but her mother would not hear of it. Consequently, Katie Anne talked of nothing else. Ethan was quite used to tuning her out on such occasions, and when they walked into the South Forty Friday evening and looked up to see Patti waving to them from the bar, Ethan knew what was in store for him. He stomped the snow off his boots and looked around for Jer.

'Said he had a date,' volunteered Whitey, who was leaning against the bar next to Patti.

'You're kiddin' me,' replied Ethan.

'No, sir.'

'With whom?'

'Wouldn't say.'

Whitey was Katie Anne's regular dance

partner. Ethan, who disliked few people, disliked Whitey. The fact that his slight five-foot-seven frame moved with sprightly agility around the dance floor and that he was particularly fond of white dress shirts with his jeans made Ethan suspect a touch of fay in his character. He had told this to Katie Anne and she had laughed at him, accusing him of jealousy.

They got their beers and joined their friends already seated at a booth in the corner. The guys argued K.U.'s chances of going to the Orange Bowl that year; the girls talked of Katie Anne's wedding. Ethan, being a K.U. alum and Katie Anne's fiancé, was partner to both conversations, and he slid easily in and out of both with the same agility Whitey displayed on the dance floor. Ethan was a fine conversationalist; he had an uncanny ability to adapt himself to the comfort level of his interlocutor. The same man who impressed his clients with his breadth of legal knowledge, and the state politicians with his persuasive and articulate arguments against federal management of the Flint Hills, also was at ease in the superficial and limited arena of conversation that flowed around this same booth every Friday night at the South Forty, where trucks outnumbered cars six to one in the parking lot, and country and western music was only a little less sacred than the word of God.

But something unusual happened this evening: Ethan became acutely aware of the tedium of the conversation.

Something hovered in the air, a cloud of discontent that had been growing since the evening he had asked Katie Anne to marry him. The thought of committing once again to married life had a strange effect on him. He found himself growing irritated with Katie Anne over little things, the things he normally tolerated with humor. He had always been a master at hiding his more unseemly emotions behind his twinkling brown eyes, but tonight those eyes wandered around the room with a bored, unsettled gaze. When Katie Anne asked him what was wrong, he answered that he was looking for Jer.

'Jer's got a date,' she reminded him.

'I wonder with whom.'

'Can't you say "Who with?" like other people?' she teased and dived back into the sea of chatter.

A man more in tune with his feelings might have suspected that his discontent had as much to do with the specter of Mrs Zeldin as with anything else. Like all men of his class and upbringing, even the ones of exceptional intelligence like himself, he viewed women like Mrs Zeldin with a faint air of contempt. Women's liberation may have altered their social condition, but it had very little effect on the way most men in these parts viewed women. Those like Mrs Zeldin – brilliant, talented and successful – did not tread the earth with a light step.

Consequently, when Whitey looked up and saw Jer

approaching their booth with Mrs Zeldin at his side, the earth trembled.

'Oh, shit,' drawled Patti. 'I hope he doesn't bring her over here.'

'Sure he will,' countered Whitey, who was eager to meet the acclaimed terror.

'I won't sit at the same table with that bitch,' snarled Patti. 'If he brings her over here ...'

They approached slowly, stopping to chat with Jer's pals, who sidled up to him, eager for an introduction to the stranger. Ethan was struck by Annette's ease and graciousness as Jer introduced her to one man after another. She wore a loose, soft white blouse unbuttoned provocatively low and tucked into a black slim skirt which, although not as short as the swinging dance skirts worn by Katie Anne and Patti, molded her hips and thighs and accentuated the sensuality of her slow, unhurried movements.

Jer seemed to be under a spell. He guided Annette through the crowd to their table with a tender pro-tectiveness he normally reserved for his animals. Ethan caught his eye and threw him a 'What the hell ...?' look which Jer pretended to ignore. He eagerly introduced her to everyone at the table. Annette smiled warmly at Patti, and if she recognized her from the restaurant she gave no sign of it. Patti, however, was not so gracious. When Ethan asked them to move down to make more room on the booth, Patti, suddenly engrossed in low conversation with Katie Anne, pretended not to hear. Jer settled the impasse by seating Annette on the booth next to Ethan and drawing up a chair for himself at the end of the table. There were furtive glances and whispers, then, with an abruptness both rude and obvious, the girls hauled their partners out to the dance floor. Ethan, however, staunchly refused to budge.

'You know I never dance,' he replied audibly to Katie Anne's strident urging.

'Well, you can do it this once.'

'Where's Whitey?'

'Dancing with Patti.'

'Then stay here with me.'

'I will not,' she whispered emphatically in his ear. She rose from the table and stormed off. Jer, who had been looking around for their waitress while the exodus had taken place, turned back and noticed the empty table.

'Where'd everybody go?'

Ethan gestured to the dance floor.

'Oh,' Jer mumbled. He glanced nervously at Annette. 'Would you like to dance?' he asked. Jer hated to dance. Annette declined and he breathed relief. 'What'll you have? I'll go up to the bar to get it,' he said.

'Whatever you're having,' replied Annette. She smiled warmly at him, which only aggravated his nervousness.

'Be right back,' he said, patting her hand as he got up.

Annette and Ethan sat stiffly in each other's presence for a moment. Neither of them wished to remark on the unpleasant incident that had just transpired. Ethan felt some kind of apology was in order but he normally dealt with unpleasantness by ignoring it. He found himself at a rare loss for words. Annette finally broke the uncomfortable silence.

'Jer's offered to give Eliana riding lessons.'

'Jer's a good man.'

'Yes, he is.'

'I was a little surprised to hear you'd decided to stay.'

'Just until spring.'

'I see.'

'But that doesn't change anything about the land. I'm still selling if you're still buying.'

'I'm still buying.'

'Good.'

'The documents are ready. You can stop by the office to sign them whenever you like.'

'I have that book, too. I need to return it.'

'There's no rush.'

'Are you sure?'

'I have plenty more.'

'Are they yours?'

Ethan wasn't quite sure he understood. 'Are they mine?'

'Yes. I mean, I thought maybe you were sharing the space ... Isn't it a library book?'

Ethan began to laugh. Jer sat down and placed a beer in front of Annette. Annette, who hated beer, smiled and thanked him.

'What's so funny?' asked Jer.

'She thinks my office is the town library.'

Jer grinned. 'Hell, Ethan's got a better library than Strong City. Only he don't lend 'em out.' Jer shook his head emphatically. 'Gettin' a book out of Ethan's harder 'n pullin' a tick out of a mad dog.' Annette stole a questioning glance at Ethan, who was examining the sticky rings on the table. 'Ethan got his Ph.D. from Yale. Had one of those big scholarships. What'd ya call it?'

'Fullbright,' mumbled Ethan.

'Yeah. He got an offer to go teach at Berkeley.'

'Teach what?' asked Annette.

'English,' answered Jer.

'Nineteenth century. The poets mainly,' offered Ethan, finally warming, but only reluctantly, to the conversation.

'Wordsworth.' Annette smiled.

Ethan nodded and returned her smile. 'And Yeats.' It was the first time their eyes had met since that moment on the hillside several weeks before.

They were both silent. Ethan played absentmindedly with his beer glass. Annette stared at the back of some-one's head at the table in front of them. Jer, who misinterpreted their silence as animosity, searched for something to say and came up blank.

'And did you?' asked Annette.

'Did I what?'

'Go to Berkeley.'

Ethan shook his head. 'I got homesick.'

'So he threw it all in and came back here and went to law school at K.U. Finished in ... how many years was it?'

'You got homesick?' asked Annette.

'What was it, two years instead of three?' pursued Jer.

'I got homesick.'

'Wasn't it two years?'

'Two and a half.'

Ethan was so acutely uncomfortable he seized upon the first thought that rattled through his brain.

'Would you like to dance, Mrs Zeldin?'

Annette's mouth opened to refuse. She hesitated, then spoke very softly. 'Yes.'

Jer watched them move onto the dance floor with a relieved smile. He was glad to see them warming toward each other. He had been a little afraid to tell Ethan about his date, knowing how he felt about her.

Once on his feet, Ethan's senses returned to him. He took Annette by the hand and she followed him to the DJ's booth, where Ethan exchanged a few brief words with his friend. As they moved onto the floor the music suddenly segued into a slow dance.

'There. That'll make it a little less painful for you,' said Ethan as he took her in his arms. Annette laid her hand on his shoulder. Underneath the wool flannel shirt was hard muscle. It had been many years since she had felt such strength in a man. His heat was tremendous. She felt it float over her as he wrapped his arm around her waist.

'You don't dance and you don't lend books,' she said, rather more soberly than she had intended. She looked up into his face.

He replied, not as lightly as he would have wished, 'That's right, ma'am,' and tightened his arm around her.

Ethan was saved from the consequences of his rash behaviour by a series of fortunate incidents.

At just the moment he and Annette rose from the table to dance, Katie Anne and Patti left the dance floor for the ladies' room, and when they came out Whitey caught them in the hallway and proposed they all go over to the Denim and Diamonds, where Whitey's favorite band was playing. By the time they had reached an agreement, Ethan was back and sitting alone at the table and Jer was dancing with Annette. Ethan left with Katie Anne and the crowd. Later that night, he didn't know if the guilt he felt was for abandoning his friend or for dancing with Annette. It had been a long time since he had felt guilty about anything.

Twelve

Despite his education in the hallowed halls of learning and his exposure to more sophisticated tastes at Yale, Ethan had never been able to overcome his prejudice against classical music. Once returned to his native soil, he felt no more compunction toward pretense, and he grew stubbornly reactionary in his tastes. It was undoubtedly a long-overdue response to all those moments of forced appreciation of something he was just not akin to.

Ethan's change of heart came in an odd and unexpected way. His attic office looked down onto the house of the Winegarner family, whose little boy had been severely burned in a prairie fire. After two years of painful plastic surgery and rehabilitation, the boy could just begin to use his hands and arms. He was still confined to a wheelchair. On sunny days his mother, who had taken over his education as best she could, wheeled him into the backyard, where she read to him and helped him with lessons made out for him by a teacher who came in from Council Grove once a week. One Friday in late November Ethan noticed Mrs Zeldin entering the house with her violin. She returned the following Friday at the same time and left, as before, an hour later. The next morning Ethan ran into Mrs Winegarner in the hardware store. Mrs Winegarner, although younger than Ethan, had always reminded him somewhat of his own mother. This was perhaps because he often watched her hang her wash on a clothesline strung across the backyard as his mother still did, or perhaps because of her stoic silence and refusal to complain of life's hardships. He hesitated to ask about the visit from 'that French woman' as the town had taken to calling Annette. To his surprise, Mrs Winegarner brought up the subject herself.

'She's giving Matthew violin lessons,' she said quietly. Her mouth looked as though it wanted to smile. Ethan hadn't seen her smile in two years. 'I'd heard she was giving lessons. I didn't think she'd be any good with kids. I'd seen her around town and she always seemed so unfriendly.'

She looked through the trays of wing nuts as she spoke, trying them on a bolt she had taken out of her handbag.

'Here. Let me help you with that,' said Ethan.

She watched in silence as Ethan fitted the proper size for her.

'And is it working out?' he asked.

She looked away, trying to hide the emotion on her face.

'You know what she did?' She looked back at Ethan; tears glistened in her eyes. 'The first time she came, she just talked to him. She told him about this man named ... Its ... Its ...'

'Itzhak Perlman.'

'Yes, Perlman. He plays the vioin. And he's in a wheelchair. And she told us about how famous he was and how he was so loved and admired by everyone. But that wasn't what ...' She stopped and rubbed her nose with the back of her hand. 'She brought her violin along. And she played for him.' Mrs Winegarner looked up into Ethan's eyes as though she were trying to articulate the most profound secrets of the universe. 'It was ...' She stopped.

'Go on,' said Ethan gently.

'Oh, it sounds silly.'

'Tell me.'

'I'd never heard anything so beautiful in all my life. I don't think I'd ever heard anyone play the violin before. At least not like that. And when I looked over at Matthew, he had this look in his eyes that I've never seen before. I can't describe it ... it was like he was ... in heaven. Listening to the angels.'

She took a deep breath and then went on.

'You know what he said when she left? He said, "Mama, this music makes me want to live." '

She was desperately trying to hold back her tears, and she looked around her to see if anyone was watching, then dug into her handbag for a tissue.

'She brought him a violin, one she'd rented for him. And she taught him the names of all the parts and how to care for it, and the names of the strings.' She turned away from him to blow her nose.

'Well, I shouldn't go on. I must be boring you.'

Ethan laid his hand on her shoulder. 'No, you're not.'

'I was very wrong about her. She's awfully patient. And she seems to strike just that right note with kids. You know what I mean?'

She took a deep breath and smiled. 'We bought Matthew a new CD player. He can't seem to get enough of his music.'

Ethan walked her to her car and with uncharacteristic spontaniety she hugged him. She laughed and said she hoped Katie Anne wouldn't mind.

The following Friday, Ethan had it in his mind that he would run some errands in the late morning, and he thought he just might time his departure to coincide with the end of Matthew Winegarner's violin lesson, but as Mrs Zeldin was on the front porch bidding good-bye to

Mrs Winegarner, and he was hastily pulling on his coat and rushing down the stairs, his phone rang. His first inclination was to ignore it, but Bonnie caught him at the reception to tell him it was Mrs Peters, who was in hysterics after finding out her husband, deceased as of Thursday evening, had donated his body to the medical center at K.U. Ethan's good sense got the better of him, and he turned to his office and took the call. From his window he watched Mrs Zeldin walk down the street, her violin case in her hand.

December was a tumultuous month for Ethan. The foundation for his house was laid, and because the weather had continued mild, with only a few cold spells and one brief snow, he was able to start construction. Katie Anne set the date of their wedding for April 23, and the preliminary guest list totaled 630. Ethan tried to stay out of it as much as possible, but whenever there was a disagreement between Katie Anne and her mother, he was dragged in to cast the deciding vote. At first he tried to give his honest opinion on things, but he soon learned the best strategy was to side with his bride. But all this was no more than petty and worrisome; Ethan's real tribulation came when Paula called from California to say their son, Jeremy, had run away from home.

Ethan's perfect life suddenly caved in. That Katie Anne was no help to him in the matter came as no surprise. He remembered the way she had been through his father's illness and death, and his instinct told him to place no great burden of comfort on her shoulders. He merely mentioned the matter over dinner one evening, and in the midst of her prattle about a wedding shower she paused, holding her fork in midair, said sweetly, 'Oh, honey, I'm so sorry. But you know he'll come back. Kids always do,' and went on to ask him if his sister would be able to come in from Abilene for the wedding shower.

That's when the nagging began to come back. The same uneasiness that had stayed with him for so long after the death of his father. He recognized it instantly, like an old injury that flares up with a sudden change in the weather, but this time he had nothing to hide behind. Katie Anne was no longer a mask for his pain, but neither had she become a balm. Ethan's soul paced through the day in anguish. Even Jer was of little comfort. Jer hid an extraordinary sensitivity underneath his tough sunburned skin. You could see it in his eyes, and you heard it in his silences. It showed in the way he sat with his colicky horses and his laboring cows through long, bonechilling nights in snow and rain. And he would do the same for his friends. But Ethan needed more than that.

Not long before they discovered the cancer, Ethan's father had written him a letter. It was the only time his father had ever mentioned the subject after Ethan's divorce from Paula. He wrote, 'Ethan, I hope you'll find a way to return to the Holy Mother Church. I'd like to think you would do this in my lifetime. But you're a stubborn kid and I can't think you'd ever do anything like this because your dad asked you to do it. Besides I really wouldn't want that anyway. You need to find your own way back.'

Ethan never answered the letter, and his father never mentioned it and never wrote him again. Sometimes Ethan thought that if he had answered that letter, perhaps this nagging guilt wouldn't be bothering him now. Anyway, it was too late to do anything about it.

On Wednesday after his call from Paula, Ethan went into Wichita to take care of some business at the courthouse. He was day-dreaming and missed the turn onto Third Street and ended up on Central. The street took him by the big cathedral where he and Paula had been married and Jeremy had been baptized and had taken his first communion. He pulled over to the curb and stared at the pillared entrance and high, wide steps for a long time. There was no sign of activity. He got out of his truck and went in.

The old familiar ritual seized him as soon as he entered, and as he dipped his fingers into the marble font of cool water and touched his forehead, he began to smile inside. As he walked slowly down the center aisle, genuflected, slipped onto a bench and kneeled, folding his hands in prayer the way he had done thousands of times as a child, he felt his mind grow as still and light as the airy dome above. As a child he had often wondered how to pray in those silences, and it was the silences that had confused him the most. He used to drive one thought after another from his head, because it was too selfish or not what he thought God wanted, until his mind had become tired with chasing away all those evil thoughts, and he had given up and fallen into the cant which always made it so much easier for him. But now there was no cant, no priest telling him what to pray, no words for him to climb up to heaven on, and he sat in the silence, the brilliant, sun-gloried silence, and felt at peace. When he had been there several minutes, he heard someone enter the cathedral from the side door and kneel in a pew near the front.

After a while the peace began to fragment and his worldly thoughts began clamoring for admission. Ethan stood, a little reluctantly, and as he did the person at the front stood also. When she turned and came toward him, he recognized Mrs Zeldin. She saw him and smiled warmly. He waited as she approached him.

'Mr Brown,' she said, and shook his hand.

'Mrs Zeldin.'

'Don't forget your hat,' she said, smiling, and took it from the pew where he had left it.

'Thank you, ma'am.'

Then she did an extraordinary thing. Instead of

bursting into chatter, she took his arm and gently leaned on him as they walked silently together down the long aisle toward the door.

Outside, at the top of the steps, they paused. She released his arm and Ethan turned to her and asked, 'What's the daughter of a Methodist minister doing in a Catholic church?'

'I joined right after Eliana was born.'

'Why'd you do that?'

'To annoy my father.'

At first he thought she was serious, she had a dead-sober look on her face, then she broke into laughter. It was the first time he had seen her laugh.

She quickly changed the subject, asking him questions about his house and the wedding plans. She said she was in town to do some Christmas shopping and run some errands, but she was having trouble finding a repair shop where she had left her violin lask week.

'I forgot to bring the address with me. I thought I could find it again.'

'What's the name of the place?'

'Goldman's Antiques.'

He led her to his truck and pulled out a telephone directory from underneath the seat. He flipped through the pages.

'Here. Three twelve North Ellis.'

'That's it.'

'Hop in. I'll drive you. It's not far.'

Annette couldn't make it into the truck with her tight skirt, and she laughed as Ethan hoisted her up.

'I'm just not made for this kind of life,' she said as he closed the door for her.

'Sure you are,' he answered as he got in. 'The clothes are the problem. Not the lady.'

A bell tinkled over the door as they entered the antique shop and a voice from the back called out, 'Be with you in a minute. I'm working with some glue right now. Can't leave it.'

It was not much of an antique shop. There was very little furniture, only a buffet and a few chairs that'd seen better days. Everything in the shop was covered with dust. Along the back wall hung shelves cluttered with violin cases. Annette approached them and casually opened a case, examining the violin.

A very thin and grizzled old man with bent shoulders, whose skin and clothing were covered with the same gray dust that covered his shop, appeared from the back.

'Mrs Zeldin!' he cried, and came toward her, wiping his hands on his apron. He spoke to her in a language Ethan took to be German. Annette replied in the same language. The old man disappeared in the back, then returned with a violin cradled in his arms. He spoke to her at some length, and she examined it closely, then replaced the violin in its case. He took Annette's check and held the door for them as they left.

'How about something to eat? You haven't eaten, have you?' Ethan asked as he opened the truck door for her.

'I'm starved,' she replied as she laid the violin on the seat and turned to him. 'Lift?' she said, smiling, taking a hold of his arm. This time he made no attempt to avert his eyes from her legs when she stepped up.

'What sounds good?' he asked as he started up the truck.

'Mr Brown' – she grinned – 'I don't expect we'll have the same taste in food either, so just take me wherever you normally eat.'

They settled on a Sonic Drive-In that took Annette's fancy as they drove by. She thought it would be fun to eat in the truck and have the waitress set their food on their window the way they used to do when she was a kid. Ethan, who was always beset with moral indigestion when he ate anything but beef, was content. From the moment she leaned on his arm in the cathedral, the awkwardness between them was swept away. Their conversation flowed easily now, and much to his surprise, Ethan found her an eager listener. She asked him questions about cattle ranching, and he talked at length about the soil of the Flint Hills and bluestem grass, its special properties that made it unique in the country, on par with the renowned pampas grass in Argentina that fed the beef she ate in France.

Ethan got a kick out of the way she handled the chilli dog. She set on her lap and used a knife and fork, cutting it up, bun and all, into bite-sized pieces.

'You've gone quiet on me,' said Ethan.

'Hmmm,' she replied as she dangled a greasy onion ring from her fingers.

Ethan finished long ahead of her.

'Was that German you were speaking back there?' he asked.

'Yiddish,' she replied. She was peering out the window at the menu. 'I think I'll have a chocolate milk shake.'

Ethan punched the button and ordered it for her.

'How'd you learn Yiddish?'

'My husband was a Belgian Jew.'

'Is he still in Paris?'

'No. He conducts the Dallas Philharmonic now.'

'Well, there you go. Another reason to stay around. Eliana's closer to her dad.'

Annette's quick look told him he had stepped into forbidden waters. 'Eliana doesn't ever see David.' She paused, looking out the window, and said, 'There's no need for her to.'

She looked back quickly at him, and her eyes held his

in a gentle pleading look. 'You mustn't judge me by that. It's not as it seems.'

'I don't get to see my son much,' he said after a moment.

Annette looked surprised. 'You have a son?'

'Jeremy. He's fifteen. He lives in Los Angeles with his mom. She moved out there after we got divorced.'

'That's a dreadful place to raise kids. Especially when they reach fifteen.'

The chocolate milk shake came. Ethan passed it to her and she took it and stirred it slowly with the straw. There was a long, hovering silence while Ethan stared at his steering wheel.

'He's run away from home,' he said suddenly.

'Oh, Lord, no.' She lifted her head, engaging his eyes with a look that held the promise of such comfort that Ethan blurted out all his misery. He was not accustomed to talking about himself, but Mrs Zeldin's eyes were never more focused than when he spoke to her about his son. The milk shake sat untouched in her lap. He told her about how the unsettled business with his father had come back to haunt him, and when Jeremy ran away all he could think of was his father. She urged him to go to California.

'I wouldn't be able to do anything. I don't know who his friends are. I don't know where he hangs out ... nothing. Anyway, Paula's already tried all that. She thinks he's with a friend, but the friend's not talking.'

'It doesn't make any difference. You're not a detective – you're his father. He needs to know you're out there, looking for him. That's what's important.'

Ethan studied her dark, luminous eyes, and saw in them all the intense emotion he had so assiduously trained himself to avoid. He noticed her milk shake. She had not touched it.

'Too much?'

She looked down at it, as though she had forgotten it was there.

'Yes,' she said softly, and handed it back to him to put on the tray.

Even the silence between them as he drove her back to her car was free of the discomfort of their previous moments together; it was a different kind of silence, an inquisitive, suggestive silence, a fallow silence, preparing their hearts for the germination of thoughts and feelings to come. It was a silence that linked them in ways they did not yet know, or even guess, with a bond that was not palpable, yet felt as strong and assured as a touch, a caress, a kiss.

Thirteen

Every Friday after Matthew Winegarner's violin lesson, Annette Zeldin dropped in at Ethan Brown's office. Ostensibly she came to borrow his books. Much to Ethan's surprise, she had read many of them already. Initially, their friendship seemed to be rooted in this mutual love of literature, but the seed of trust that had been planted over a melting milk shake at the Sonic Drive-In was buried much deeper than Tennyson and Yeats. Jeremy had returned home the day after their conversation, and Ethan was spared the anguish of flying to California. Instead, he was harboring the idea of bringing Jeremy to live with him. He had not spoken about it to Paula or to Katie Anne; he was not eager to wage those wars quite yet. He did speak freely about it to Annette.

'I think it's a fabulous idea,' she said, sitting

in his office, flipping through the pages of Cather's *Great Short Works*.

'Any place is better than LA.' She laid the book next to her violin and looked up at him. 'Do you think Paula would go for it?'

'Frankly, I think she'd jump at the chance. Jeremy's the problem. He'd have to give up his basketball. His friends.'

'When's the last time he was out here?'

'Last Christmas. He'll be out here this Christmas, I hope. We're plannin' on it.'

She got up and poured herself another cup of coffee.

'I can't imagine your fiancée is the type of woman who'd like to share you with a fifteen-year-old boy.' Annette never referred to Katie Anne by name.

'It won't be a problem.'

Annette looked at him over her coffee cup.

That night he brought up the subject with Katie Anne. Katie Anne, who never for a moment imgained that Ethan's mind was on anything except the wedding, stared at him in frozen horror for a long minute, then rose without a word and went into the bedroom. Ethan knew she wanted him to follow her, but he loathed these histrionics, and since he stubbornly refused to follow the scenario, he was repaid in kind. After a few minutes of silence, he heard her on the phone with Whitey making plans to go out dancing. Finally, reluctantly, Ethan went to find her. She was thrashing around in her closet.

'Damn, where's my red skirt?'

'We need to talk about this.'

She rummaged through a pile of clothes at the foot of their bed. 'I don't know what there is to talk about. I mean, how can anybody be so ... so dense as to think I'd want to spend my honeymoon with a fifteen-year-old brat.'

'Jeremy's not a brat.' There was an edge to his voice that warned her to pull back.

'All fifteen-year-old kids are brats, Ethan. It goes with the territory,' she said, a little more gently.

'We've been living together for nearly two years now. It's not as if we haven't had time alone,' he replied.

She had a sudden urge to slap him, for his insensitivity, his stubborn, bullish refusal to understand. 'Ethan, if Jeremy comes out here, I honestly don't think our marriage will last very long.'

She turned her back to him, unzipped her jeans and slowly slid them down over her hips. Then she tugged her sweater up over her head. Suddenly, Ethan was acutely aware of every curve of her back, the sharp angle of her shoulder blades, the ripple of her muscles as she tried to wriggle out of the tightly knit clothing. Her thick dark hair caught in the sweater, and he watched her struggle, momentarily trapped. Ethan touched her breast, and the struggling ceased. He could feel the tension that ran through her into him. She stood frozen, waiting, while he unfastened her bra, letting it hang from her shoulders. He touched his lips to the back of her neck and felt her shudder. With his eyes closed he felt the weight of her breasts in his hands; he explored the delicate details of her body with his fingertips; he listened to her breath and the little whimpering sounds she made. And he smelled her, the feminine odor of her sweat mixed with a faint lingering trace of perfume. He moved closer and pressed her against the wall.

Moments later when she cried out his name he barely heard her; her voice seemed far away, remote, distanced from that dark, mysterious thing that gripped him so steadfastly.

He didn't bring up the subject of Jeremy's visit again. He didn't really need to. Jeremy wrote him a stinging letter saying he didn't want to spend Christmas with them this year. The next Sunday, instead of getting up and fixing his traditional Sunday breakfast of scrambled eggs with sausage and homemade hash browns, Ethan quietly got dressed and drove twenty-eight miles to Council Grove to attend mass. Annette Zeldin was there, as he had anticipated. When he walked in and kneeled behind her and her daughter and poked her in the back, she turned to him and grinned.

'Ah, my prayers are working.'

'Don't tell me I'm in your prayers.'

'Of course you are.'

They didn't speak to each other throughout mass, except when Ethan whispered a comment about the soloist's resemblance to Kermit the Frog, which made Eliana giggle. Annette threw him a warning glance and he was quiet after that, but Annette felt his presence, and he felt hers.

What he had not anticipated was Katie Anne's reaction to this new habit of his.

'You're not goin' all religious on me, are you?' she yelled from the shower the next day. Ethan was shaving at the time, and the question caught him at an awkward moment, while he was looking closely at his reflection in the mirror. It made him take the question a little more seriously than he might have had he been, say, making breakfast or cleaning his boots. He paused, inspecting his cheek for bristles.

'I mean, you're not gonna make me become Catholic or anything like that, are you?'

'Course not,' he mumbled. 'But you're welcome to come with me.'

There was a loud thud when she dropped the bar of soap, then a litany of curses as she chased it around the tub with her foot.

'I take it you're not interested,' he said.

'What?'

'Nothing.'

∽ Nonetheless, when she saw he intended to make a regular habit out of what she had thought was merely a seasonal twinge of conscience, she began to complain in earnest. Their Sunday mornings were now disrupted by Ethan who got up early, by Ethan who wasn't there to make Sunday-morning love, by Ethan who made his ritual breakfast closer to noon, by which time she wasn't very hungry, having already fixed something for herself while he was out.

But for Ethan it was worth it. Katie Anne's grumbling was a small price to pay for the inexpressible comfort he experienced every week sitting with Annette, Eliana between them, on a pew near the back of the little church in Council Grove. There was something undeniably familial about it, and at times he found himself wishing Jeremy were with them. Ethan who generally noticed children only if they were his or if they were ill mannered, found himself a victim, like many others before him, of Eliana's buoyant enthusiasm. She invariably drew him into a conversation about horses, and her face took on a lightness, a near etheral quality, as though gravity were turned on end and some great joyous power were being exerted on her, charging her every look and gesture, lighting her eyes and tugging at her mouth in an all-out determined effort to lift her up. At first he was concerned that his presence, next to Annette, might make tongues waggle, but Council Grove was just far enough removed from Cottonwood Falls to afford a modicum of anonymity, and the scattering of tourists who straggled in during the winter and came in hordes in the summer kept the parish free from the kind of complicated familiarities and liberties bred in small, insular towns. Annette came this far to mass to avoid the inevitable gossip that would plague Charlie if it were known that his daughter and granddaughter were faithful Catholics. Ethan, on the other hand, divorced, engaged to remarry, estranged from the church, was drawn to this little enclave by its renegade spirit. The priest was an old Irishman who had long since pruned himself of his stern ways and had mellowed into a witty, self-deprecating and deeply loving old buzzard whose deafness seemed particularly acute in the confessional. In all, Ethan liked his Sunday mornings. He soon began to look forward to them.

But the worst complication about December was Christmas. Christmas baffled Ethan. He was a deeply caring man, but he was also tight with his money. His gifts to others were thoughtful, practical, greatly appreciated, but always slightly off target. He never seemed to get it quite right. Lacking the spontaniety of his romantic poetic idols, he gave sides of beef to his parents and sheepskin-lined gloves to his girlfriends. He'd given flowers only once in his life, to Paula on the occasion of his son's birth, and things like perfume and chocolates and jewelry seemed tarnished by a vague notion of self-indulgence, something close enough to sin so that, hovering in his unconscious, it steered him clear of such luxuries with the same moral determination that kept him ever faithful to a slab of beef on his plate every night (fish and chicken be damned). Ethan's father had raised him on the proverb, 'He who feasts will never be rich,' and Ethan took the maxim to heart. He worked hard for his money, and the first year he earned a six-figure income, he celebrated by taking Jer out for a beer. Jer ordered a Chivas, but Ethan stuck to his Bud. In the days of consumer debt and gluttonous overspending, Ethan was a dinosaur. He had $10,000 stashed away in a catastrophic medical fund, almost $22,000 in a college fund for Jeremy, $53,000 in a mutual fund earmarked for retirement, a little over $8,000 in an unspecified savings account, and he had purchased his land outright in cash. He borrowed money only for the construction of his house, but he was ready with a hefty down payment and much of the finishing work he paid for in cash. Except when traveling, Ethan operated without the benefit of credit cards, and apart from his soon-to-be finished house, he owed not a penny to anyone.

Katie Anne, blessed with her own family fortune, took little interest in Ethan's wealth. She was used to his frugal ways by now and his miserliness annoyed her only around the time of her birthday and Christmas, when her expectations ran exceedingly high. This Christmas she was expecting an engagement ring. She had given up waiting for Ethan to take her into Kansas City to look for rings, and she had driven in with Patti and narrowed down her selection to a half dozen gorgeous stones at two different jewelers.

Three days before Christmas, Ethan called Jer in the closest thing to panic Jer had ever seen him exhibit.

'Pal, you've gotta do this for me.'

'Ethan, you're crazy. If Katie Anne finds out, she'll be heartbroken. Worse than that, she'll call it off.'

'No, she won't.'

'No, you're right she won't. She's been waitin' too long to get you hooked. But she'll be madder'n hell.'

'She won't find out. You can tell me exactly where you went, who sold it to you . . .'

'This isn't like you, buddy. You don't pull these kind of tricks. Why don't you just do it yourself?'

'I got too much work to do.'

'You don't want to get married, do you?'

It was the closest Jer had ever come to psychoanalysis, and the startling effect of this straightforward cowboy reading between the lines of Ethan's muddled inner dialogue jolted Ethan into silence.

Ethan replied after a long hesitation, and his voice was unusually high, as if someone had him by the throat.

'Well ... will you come with me at least?'

'Sure. I'll come with ya.'

Ethan picked him up an hour later and they reached the plaza a little after four o'clock. In the first store, Ethan glanced cursorily at the rings Katie Anne had chosen, cutting short the salesman whose languorous movements matched his sultry speech as he carefully withdrew each ring and replaced it, habituated after long years of selling a product that was generally not purchased in a hurry. On the way to the second store, Ethan proposed they stop somewhere for a beer.

'After you buy the ring,' Jer said firmly. He looked down at the little square of paper in his hand. 'Take a left here. Should be right down this street ... Yeah. There it is. Helzberg's Jewelers.'

While the jeweler brought out the rings Katie Anne had selected, Jer's attention was caught by a display of gold necklaces.

'Pardon me, ma'am, but do you have any Saint Christopher medals in here?' asked Jer.

'Yes, we do,' said the jeweler as she set out three rings for Ethan to examine and turned to help Jer.

'What do you want with a Saint Christopher medal?' asked Ethan.

Jer ignored him and watched as the mild-mannered woman gently removed a display of medals and crosses.

'It's for a lady,' he said very quietly. 'Needs to be small. Something feminine.'

She selected a finely crafted solid-gold medal and arranged it on the black velvet cloth before him.

'Who are you buying this for?' demanded Ethan as he stepped up behind him.

Jer turned and whispered in his ear, 'Ethan, just go buy your goddamn ring and leave me to my business. Okay?'

Ethan only pretended to admire the rings; he was listening to Jer. The transaction was done quickly. The medal was priced at nearly $400, but Jer forked it out in cash and quietly slipped the red velvet box in his pocket.

'No, thanks, ma'am. Don't need a bag. Thank you.'

The jeweler turned back to Ethan and held up the first ring for him, describing the cut and quality of the stone, but Ethan cut her short, pointed to the largest of the three, a two-carat perfect marquis set in a ring of smaller diamonds, and said, 'I'll take this one.'

Without missing a beat, the jeweler quickly returned the other two rings to the cabinet. 'Would you like to put this on a credit card, sir?' she asked.

'Yes, ma'am,' Ethan answered.

As Ethan signed the voucher, he noticed the price. With taxes, the ring was $8,700.

'You have impeccable taste, sir,' said the lady. She said it quietly and simply, without any of the obsequious charm Ethan associated with her trade. 'That's one of the finest pieces of jewelry I've ever had in my store.'

Her commendation might as well have been a condolence, for the entire shopping episode hung over Ethan like a pall. Neither he nor Jer mentioned stopping for a beer, and they drove directly back to Cottonwood Falls that evening. They talked about cattle and ranching, and not one word was spoken about Saint Christopher medals or engagement rings.

Fourteen

~ Christmas at the Mackey ranch was one of the things that Ethan enjoyed most about his association with the family. Family and friends converged from all over the state, always to be received with gracious hospitality. Betty Sue Mackey greeted uninvited guests with the same warmth she lavished on her next of kin; she gladly squeezed in an extra plate and dusted off another chair. Tom Mackey, dressed in his hallmark Santa suspenders, a crisp starched white shirt, and brand-new jeans, moved around the house filling champagne glasses and telling jokes, and by the time they sat down to eat, everyone was infected with his exuberance.

This year, the big news was Katie Anne's engagement, and her two-carat marquis was the star of the show. She flashed it at everyone, throwing glances at Ethan that were so full of tenderness and pride that he found himself quietly commending himself for the purchase, a feeling due in part to the effects of the champagne, which made the afternoon all the more festive for him. His greatest disappointment was that Jer was not here. Jer had been invited to Annette's for Christmas dinner, but said he'd stop by later in the day for a piece of Betty Sue's pecan pie. Ethan found him in the kitchen, sitting by himself at the table piled with empty serving dishes, eating the double slice of pie that Betty Sue had put aside for him.

Ethan laughed at him. 'Didn't you get enough to eat over there?'

Jer swallowed his bite of pie and waved his fork in the air. 'I tell you, I was pretty damned surprised. That lady's one helluva cook.' The fork dived into the pie and he snapped the next bite into his mouth. Jer waggled his head in lieu of words until he could speak intelligibly. 'Except for this weird stuff she put in the turkey. Chestnuts, I think she said.'

Only then did Ethan notice the red glow on Jer's face.

'Looks like you've had a fair share to drink, haven't you, buddy?'

Jer nodded. 'Wine,' he mumbled. 'Had wine with the dinner.'

'Wine? Shit.'

Jer stabbed his fork at Ethan and shook his head indignantly. 'You've never tasted anything like this before, I swear to God. Annette went all the way to Kansas City to get it. This stuff, it just sort of ...' He paused, stared at the pie, momentarily reflecting. 'Hell, I don't even like wine. And before I know it, here I've gone and had three glasses.' He suddenly burst out in a bellow of laughter. 'Shit, that was good stuff,' he commented, almost to himself, as though still in a state of disbelief.

Jer scraped up the last crumbs, then rose and poured himself a cup of coffee.

'Well, we sure missed you over here, pal,' said Ethan. He was surprised at how sincerely he meant it. Jer sat back down next to him and pulled a pack of cigarettes out of his shirt pocket. He showed it to Ethan. It was squat and blue, with the outline of a winged helmet printed on the front.

'Look what she gave me.' He pulled out one of the cigarettes. They were short, fat, and without filters. Jer grinned. 'That's what I like about that lady. Hell, she's the first woman I've met in years who hasn't started lecturin' me on quittin' smoking.'

'Well, maybe she just doesn't love you like we do.' Ethan shook his head sadly. 'They'll kill you, Jer.'

'Maybe,' Jer said, running it under his nose, sniffing the tobacco. 'Maybe not. Maybe I'll get kicked in the head by a damned horse.'

He lit one up, took a gulp of coffee, leaned back in his chair. 'I thought I'd ride out tomorrow and help you with the fencing on your new place.'

Jer had never been one to fret much about life, but neither had he ever shown much enthusiasm for it. The contentment that shone on his face that evening, smoking his Gauloise and drinking his coffee, was as close to beatific as he had ever come.

The Sunday after Christmas, Annette and Eliana were late to mass and Ethan didn't see them until the service was over. Annette was just buttoning up her coat when he caught up with them outside but he got a glimpse of the tiny gold medal against her black sweater.

The comment that escaped Ethan's mouth was so unexpected that it seemed spirited out of him.

'Morning, ma'am. And a belated merry Christmas. Nice necklace.' A startled look appeared in Annette's eyes for only a second, then it passed, but Ethan blushed solidly all the same.

'Merry Christmas to you, too, Mr Brown.'

'Ethan, look!' Eliana waved a child's white cowboy hat and fixed it proudly on her head. 'Look what Jer gave me for Christmas!'

'Well, don't you look pretty!' In an unusual surge of playfulness, he swung her up onto his shoulders. 'How about a ride?' Ethan jogged off over the grass with Eliana squealing and giggling. After a few turns around the lawn he circled back to meet Annette as she walked toward her car.

'I hear you had one darn good Christmas dinner.'

Through Annette's mind flashed the uneasiness, the tension that sat upon them all that afternoon like an ugly, squat devil. Her father had disapproved of her expenditures, the wine, the endives, the specialty imports like the Roquefort, even though she had paid for everything herself. He scowled at her throughout the entire meal, but mostly it was the child that annoyed him. Eliana giggled and draped her napkin over her face; Eliana interrupted him when he was speaking; Eliana took a large second helping of potatoes and left them uneaten on her plate. As he said grace, Annette stole a peek at his face and wondered how such a soul, so intolerant of human frailty, so scornful of childlike behavior, could possibly have any communion with God. Then they sat down, and even the pretense of good cheer as they passed their plates and praised the meal could not lift the pall that hung over the table. She ate only a few bites of turkey and drank some wine, and she tried very hard to protect Eliana from her father's wrath and see to it that Jer and Nell were supplied with easy and pleasant conversation, and defuse her father's anger whenever she heard it rumble in the distance. Sometimes she would look up and see her mother sitting in the rocking chair in the living room, and when she did, the ugly devil squatting in the middle of the table would disappear.

'Yes,' she said to Ethan as they reached her car. 'It was nice.'

'Hey, hold on to that hat. We're dismounting.' He lowered Eliana to the ground. As he did he caught sight of the look on Annette's face. It was odd. Nothing he could figure out. But there was a lot about her he couldn't figure out.

'Will you be in Friday?' she asked as she got in and started up the engine.

'You bet.'

'Good. I'm glad. I'm looking forward to it.'

Ethan turned toward his truck and as they drove away he heard Eliana call out, ' 'Bye, Ethan!'

What happened the following week was destined to change the nature of their relationship for ever. On Tuesday, Annette was late picking up Eliana from school. She had taken the car into Strong City to have some work done on it, and when she got to the school the children had already been dismissed and the grounds were empty.

Her heart began to pound as she walked quickly down the hall toward the principal's office. The sound of her high heels clicking on the polished linoleum floor in the eerily empty hall, reverberated off the pale blue stucco walls, resounded from the glass display cases, and were thrown back at her throbbing ears to beat alongside the sound of her heart. A terrifying nausea swept over her.

'I'm looking for Eliana. Eliana Zeldin,' she said abruptly as she entered the office. 'Do you know where she is?'

The startled secretary looked up. 'I think everyone's gone. Did you try the classroom?'

'It's locked.'

She shrugged. 'I don't know. Let me ask Mrs Walters.' She rose and tapped on a closed door, then opened it and spoke softly. She turned back to Annette.

'No. No one saw her.'

'What do you mean, no one saw her. You only have fifty kids here and you're telling me no one saw her?'

The principal emerged from her office. 'I remember seeing her leave the building, Mrs Zeldin. But we had a little problem, a couple of the boys got in a scuffle on the bus and we had to bring them back inside and call their parents, so I'm afraid we were a little distracted.'

Annette spun the secretary's phone around and dialed her home. She let it ring and ring, but no one answered. Then she called Nell. No, Nell hadn't seen her. She'd been home all afternoon.

Annette raced out of the office, down the hall, and out to her car. Her hands were shaking so badly, indeed her entire body shook convulsively now, that she had difficulty fitting the key into the ignition.

And then it began again. The cries. She knew it would. She could tell it was coming on. She jammed the accelerator to the floor and the car skidded away from the curb, kicking up sand and dirt behind her. Suddenly she knew it was important she be alert, that she slow down and look around for clues, any clues, as she drove home, anything that might help the police. She braked suddenly and rolled down the window. It was beginning to rain. The sound of the crying had gone. She was alert now, although her body was still shaking. From the end of the block she could see her backyard. Was that Eliana there? Hanging over the back fence? Her eyes worked keenly to discern the outline. No, it was just the hedge, the play of shadow in the dull winter light. She pulled up out front and ran to the backyard. She called her daughter's name. There was no answer. Not even the neighbor's dog barked back at her. She opened the back door and called again. The house was dreary and silent. Her father was in Emporia for the day at a trustees meeting. She went through every room in the house but no one was home. She found some paper and scribbled a note: *Looking all over for you. So sorry I'm late. Where are you!!! If you come home, please don't go out. Wait for me.* She went outside to tape the note to the front door, but the tape stuck to the roll inside the dispenser.

Through her tears and the rain she couldn't see to find the end. The entire roll was a pale, frosty blur. It was cheap tape. Her father always bought the cheaper, generic brands. And now her daughter was dead because of it.

She angrily hurled the tape into the rosebush next to the front door, then she laid the note in a conspicuous place on the carpet and ran out. The cries had returned, incessant, startling clear, not at all like something imagined. It was frightening how clear they were.

She got in the car and drove, slowly, looking up and down each street. It was raining heavily now. When she got to Ethan Brown's office she stopped.

Ethan looked up at the sound of footsteps running up the stairs. Bonnie knocked loudly, then threw open the door.

'Ethan! Ethan! Come quickly!'

Ethan rose and followed her, but she was ahead of him by a flight of stairs, and when he got to the second landing he saw her at the foot of the staircase with Mrs Zeldin.

The woman's frailty never again struck him so forcefully as it did that afternoon, when she turned her haunted brown eyes upon him. She wore no coat, only a black cardigan sweater that was drenched with rain, and

Bonnie was carefully peeling it off her. Underneath it she wore a thin short-sleeved blouse, and the sight of her naked, pale arms against the black silk, glistening with rain; her long white neck curved downward; this vision of her in need and despair wrenched his gentle heart more violently than any misery ever had done before.

'Bonnie, do we have any blankets?' he said as he rushed down to Annette.

'There's one in my trunk, I think, but it's . . .'

'Go get it.'

He put an arm around Annette and helped her up the stairs. Her skin was like ice. She shook violently.

'What happened?'

'She's gone,' gasped Annette, and she laid her head on his arm.

'Who?'

'My daughter. She's gone.'

His nearness, his touch, his strong arm around her seemed to release the tension in her, and she stumbled up the last few steps into his office. He let her down into a chair. Bonnie appeared with the blanket, making profuse apologies about the straw struck to it, and Ethan wrapped it around her. He pulled a twenty-dollar bill from his pocket, thrust it into Bonnie's hand, and told her to run over to Carl's Liquor and get a pint of whiskey.

After she left, Ethan pulled the other chair up to Annette's and sat down, taking her hands in his. They were thin and icy, and he gently pressed them between his own callused, warm hands.

'Tell me what happened.'

Her body shook convulsively.

'Take a deep breath.'

She nodded, inhaled deeply, and looked up at him. 'I was late picking her up. She wasn't there. Nobody saw where she went. She's not at home. She's not at Nell's. I've looked all over.'

'Annette, this is Cottonwood Falls. Kids don't just disappear ...'

'It can't happen again, can it?'

'What do you mean?'

She looked down.

'What do you mean?'

'Oh, God ...'

'Could she have gone over to play with a friend? Maybe, since you weren't there, she went home with somebody else.'

'Nobody's ever invited her over to play. I wouldn't know who to call ...'

'Doesn't she have riding lessons after school sometimes, with Jer?'

'Thursday. Jer picks her up on Thursday. This is Tuesday.'

Ethan thought for a moment, then rose and went to his desk. He dialed a number, then looked over at

Annette. Her eyes hung on him.

'Jer. Hey, bud. You haven't seen Eliana this afternoon, have you?'

He listened, then a smile crept over his face. He nodded to Annette.

'Yeah, well, I guess she didn't get the message. We've got one worried mom over here.'

Bonnie showed up with the whiskey just then, and Ethan motioned for her to set it down. She threw an inquisitive look at him, then left quietly.

'Yeah, sure. I'll tell her. Thanks, Jer.' He hung up and turned to Annette.

'He said he called yesterday and left a message with your dad. He'll be gone Thursday. Said he'd pick her up today instead. I guess your dad forgot to tell you. He's got her working in the indoor arena. He'll bring her home in about an hour.'

Annette stared at him blankly.

'Hey, did you hear me? She's okay. Nothing to worry about.'

Annette nodded. Ethan poured some whiskey into a coffee mug and when he turned back to her she had her hands over her ears. He held it out to her. 'Annette?'

'Can you turn off the music?' she asked weakly.

Ethan set down the mug and gently peeled her hands away from her face.

'There isn't any music.'

He held her hands tightly in his.

'See? There's no music playing. Now, what happened? Will you tell me?'

He held the mug of whiskey out to her. This time she took it and drank a little. After a long pause, she shook her head sadly. Ethan waited patiently. She took another deep drink of the whiskey, and finally its warmth began to swim through her veins. She looked up, into the gentle eyes of the man in front of her. The whiskey mollified her, and she reached out and touched his lips, very lightly, with the tips of her fingers. Her touch electrified him. He closed his eyes for a second, and when he opened them again her hands were back in her lap, clasping the mug.

That afternoon, Annette revealed her past to Ethan. It was an intimate act tinged with eroticism, as are all revelations of past loves to new lovers, for Ethan and Annette were indeed lovers. Their love was in a nascent state, and it had been waiting this moment, like some souls await their appointed hour of bodily birth with eager delight, knowing full well it means renunciation of harmony and peace.

Fifteen

Well over a decade had passed since the evening David Zeldin had settled Annette on the sofa in his Tel Aviv apartment on the top floor of a high-rise overlooking the Mediterranean and told her about herself, but Annette's recollection of the moment had never faded. She was only twenty-three; he was over forty. Although he spoke with no sentimentality whatsoever, she went back to her hotel later that night, after he had made love to her, and cried. His life reminded her of the freakish characters and grotesque events in a Jerzy Kosinski novel. And she had been afraid to face him the next day, not only out of shame, but out of fear. One night with him had shattered her world. The bland, white-bread comfort of the Kansas town where she had grown up, its symmetry and hygiene, its self-righteous congeniality, its mediocrity, was suddenly revealed for what it was. Overnight her mind-set was obliterated and before her stood the rest of the world, variegated and factious, painted garishly with opposing forces and other truths.

She was in awe of David Zeldin, for she was young and had known only one lover before him. The most tantalizing thing about him was the odor of his body. It was pungent, fiery, and sweet at the same time, and she had carried it home with her and lay in bed that night with it on her, like a salty perfume, exciting her all over again. It was the smell of ancient Hebrew, of pale, rocky hills, of deserts and olive trees, of war, of song. She had toured Europe and played in major cities throughout the United States, but none of this, though glorious and exciting, had effected any real change in the way she saw the world. What changed her, irrevocably and implacably, was a night of intimacy with one extraordinary man. This was why, when she stepped up on the stage for rehearsal the next day and saw David Zeldin waiting, smiling, she was afraid.

David was six when he was torn out of his mother's arms and herded to the children's barracks in the Polish concentration camp, where they had been sent from their native Belgium. His mother had fought so fiercely for him that she nearly dislocated his shoulder before the Nazis finally clubbed her unconscious. He never saw her again. Three years later, when his camp was liberated by the Russians, he had no family, no homeland, and no language. The kapos beat him whenever he spoke Yiddish or French, and now the only words he comprehended were the hate-drenched German commands he had listened to with fear and humiliation for three years. For weeks after that he lived in the streets, eating rotten garbage and sleeping in rubble, until a priest found him and sent him to an orphanage in Belgium.

It was two years before David learned his father had survived Auschwitz, and in 1948 father and son emigrated to the newly independent Zionist state of Israel, where David's father remarried, this time to an American journalist. Even the Nazis, however, could not bash the boy's brilliance out of him, or his linguistic aptitude (by the time he was at university he spoke seven languages), or his gift for music. It was his American stepmother who took him out of the kibbutz every Saturday and into Tel Aviv for his violin lessons, an operation that remained clandestine for many years because there was no money to be spent on such luxuries. David kept his violin at the home of a math teacher in the nearby village of Ashdod, and every day after school he walked seven kilometers into the village, where he practiced, then walked seven kilometers back to the kibbutz to work the rest of the afternoon in the diary, mucking out the milking stalls. He skipped practice only on holidays, and on the day his baby sister, Simi, was born.

When she was eight months old, Simi was massacred, along with seventeen other children, in a terrorist raid on the kibbutz nursery. Shortly thereafter, his family left the kibbutz and moved to Tel Aviv; at that point David's lessons were no longer clandestine. His first composition was an achingly mournful lullaby dedicated to his dead sister.

When Annette met him, he was finishing his season in Tel Aviv before taking up the baton as conductor of l'Orchestre de Paris. Although his career was to be envied, personal fulfillment had continued to escape him. He was forty-three, divorced, and childless. The morning he greeted Annette at the airport in Tel Aviv and guided her to his car, intimations of a future began to trouble him, intimations that shaped themselves into clear thought when he awakened in the middle of the night and found that they had been pieced together during sleep, where the unconscious does its handiwork. These thoughts were nurtured during the week as they rehearsed Mendelssohn's and Sibelius's violin concertos, as their music began to meld into a uniquely beautiful expression, and with it their hearts and souls. David had never seen an artist respond so fully and passionately to his direction, and Annette had never met a conductor who could draw genius from her with such gentle ease. The morning after their first night together, which was the day of their final matinee performance, she approached him onstage, averting her eyes darkened with fear and doubt, and he saw in her countenance his own personal messiah. He took her back to his apartment after the performance that afternoon and they made love again, and as they lay there in the faded light of dusk, sharing a single cigarette, listening to the gentle waves rushing onto the beach below, they both believed in happiness.

The next day he drove her to the airport, and Annette changed her ticket so that she could stay with him another week. The week turned into three, and she stayed to help him pack his books and paintings and watched as the movers crated up his furniture for the move to Paris. After the apartment was emptied, they took David's car and toured the Negev and Jerusalem, and they flew together to Athens, where David was to transfer for his flight to Paris and she to New York. On their third day in Athens they were married by an American naval chaplain. A week later they arrived in Paris as husband and wife.

How two beings of such divergent pasts could live in such congruence was a testament to the power of their unusual devotion. Although arrogant and inflexible by nature, David recognized his felicity as a rare gift, and he strove to grant his young wife the esteem and recognition she merited. His task was facilitated by Annette's ability to detach herself from a past she had always considered ill fitting. She shed her native skin and emerged the creature she was always meant to be. The limited French she had learned as part of her training soon became her dominant language; she spoke it, argued in it, made love in it, and dreamed in it. And the uncomfortable memories of her childhood receded into that part of her brain where the English language sat dormant. Now the only English she heard was that spoken by South Africans or Londoners or Irish, and she gradually took on those expressions and intonations until she eventually sounded more British than American. Only when she spoke to her parents on the telephone did she unconsciously revert to her mid-western drawl.

When Violette was born to them four years later, Annette, who was a vibrant twenty-seven, took it in stride; David, then in his late forties, was profoundly altered. David Zeldin was not a nurturing man; rather, he was intensely cerebral. Yet some atavistic instinct emerged in him with the birth of his daughter, and his immense love for her found its way to expression in a confusion of behaviors. For four years Annette had been trying to no avail to get him to cut back on his two packs of cigarettes a day but the day after Violette's birth he quit smoking cold turkey. His nights, which had always been more sleepless than not, were now a bustle of activity. A deep, visceral envy arose in him as he watched Annette nurse the infant, and when, after four months, she started the child on formula so she could do a short European tour, he eagerly took over the night feedings. If the weather was pleasant, he would come back early from rehearsals, command Maria, their Portuguese nanny, to ready the pram, and stroll off with his baby down Avenue Victor Hugo to the park, where he would sit among all the mothers and nannies, gazing lovingly into his daughter's pale blue eyes as he rocked the pram in gentle, rhythmic motions, humming bars from Mozart or Strauss, oblivious to the amused whispers of the women seated on the benches around him.

Even though he now had the means, he had never acquired the habit of extravagant spending, and his tastes were quite simple. He wandered through toy stores, marveling at all the wondrous fancies of childhood. He queried sales clerks in great detail about the suitability of certain toys, learning how this game or that toy would assist in child development, how the brain would be stimulated or the motor skills enhanced, and then he would come home with a small pale blue stuffed bear because it matched the color of Violette's eyes. And in his odd, confused manner, he always managed to please the child. It was as if the infant still saw with her soul, and she saw into his heart and loved him for all his pain, for his starved fatherhood, for his butchered youth. All the things he had lost were mourned in this passionate cele-bration of Violette's birth, and in his strange, misguided manner, he took on the mantle of parenthood as though it were both cross and crown.

When Violette was not yet one year old, Annette and David were invited to return to Israel as guest artists with the symphony orchestra for a special performance to celebrate the opening of the new School of Music at the Hebrew University in Jerusalem. Some of the greatest classical recording artists of the century would be performing. Since Violette's birth, David had turned down all engagements that required travel away from home, but this opportunity sorely tempted him. It would be his first trip back in five years. He was not the type of man to indulge in nostalgia, but he found himself lying in bed at night imagining the warm fingers of the khamsin on his bare chest and the scent of orange blossoms on the wind. When Violette awakened at night he sang old Hebrew songs to her. He missed his country. Finally they accepted. They would, of course, take the baby and Maria with them.

But Maria would not go. She was old and dreaded planes, and she was frightened of the war, she said. Annette tried to explain to her that there was no war, that it was no more dangerous than Paris, but she would only shake her head and pound away at the dish towels with her iron (she had never gotten used to lightweight aluminum irons), muttering to herself in a peasant Portuguese that even David could not understand. They finally gave up and began looking for a nanny to accompany them, which proved even more difficult than finding Maria had been. At last they settled on Magda, a young Argentine girl who came highly recommended by the Australian ambassador to the OECD.

Violette did not take kindly to this changing of the guards. She was deeply attached to Maria, to her throaty chatter, her wiry gray hair, her worn black dresses smelling of musky perfume. The new girl smiled and cooed, and carried on so easily around the baby (she had raised her five young siblings), but she was a stranger. Once they were airborne, Violette would have nothing to do with her.

In retrospect, Annette thought there was something uncannily perceptive about the baby's dislike for Magda, but at the time they read all these things quite differently. Annette was eagerly anticipating this visit to the place where they had been lovers, and David was looking forward to showing off his wife and child to his old friends and colleagues. When Violette mashed her plump little fist into Magda's smiling face, when she twisted her little body around and looked frantically for the faces of her mother or father or Maria, squirming to free herself from those snakelike arms coiled around her so tightly, they said to each other and to themselves, 'It's just a question of time. She'll adjust in a day or two.' They reasoned away their worries. But then they would hear her cry again, and Annette would break down and say, 'Oh, my God, David, give her to me. She sounds like she's in pain. Could it be her tummy? Or her ears?'

As soon as they arrived at their suite at the King David Hotel in Jerusalem, David called in a doctor. Yes, she did indeed have an ear infection. The change in air pressure must have been very painful. Of course. That was why she had wailed and fussed and sobbed so. She fell asleep then, driven into deep slumber by the drugs, and Magda assured them it would be all right, that they could go off to their cocktail reception and not to worry. In the back of the taxi, dressed elegantly in black, bathed and perfumed, they reassured each other with observations about Magda's maturity, her poise. She had never been ruffled, even during the nerve-wracking flight; she seemed much older than her twenty years, but that came from the experience of handling all those younger siblings. She came from a good family – her father was mayor of a small town in Argentina. If an emergency should arise, she would handle it. She knew where to find them. The concierge had been alerted.

They were happy that evening. It was spring, and the air smelled of warm, rain-fed earth. In the taxi Annette draped her long, silky leg over David's and took his hand and ran it up the inside of her thigh. At the reception he kept noticing how beautiful she was, how motherhood had rounded out her body, added a slight fullness to her hips and breasts, and when they returned home that evening and found Violette sleeping peacefully and

Magda reading quietly, they slipped away to their bedroom and made wide-eyed, brutal love to one another.
They did things they had never done before, things they
would never speak of later, but would suggest to each
other by a brief word, a glance, or a touch, things that
bound them to each other in silent guilty pleasure.

The next day, Violette began running a fever. By late
afternoon it ran high. They called in the doctor again,
who reassured them it was a result of the ear infection
and that the antibiotics would soon get it under control,
that they were not to worry, but keep her cool. Annette,
dressed in her long black gown, bathed the baby con-
tinually during the hour before they left for the concert
hall. She kept Magda running back and forth for ice, for
fresh clothes, for dry towels, and clean diapers. She
refused to leave until the last possible moment, and until
then she would care for Violette herself. David looked on,
and for once he could offer no soothing platitudes; his
anxiety was as great as hers. Violette's eyes seemed a
darker shade of blue, and he told himself this was not the
color of death, that it was his imagination, nothing more.
She was awake, and she would slowly turn her darkened
gaze to him, then back to her mother. It was a strikingly
eloquent gaze, he thought. As if she wanted them to read
something in her feverish eyes. Only much later did he
find out that Annette had seen the same thing. When
they finally left for the concert, Violette did not cry or

fuss as they had feared; she was quiet. But she sat up and gripped the side of the crib, and her darkened eyes silently followed them as they gathered up their coats and keys, their music, her mother's violin. Her eyes rested solemnly on their faces as they gave last-minute directives to Magda, and then closed the door.

Annette didn't have time to call until intermission. Despite her anxiety, she had played well. Her remarkable powers of concentration had carried her through. She was playing before a tough audience of peers and academicians, and she had moved them, swept them into Mahler's tender, mournful world and locked them there until the end. The final notes were followed by a deep silence, then a cannonade of applause. David smiled at her from the podium, his brow slick and shiny with perspiration.

They had given Magda the program and she was to expect their call shortly after nine o'clock. She answered immediately, in a whisper. Yes, Violette was finally sleeping. Her fever had finally broken. All was well.

Backstage during intermission, David and Annette were showered with attention from David's old friends who were eager to meet Annette and see photographs of their daughter. David, usually so restrained, drank a glass of champagne and held his wife's hand.

The Sibelius concerto on the second half of the program that night had always been Annette's favorite piece, but since she had met David, it had acquired a very personal significance. She had performed it with the Tel Aviv Symphony under David's direction when they first met five years before, and tonight she expected his love to be the signature inspiration as it had been every time she had performed it since then. Instead, she found the piece sang of her daughter. She had not the time to rationalize this, and if she had, she would have found it strange, for there were moments when the music soared into an ominous delirium and the orchestra whirled along with her in a great pounding gallop, spinning the air into plaintive frenzied motion.

Violette, awakened, looked up at the face that no longer smiled, felt the damp, cold cloth on her nose, and breathed in the burning fumes. For one brief moment before she succumbed, her little heart pounded like a drum in her chest.

When David and Annette returned to their room that evening, their child was gone. Within minutes of David's call the King David Hotel was invaded by detectives from every branch of service. There was a stealth about their manner of operation that underscored the urgency of the affair. Guests and employees were interrogated; a scenario was pieced together. Magda had left the hotel at approximately 9:20 p.m. with the stroller. The stroller was found abandoned in a side street several blocks away. Residents were interrogated. And then nothing. There were no witnesses. Nothing to lead them anywhere. Just the abandoned stroller. Their lives stopped there.

David made calls late into the night. Then, after Annette fell asleep on the sofa, he went out on the streets. Jerusalem was such a quiet city after dark. All the excitement, the nightlife, the cafes, were to be found in Tel Aviv. Jerusalem seemed to be weighted down by prayer. The Jews, the Christians, the Muslims, all fighting over the land, supplicating their gods. It was such a beautiful city, tantalizing, full of light in the day, but at night it became a solemn place. Laughter seemed like blasphemy piercing the air.

David stood at the spot where they had found the stroller and stared helplessly into the darkened windows, willing them to give up their silent stony knowledge. Once he heard a child's cry and he followed it, but it eluded him, and then it ceased.

The ransom note they were awaiting never arrived. No demands were made, no communication was ever attempted, and there was never a trace of Violette or

Magda. The police had theories, but they were so distasteful they hesitated sharing them with the baby's parents. After two weeks of futile waiting, all the while suffering the intense scrutiny of the press, David and Annette returned to Paris. Only much later, when David was able to obtain a copy of the complete dossier, did they learn all the police suspected. There had been other cases similar to this, one in Greece and two in Italy; they offered no connections clear enough to lead them anywhere, but enough sordid details to feed the imagination.

The contents of the dossier came as no surprise to Annette; she had already surmised her child's fate. The last night she spent in the King David Hotel she dreamed of a strange and unknown place, and she awakened to the sound of a baby's cry. That same night, far away, in a dark and dirty place, Violette opened her eyes. The cold and stench told her she was far from home. Her stricken soul grieved for her parents, and her tiny heart sent up such a desperate wail that even the angels cried.

Sixteen

Ethan Brown rose and went into the bathroom. He poured the cold coffee out of his mug and rinsed it. He took a deep breath before returning to his office.

Annette Zeldin was leaning back in her chair, taking a long drag on the cigarette she had just lit. It had been months since she had smoked.

'I'm sorry,' she said, suddenly sitting forward. 'I forgot. You should have said something. I'll go out on the balcony.'

'It's raining,' replied Ethan.

'I don't mind.'

'Sit down.'

She took the ashtray he held out to her and leaned back in the chair.

Ethan didn't care much for scotch, but he poured a couple of fingers into his mug and took a drink. He studied the woman closely, without inhibition. She was calm now. The blanket had fallen from her shoulders, and there was an illusion of nakedness about her. He walked around behind her and quietly pulled the blanket up over her arms. She reached for his hand.

'Ethan, she may have been adopted. Not a day goes by when I don't pray for her. I pray she is in a family, a good family. Someone who loves her. But then at times I have this feeling, this gut feeling, that the police were right. That she was sold. For awful reasons. And then I pray ... Oh, God, I pray ...'

She told him how David had wanted another child. Right away. But she only wanted to keep moving. She took any engagement she could get. She would go anywhere in the world. She found respite from her misery only when she was performing. And she looked for her daughter everywhere. In every country, every city, she approached the consulates and embassies. She took pictures of Violette with her. She located authorities and filled out papers, wrote letters, opened files.

Steadily, quietly, their marriage fell apart. When they were home together, an inescapable emptiness blanketed their conversations. Overnight, it seemed, they became strangers. As suddenly and inexplicably as they had become lovers. A year after Violette's disappearance, Annette filed for divorce.

It was in Johannesburg that she was asked to perform Sibelius's violin concerto again. When Ernst Rodine saw her, he hardly recognized her as the same woman who had played with his orchestra several years before. When she took her place up onstage he noticed the thin arms as she raised her instrument to her chin, the sunken, empty eyes, the raw smile. During the first part of the performance, the shoulder of her black satin gown kept slipping, and backstage during intermission he found a safety pin and pinned it back for her. With an embarrassed laugh she told him she had dropped two dress sizes and had already had the gown altered once.

He first noticed something was wrong when they returned to the stage and Annette suddenly turned to look at the audience just as he lifted his baton. She was just a breath slow on the pickup. Then he noticed the way she was holding her head, as if she were listening for something beyond the music.

Annette first heard it in the seconds of silence preceding the opening chords. It was faint, but distant. From that moment on her hands and her heart were separate. Her bow danced across the strings as if seized by a spirit, and with her whole soul, detached, she turned to the air and listened. Then, early on in the allegro she heard it again. Her heart leapt. From his podium, over his swaying arms, Ernst threw her an alarmed look. She was picking up tempo. He tried to catch her eye, but she

would not look at him. During a pause, she listened. Her
acutely trained ear searched the audience, the balcony,
and her eyes swept the shadowy faces in the deep
cavernous hall before her, but she knew the cry did not
come from this place. Then came her solo. She watched
her fingers and her bow flying over the strings, but she
heard not one note of the music she played; she heard
only the sound of her baby's piercing cry. She remembered all the times she had heard that heart-wrenching
wail, and the ways she had rushed to calm it. The way she
had brought the baby to her breast, hurriedly, eagerly,
fumbling with the buttons on her blouse, her nipples
taut, warm, and full, barely able to hold back their milk.
She remembered looking down at Violette's eyes, bright
and alert in the middle of the night as she rocked her and
sang to her. She remembered those eyes. Their lightness,
their intelligence, their inarticulate knowledge. But now
the cries would not cease. There was nothing more she
could do. So she listened, and she played on.

*Violette felt only the first shaft of pain, and then,
mercifully, her little body was numbed to the torture.
Her cries turned to long staccato sobs, and her heart
fluttered as rapidly and perfectly as a bird's. Her lashes,
heavy with tears, closed upon her blinded eyes. Then
her tiny hand released its prisoner, her delicate body
shuddered, and her heart ceased to beat.*

The orchestra had stopped. Many had their heads

lowered. Some whispered to each other. An embarrassed murmur passed through the audience. Someone laughed nervously. The conductor's hands hung defeated at his sides. In the back of his mind he thought it rather amazing, really, that she was still going on, at a tempo none of them could match, a delirious speed, and yet she was playing impeccably. Suddenly she stopped. She lowered her violin and her bow slid from her hand. It clattered to the stage and all the whispers and murmurs stopped. She raised her eyes to his and stepped toward him, her hand outstretched for help, and then she collapsed.

Annette fidgeted with the silky blue binding on the blanket.

'I don't know if she died then, or later, or maybe before. But I believe it was her spirit crying to me. I heard her, Ethan, as clearly as you hear my voice now, I heard her. Why it was given to me, that awful punishment of hearing her suffer, I don't know. But I believe she's at peace now.' She looked up at him. 'I know you think I'm crazy. Everyone else did.'

Ethan poured a little more scotch in her mug and held it out to her. 'No,' he said softly. 'No, that's not what I think at all.'

She told him how she went away to Switzerland after Johannesburg. It was a rest cure more than anything else. Her hotel room had a small balcony overlooking Lac Leman and the Alps, and she would sit there and read, wrapped in blankets against the chill, steeping herself in long, ponderous works by Flaubert and Tolstoy. She read voraciously and, through the power of words, was able to keep the ghosts of her own life in abeyance. Most important, she read stories that were situated in worlds and times vastly different from her own. Music was conspicuously absent from her life. The hotel was old, elegant, and comfortable, but decidedly lacking in technology. There were no radios or televisions in the rooms. She had wanted it like that. At night she slept soundly, deeply, and her dreams were pleasant. She wrote no letters; she could not bear the pretense. She kept a journal, however, and in it she recorded the banal and trivial incidents of her days. The books she read, what she ate for breakfast, and lunch, and dinner, the disposition of her room, her walks in the mountains, her morning excursions by bus into Montreaux, where she purchased more books and browsed through the open-air markets, her afternoons in a large and busy cafe opposite the lake where she read newspapers and drank tea, and no one noticed her.

Then, one Saturday morning, sometime after her third week there, she woke up restless. She dressed and went down into the town for her coffee instead of taking it in her room as she usually did. It was still very early, and the cafe in Montreaux was deserted. She stared out over the lake, at the blue mountains on the other shore, and for perhaps the first time in her life she experienced a pang of wanderlust. Purpose had always guided her movements, and her purpose had been her music, ever since she could remember. Nothing had ever appealed to her for its own sake, but only through its relationship to her music. When she had left Kansas, it was to study at Juilliard in New York. When she had traveled, it was to perform. Music had even been central to her marriage. But for over a month now, she had neither lifted a violin nor attended a concert. She had shut music out of her life as she had shut out David. It was the last link to the nightmare, and the nightmare was finally beginning to fade.

What took its place that morning as she looked out over Lac Leman was a vague curiosity about life as she had never known it. She did not know how to approach it, but she did something that seemed reasonable to her at the time. She walked to the train station and stood for a long time looking at the schedule of departures. As she stood there, a train pulled into the station. It was a sleek silver machine, fast, smooth, and silent, and with an impulse that made her smile to herself, she stepped up into it. It was crowded, and she walked through several wagons until she came to a first-class compartment and found an empty seat near the window opposite a young man. With a barely perceptible motion the train began to glide out of the station. It was too late to get off. She turned her eyes to the station as it slid away, and she watched the city pass her by. As the train curved around the lake and she saw her hotel perched on the side of the mountain above the city, an exhilarating sense of freedom hit her. She suppressed a smile at the thought of all her belongings back at the hotel room, at the maid who would turn back her bed that night, at the small, round table in the corner of the dining room which was always reserved for her and which would be empty this evening.

They were well out of Montreaux when the conductor came for her ticket.

'I don't have a ticket,' she said. 'Where's this train going?'

'Lausanne,' he replied curtly.

'Lausanne,' she repeated. 'Lausanne will be fine.'

'You'll have to pay a surcharge.'

'That's quite all right.'

He was annoyed. Boarding the train without a ticket. It meant filling out forms in duplicate. He flipped through his receipt book and a little square of carbon paper fluttered through the air and landed in the lap of the young man opposite Annette. The young man picked it up and handed it to the conductor.

When the conductor had moved on, Annette turned

toward the window. The reflection of the young man opposite her drew her attention. He was resting his chin on his hand, his deep brown eyes fixed intently on the passing landscape, his long, slender fingers absent-mindedly tapping his lips. There was an air of dignity about the way he held himself and the way he moved, an unusual quality for someone his age, which she guessed to be about twenty. A folded newspaper, *Le Monde,* lay on the seat next to him.

As the train wound through the verdant Swiss hills, she found her thoughts drawn to him. Each time her eyes dared a glimpse of him, or rested on his reflection in the window, when he excused himself to get up, or when he returned to his seat, her curiosity only grew stronger. He spoke only a few words to her, but she sensed his restraint was affected. As surely as she was making invisible claims upon him, he was making claims upon her.

The train emptied at Lausanne. With a polite nod to her, he stood, took his raincoat and small suitcase from the overhead rack, and inched his way down the aisle with the other passengers. When she got off the train, she looked for him, but he had disappeared into the crowd.

She made her way to the exit. It was raining, and she stood at the top of the steps and looked at the city rising up on the mountainside before her. Even in the gray rain, the city sparkled with color; balls of fiery red geraniums dangled from every balcony, bushes of blue and pink hydrangea stood like dazzling sentries around the cafes, yellow pansies flooded the parks. Her senses were over-whelmed. Reason was lost, abandoned, in this muddle of glorious feeling.

Suddenly he stood beside her.

'Excuse me,' he muttered, a little shyly and very respectfully, 'I can suggest a hotel if ...'

'Yes, thank you,' she said. 'I would appreciate that.'

He looked at her then, in her eyes, not curiously, but warmly, an intensely honest gaze. His eyes were very dark and very bright. A lock of tawny brown hair dangled over his forehead and he swept it back with a toss of his head. He opened his wide black umbrella over them.

'It's not far, just up the hill. The taxis won't take us. It's not enough fare.'

'I don't mind. I don't have anything to carry.'

They both dined at the hotel that evening, and he asked the waiter to invite her to his table for coffee. He was an engineering student, and he had come to Lausanne to meet his mother, who would be arriving the next day from St. Moritz. Annette gave him her maiden name and told him she was on vacation. He was a mature young man, very well bred, intelligent and gracious in his conversation. Over cognac they energetically argued politics, and they were the last ones to leave the dining room. On the way up the stairs, he slipped his hand into hers. There was something reassuring about his decisiveness, and she did not hesitate when he drew her into his room.

She never saw him again after that night. He asked for her address in Paris, but she would not give it to him. He seemed sincerely hurt. She was surprised to find herself crying as she took the early train back to Montreux the next morning.

Three weeks later she learned she was pregnant. She did not greet the news with elation, as she had her previous pregnancy. Instead, a profound peace settled over her, a kind of prophetic serenity. She questioned nothing, and she had no fears. She named the baby Eliana, which in Hebrew meant 'God has answered me.'

When she had finished telling Ethan all these things they sat quietly for a long while. Ethan didn't know what to say. And she looked so tired. Without thinking, he leaned forward and kissed her silently on the lips. A light came into her eyes.

Seventeen

Annette was holding on the line for Ethan when he walked in the front door of the Salmon P. Chase House the next morning. He plodded leisurely up the steps with feigned casualness, ignoring Bonnie's look. He closed the door to his office and picked up the telephone.

'Ethan?' Her voice was bright.

'Mornin',' he answered. His heart beat rapidly.

'Ethan, can I still get in that house? My mother's old house?'

'Sure. I haven't done a thing to it.'

'Would you mind terribly if I . . . if I went out there sometimes?'

'Course not. I keep it locked, though. There's still some stuff up in the attic.'

'I didn't know that.'

'Just a few boxes. There's not anything your

mother cared much about. Stuff for a garage sale, she said. She didn't want to bother moving it. But I always kept it locked anyway.'

'Could I come by and get the key?'

'Anytime. I'm here.'

She entered his office dressed in jeans and wearing her sable coat. Ethan thought she looked like a movie star, but all he said was, 'Lady, you could use a good old sheepskin-lined parka.'

'You're such a cowboy,' she replied. The fondness in her voice was unmistakable.

'So what's all the excitement?' he asked.

'I can't tell you. If I do, it might go away.'

'Come on now, you're not superstitious.'

'No. But I get very nervous when good things happen.'

She smiled and took the key he held out to her.

Annette enjoyed the drive out to the old house. Even the bleakness of the winter landscape didn't seem to oppress her, and as she slid the key into the lock and opened the front door of her mother's family home, it struck her that she was falling in love with Ethan Brown. She stood motionless in the doorway for a moment with the cold February wind blowing at her back, then she walked inside. The wind shrieked around the corners of the house. It was a terrifying sound. The wind never sounded this way out on the open plains, only when it was confronted with an obstacle of some sort, a dwelling, a shelter, something built up in the midst of the vast emptiness. She closed the door behind her and laid her violin case on the dusty table, then she carefully removed the instrument. As she turned it and tightened the bow, thoughts of Ethan crowded her mind. She marveled at how such an extraordinary man could be so much at home in this place. And yet she could envision him nowhere else. He loved his land, his cows, and his truck with the simpleminded devotion of an illiterate cowhand, but he had a passion for things of the mind that set him apart from anyone she had ever met. He could have been a partner in a prestigious law firm, or taken his place among the academics at Harvard and Yale. Instead, he collected books, and read them late into the night, when his pretty girlfriend was asleep, enjoying communion with minds like his own in silence and solitude.

She began to play, and gradually the wind ceased its roar. The demons withdrew into silence, and music calmed the land.

* * *

Just that week Ethan had hired a couple of guys to help him tear down the fences that bordered Emma Fergusen's property. It was a long, slow process, and stray wire was always a potential hazard to the animals. Ethan thought it was about time to check on it, so the next day he rode out to visit the property. He finished a little before noon, and he thought he just might ride over to see if Annette Zeldin was out at the old house.

He reined in his mare at the top of Jacob's Mound and looked down at the old Reilly house. How many times had he ridden by the place over the years, glancing at it without so much as a passing thought for its past or its future? He saw only the land and its place in his scheme of things. When old man Norton died and his ranch went up for sale, Ethan saw a chance to realize his wildest dreams. He bought up the Norton place, knowing that all the Mackey land would go to Katie Anne, and if he could ever get his hands on Mrs Fergusen's little strip of prairie that cut like a ribbon between the Mackey land and his own, then his cattle would have access to the richest and biggest holding of bluestem in the state of Kansas.

Now, as he looked down at the weathered old house, such thoughts were far from his mind. This strip of land was his, and Katie Anne would soon be his wife. Another

obstacle, much more threatening, now stood here. For a
moment he cursed the fate that had brought her here,
and then he pressed his heels into his horse's flanks and
rode at full gallop down the hill.

When Annette heard the sound of his boots on the
porch, she stopped playing and lowered her violin. She
waited for him to knock, and when he didn't she called
for him to come in. Ethan opened the door hesitantly and
removed his hat. She was smiling at him, and he thought
her eyes looked different, happier maybe, but he wasn't
sure.

'Don't stop,' he said quietly, a shade embarrassed. He
sat down at the table and laid his hat next to the violin
case. Then he listened, and gave himself up to the
unbearable sweetness of the sound.

When she had finished, she laid the instrument back
in its case. Ethan sat quietly with his hands folded
between his knees.

'I have some hot coffee in a Thermos. You want some?'
she asked.

'Sure.'

'I've only got this one cup.'

'No problem.'

She poured some coffee and passed it to him. As he
took the cup he commented on her gloves.

'I thought those things went out with Charles
Dickens.'

'We wore them quite a lot in Europe. Places like Prague and Budapest. The concert halls were never heated.'

He reached out and took her hand and turned it over, examining the glove. He grazed the tips of her naked fingers with his thumb and desire swept through her.

'Are you going to make a habit out of this?' he asked.

'Out of what?'

He grinned. 'Coming out here in the cold and serenading my cows.'

She replied brightly, 'I'm planning on it.'

'Then I guess I'd better call the electric company and have them turn on the juice.'

'You don't need to do that. I've rehearsed under worse conditions.'

'I'm not competing for first place with the worst. I'll call them this afternoon.'

He was still holding her hand.

'You said you were rehearsing,' he said.

'Yes.'

'That means you're going to start performing again.'

She smiled.

'Was that your secret?'

'Yes.'

'Headed back to the big time?'

'I hope so.'

166

'The good old talking cure. Maybe Freud was on to something, after all.'

'I don't know if it's as simple as all that.'

'I know it's not.'

Her hand had settled in his, comfortably, without restraint.

'But you're right. It did change things. I don't know why. This morning I called my old booking agent in London. I didn't know if I was still worth anything. She seems to think I am. She's going to line up some engagements for next winter. I told her I wanted to stay in Europe. I don't want to travel far. Places I can do in a day or two.'

As she spoke, her face came alive, and it struck him how emotions danced across her face like the shadows of the clouds across the plains.

'What was that you were playing?'

'Beethoven's violin concerto.'

He shook his head slowly. 'You're a pretty amazing woman.'

'And you're a pretty amazing man.'

'I'm just a cowboy.'

'Sure.'

'I think the phone lines are still working. You want the phone connected?' he asked.

'Oh, heavens no. That's the last thing I want. I don't want anyone to find me out here.'

'Even me?'

'Except you.'

For a long while they sat without speaking. They stared silently at their intertwined hands, heads lowered, their faces so close they could smell the skin of the other.

'I love you,' he said softly.

She grew very still. He could not see her face.

'Annette?'

He lifted her chin.

'Look at me.'

A smile trembled on her lips, and her eyes told him all he needed to know.

After that day Ethan rode out to see her several times a week, and in those bleak, bare surroundings they looked upon each other with new eyes. There were only the one table and two stiff wooden chairs. And her violin stand with her music. She said she liked the acoustics of an empty room. But it was more than that. So when they were together they sat in stiff-backed chairs and talked about reviews of films they wished they could see, about articles Ethan had read in the *New Yorker*, about Annette's father and Ethan's mother, about medieval mystics, and *The Ascent of Man*. And when Ethan could bear it no longer, he would lean across the table and kiss her face, or stand and hold her for long, painful minutes. And then he would leave.

This willful confinement of their love only served to deepen it. As Ethan kneeled beside Annette during mass every Sunday, he recognized that something wordless was deep at work in him. He believed he was coming closer to God through loving her. At times he thought of his father, and he thought if Annette had been here at the time of his death, if he had been able to turn to her instead of Katie Anne, he would have something to hold on to now, rather than this vague, shifting guilt that sifted through his soul whenever he thought of the old man.

Ethan did not know how to position this love within the framework of his morality. It was an unearthly plant nurtured by things of the mind and the spirit; it seemed neither of their own choosing, nor could they find the heart to destroy it. Desire took root long after the blossom had opened, and when it did, it burrowed long and deep, straight down into the rocky bosom of the flinty hills, down into the core.

When they were apart, they blindly planned their futures. Responses to Annette's comeback were overwhelming, far beyond her modest hopes. Her winter schedule was already shaping up with guest performances in Lyons, The Hague, Heidelberg, and Munich, and her agent was pushing her to start as early as October.

Ethan began to focus on the details of his house. Evenings he would sit Katie Anne down at the kitchen table and earnestly solicit her advice on kitchen countertops and cabinet finishes. She was flattered, and took it as a sign of his growing commitment. His lovemaking became more urgent, more passionate, and afterward he was more reflective. Katie Anne fell in love with him all over again.

Eighteen

Ethan got a cold blast of reality one evening while playing pool with Jer at the Beto Junction Truck Stop. It was late at night and the empty beer bottles stood in a row on the windowsill behind their table. Ethan was doing most of the drinking. Jer had wanted to quit much earlier, but Ethan had begged him to stay, so Jer kept his buddy company, silently and without question. When Ethan reached a stage of very real inebriation, Jer thought it was time to step in. He chalked up his stick and leaned over the table.

'Six ball in the side pocket,' he said. He made the shot and walked around to the other side of the table. 'You're gonna get yourself in deep, deep shit if you let this thing go on.'

'What can I do, buddy? You're on a roll,' Ethan laughed. His speech was only slightly thick, but Jer could hear the difference.

'That's not what I mean.'

Jer hovered over the seven ball, calculating his next move.

'What're you talkin' about, pal?'

'You know what I'm talkin' about. Don't play dumb ass on me.' Jer bent down to eyeball his next shot. 'Unless you're so shitfaced drunk right now you really don't know.'

The balls cracked and the seven ball dropped into the corner pocket.

'Are you fuckin' her?' Jer said.

Ethan laid his cue across the table and bent down to look Jer in the eye.

'Don't even use that word in the same breath with her.'

Jer peeled Ethan's stick off the table. 'Yeah, I don't much like the sound of it, either.' He sighted down his cue. 'But I guess I got my answer.'

Ethan tore Jer's cue out of his hands and slammed it down on the table.

'You've got nothin'. Don't mess with me, Jer.'

Jer glared back at him. 'You can't make enemies around here,' he said. 'You make enemies with Tom Mackey and you're dead meat. You're a canner. You won't have a friend in all of Chase County. And you can't survive out here without friends.'

Jer took his coat and hat from the rack. As he buttoned up his coat, he said, 'Katie Anne's been askin' questions. She ain't as blind as you think.'

After Jer left, Ethan sat at the counter drinking coffee with the truckers. But the coffee was just to warm him and give him something to play with. He didn't really need it. Jer's comment about Katie Anne had sobered him up immediately. Wham. Just like that. His brain triggered a flood of something into his system, darn near drowning him in sobriety.

When he got home Katie Anne was asleep, but there was a note on the kitchen table: *Daddy called. Just wanted to make sure you hadn't forgotten about tomorrow. He'll pick you up at seven.*

Ethan liked working cattle with Tom Mackey. He liked the man, envied him his down-to-earth simplicity. If ever any esoteric or abstract thoughts entered his mind, Tom wrestled them to the ground. He dealt in numbers, in deeds, in blood and dander, hide and meat. He set his mind to the objective necessities of livestock, the branding and vaccinating and castrating, the feeding and moving. When Ethan was riding the range with Tom Mackey he was able to laugh at that other side of himself that sat up in his office late at night reading Rilke and Yeats. He stole a glance at the man now and wondered what reveries ever passed through his mind, and what he'd done with them.

'There he is,' said Tom Mackey, pointing to a big black Angus bull staring at them.

'You're not figurin' on sellin' him, are you?' asked Ethan.

'Hell no. Old Paco's the best breeding bull I've ever had.'

The two men slowly eased their horses through the herd, scattering the cows.

'I'm gonna give him away.'

Ethan felt his horse shudder.

'Give him away?'

'Well, I figure now you've got your fencin' finished on Emma Fergusen's property I could go ahead and give you your wedding present. I want you and Katie Anne to come out here tomorrow and cut fifteen cows outta this herd and put 'em to pasture with Old Paco on your place.'

Tom reached over and slapped Ethan firmly on the back.

'Welcome to Chase County,' he said.

Katie Anne said she wasn't feeling well the next morning, so Ethan cut the cows with Tom and one of the Mackey cowhands. They drove the small herd back over Jacob's Mound and at the top of the hill Ethan thought he could hear the faint strains of a violin in the distance. But he kept his eyes fastened to the cow rumps and would not look toward the east. His heart pounded in his chest like the horses' hooves pounded the dry winter ground, and he laughed a strangled, miserable laugh when he thought of Ulysses lashing himself to the mast. Tom Mackey must have heard him laugh because he looked over at him and grinned. Ethan was drowned in guilt.

He spent the rest of the day on his property. The house was nearing completion, thanks to the unseasonably warm and dry winter, and Ethan poked around the construction site, inspecting tiles and moldings and insulation and anything else that could possibly need his attention. By the time he got home, Katie Anne had already gone down to the main ranch, where they were to dine with her parents.

Tom Mackey was unusually voluble that evening. He had just taken delivery on a new Cessna, and when Ethan arrived he opened up a bottle of champagne he'd chilled just for the occasion. Ethan didn't particularly care for champagne but he drank to keep Tom company and to muddle his brain. Katie Anne looked especially pretty. She had gone into Strong City that afternoon to have her hair cut and her nails done, and she threw shy, seductive smiles at him when her parents weren't looking. It reminded Ethan of the evenings they had spent together when they first met, flirtatious and hesitant.

During dinner Ethan drank too much champagne and Katie Anne drank nothing at all. He got the impression she was watching him without looking at him, and the more he drank, the more uncomfortable he became. He listened to Tom talk about his basic training as a pilot during World War II out at Luke Field in Arizona. How the guys used to fly their little propeller-driven Steerman planes out over the desert in 125-degree weather. How they would buzz the saguaro cacti, flying so low they'd make the tall gangly things sway. Tom Mackey was his savior. His father. Tom was all he had now. Tom wouldn't abandon him.

He glanced over at Katie Anne. She hadn't eaten much. She was scratching at something on the tablecloth with a pale frosted pink nail. He looked away, back at Tom, because he was acutely aware of the dryness he felt as he looked at her. Damn. What would he do without Tom?

After dinner Ethan glued himself to the old man. They went into Tom's office to look over the prospectus on the new Cessna, and Katie Anne stood in the doorway, watching them. After a moment, she walked over to where her father sat and wrapped her arms around his neck.

'Guys, I'm tired. I'm gonna take my Jeep and go on home.' She glanced up at Ethan. 'You mind, honey?'

He looked up at her and found himself trapped in a

gaze of startling transparency. Her eyes appeared to him as pools of astonishing sharpness and clarity, and at their depths shimmered all those confounding things of the heart that Ethan so feared. He looked quickly away.

'I'll take you home,' he muttered and started to rise.

'No,' she answered quickly. 'Stay with Dad.' She kissed her father's cheek. 'You guys look like you're havin' fun.'

Tom Mackey patted his daughter's hand. 'You feelin' okay?'

'I'm fine. Just tired, that's all.'

'You sure are lookin' pretty tonight.'

'Thanks, Daddy,' she whispered.

After she left, Ethan had a hard time focusing on his conversation with Tom. Betty Sue made him down several cups of hot coffee before she let him go home.

When Ethan walked up the front steps to the guest ranch the lights were off, but he saw a ghostly flicker from the television set coming from the bedroom and he knew she was still awake. He was just hoping to get through another evening. Just one more evening. He'd get through this.

He undressed and got into bed next to her.

'You want me to turn this off?' she asked.

'What is it?'

'I don't know. Some old movie.'

'Who's in it?'

She shrugged. 'I don't know.'

The remote control was lying on her stomach. For a long time he watched the thin black rectangular box rise and fall with her breathing.

'Katie Anne?'

'Yeah?'

'We need to talk.'

She picked up the remote control and turned off the television. Then, without a word, she pulled the blankets up around her neck and curled up with her back to him.

Ethan was quiet. He lay staring at the dark ceiling for a long time, then he turned his back to her and fell asleep.

Thunder woke him in the night, and he looked over and saw she wasn't there. He found her sitting on the front porch steps, her knees pulled up under her chin and her robe wrapped around her legs.

'What're you doing out here? It's cold,' he said from the doorway.

Lightning crackled in the distance, momentarily lighting up the sky, revealing the high, heavy clouds slowly rolling across the southern sky.

'God, we need this rain,' she said.

Thunder shook the earth. Ethan looked down to see

Traveler come padding up and quietly sit down next to him. He reached down and scratched the animal behind his ears. Katie Anne had never taken much of a liking to the dog, and so he never went to her, even if he was hungry or thirsty or worried. He always sat and watched her from a distance. But tonight he did something extra-ordinary. He left Ethan and went and lay down next to Katie Anne. Absentmindedly, without thinking, she reached out her hand and stroked his back. Ethan saw her shoulders shake and he knew she was crying. He looked away, back at the sky, at the dramatic struggle of the elements, but out of the corner of his eye he could still see her shoulders moving.

'I'm sorry, hon,' he said quietly. That's all he said. He thought maybe he should say more, but he couldn't find the words.

Ethan turned and went back inside. Traveler watched him go, but he stayed next to Katie Anne. Only when he heard the truck engine start up did he jump up and trot around the house and wait, sitting, alert, until Ethan whistled and he sailed over the tailgate into the back of the truck.

Ethan threw down his sleeping bag on the hard wooden floor of his new house and Traveler lay down beside him. He slept late, long after sunrise, and was awakened by one of the construction workers. He went down to the old Reilly house and took a cold shower, then he sat on the porch in the cold March wind and waited for Annette.

'Mornin', ma'am,' he said as she got out of the car and walked toward him, violin case in one hand and a Thermos in the other. She wore an old sheepskin jacket he had found at the back of his closet and given her. It was stained and dirty but she said she didn't mind. He loved seeing her in it. It made her belong to him.

'You haven't shaved,' she said as she stood over him.

'Nope,' he said.

She drew her fingers down his cheek. He caught her hand and pressed the open palm to his lips. A wave of desire passed through her, and she pulled her hand away. He rose and followed her inside the house.

She unscrewed the Thermos and poured a cup of steaming coffee for him. They sat at the kitchen table and looked at each other as they sipped their coffee.

'You've never seen the house I'm building, have you?'

She smiled. 'I've sneaked a look from time to time.'

'What do you think of it?'

'It's big. It's not finished. What can I say?' she teased.

He looked down at the placid surface of the coffee, feeling the blood pounding through his veins.

'Why?' she asked softly. 'Is it important what I think?'

Thunder rolled in the distance, and Ethan looked out the window to see dark, heavy clouds scudding swiftly through the sky, covering the sun.

'We sure need some rain,' he sighed.

'Ethan. Why is it important?'

Suddenly his face drew up, as if he were in great pain. She reached out and touched his cheek.

'Ethan,' she whispered.

'I've done more soul searchin' these past few months than I've ever done in my life.'

'Ethan, what have you done?'

Now she held his hand, running her fingers through his. The feel of his skin against hers made her ache. Her eyelids grew heavy, drugged by desire.

Ethan withdrew his hand from hers and reached over to unbutton her blouse.

'Ethan,' she murmured. Her eyes were nearly closed. 'Ethan, I can't stop you.'

Purposefully, without the slightest hesitation, he stood and came around the table to her. He lifted her out of her chair, and in a flurry of movement, with her hands fluttering helplessly about his, he undressed her. As he fumbled with his shirt, he was swallowed up by a wave of outrage toward every person and every thing that had kept him away from her, and he tore at their clothing with the urgency of a prisoner hacking at his chains. When he was finally free, he laid her back on the table, gathering her up tightly in his arms, and it seemed that she was drawing him in with her whole body. All of a sudden he felt her wince and grab the table.

'I'm sorry,' he whispered as he pulled back. 'God, I'm sorry.' He looked down at her milky white skin against the dark stained wood. 'I didn't want it to happen like this.'

She kissed the top of his head. His hair was damp and cool against her lips.

'Is this ...' She paused. Her voice was a throaty whisper. 'Is this all we'll ever have?'

He lifted his eyes to meet hers.

'Do you want more?' he asked, and he began to move again, very gently.

Suddenly, her face became like a child's, full of tenderness and vulnerability, and in those terrible moments Ethan felt bound to her like to no other thing on the face of the earth. It came upon her without warning, and Ethan felt himself go with her. He heard her cry out, and from his own lungs burst forth strange deep savage sounds he did not recognize as his own.

A cold rain had begun to fall so lightly that it landed with all the stillness of snow. Ethan and Annette, wrapped in their coats, lay together on the floor in front of the dark fireplace. The air was cold, and Annette burrowed into Ethan's arms.

'What are you going to do with the house?' she asked.

'Nothing.'

'You're not going to tear it down?'

'I wasn't planning on it.'

'Good.'

She laid her head on his chest.

'This has changed everything,' she said in a low voice. 'That's why I was hoping to get away. To get out of here. Before this happened.'

Ethan was quiet for a long time, but he held her close to him.

'How has it changed things?' he asked finally.

She shook her head. 'Don't make me make a fool of myself.'

'Ah, yes. We're so afraid of looking like fools, aren't we?'

'Don't torture me. Please.'

'What's changed?' he asked.

She hesitated. 'The way I see this place. Maybe I'm beginning to see it the way you do.'

'Annette,' he began. His voice was tight in his throat. 'Annette, could you live here? With me?'

She shivered. 'I'm cold.' She started to get up, but he stopped her.

'Answer me.'

'I think I could,' she said as she knelt before him.

Suddenly Ethan felt tears sting his eyes. He turned

away and stared out the window. Fat raindrops hung on the glass panes.

'Then I'm yours,' he said quietly. 'You've had my heart and soul for a long time. Now I'm all yours. Just give me some time to work things out.'

She looked down at him, but she didn't ask any questions.

'I want you again,' she whispered.

'You can have me,' he answered with a kiss. 'Every damn day from here on, you can have me.'

'Will you come here again?'

'Every day. And I'll bring a bed next time I come.'

'Don't wait. Do it today,' she replied.

'You know, I think I just might do that,' he said, grinning. 'Say, would you mind if I slept out here?'

She laughed. 'For heaven's sake, Ethan, it's your house.'

'But will I disturb you?'

'I'm only out here in the mornings. It's not like I sleep out here.'

She caught the look in his eyes, and she kissed his face tenderly. 'I love you, Ethan,' she whispered.

'Could you?' he asked. 'Sleep out here sometimes?'

'I'd have to come late. And leave early.'

'Would you do it?'

'Yes.'

The rain began to come down heavily now and they

184

fell silent. Ethan thought what a mess his life was, and how gloriously happy he was.

He got into the office around ten. He was unshaven and his shirt was wrinkled, and Bonnie stared at him, but he kept her busy enough to divert her attention, and he got away at noon without having to answer any questions. He got up his courage to go back to the guest ranch to pick up some clothing and some of his things, and his heart pounded so hard on the way over there that he almost turned back. He relaxed when he saw Katie Anne's Wrangler was gone, and he quickly threw a few things in a duffel bag, snatched up Traveler's dishes and his bag of food, grabbed a few books and some CDs and hurried out again. He didn't want to run into her like this, like a thief in the night. He wanted her to sit down and listen to him. To what he'd been trying to say and couldn't.

He had to drive up to Emporia to get the bed. He had called around from his office that morning and located a place that could get him what he wanted that very day, and with the help of the warehouse man he loaded the thing onto his truck and drove the back roads through the hills to the Reilly house, hoping he wouldn't pass anyone he knew along the way. As he drove along he had a sudden flash of what his life would be. How all the habits and customs he'd built over the years would be halted, abruptly, dealt a deathblow. His ordered life was in upheaval. He thought how he had so deftly evaded this storm for so many years, how he had hidden from it, and then it sat down right on top of him. Right out here in the middle of nowhere.

After he'd set up the bed he went back to work in his office. It was quiet and Bonnie was gone, and there was no one to ask him any questions. When he came back to the old house it was almost eleven at night, and Annette was sitting on the bed reading a book.

'This is brand new, isn't it?' she commented as he walked in.

'You bet. It's ours.'

'Well. That's quite a commitment,' she said with a grin. 'Why'd you get such a big one?'

'Don't you think we'll use it?'

'Is it for sleeping?'

'Eventually. When we're old and gray.'

' "And full of sleep / And nodding by the fire..." ' He took the book from her hands and stretched out alongside her.

' "Take down this book / And slowly read, and dream of the soft look / Your eyes had once..." '

For a long while they looked at each other in silence. The night was black around them, and it stared in through the naked windows at the two figures in heavy winter coats lying together on an unclothed bed. A bare bulb in the kitchen shed its faint light on them. The setting lent an air of fragility to them, although there was nothing fragile about their love; it was cast for eternity. It was their bodies that seemed vulnerable to all this nakedness surrounding them, as if the night might reach in with its dark fingers and pluck them apart.

They felt it, this ominous presence of the night, and so they turned off the light and pulled the sleeping bag over them, and buried themselves deep in each other's warmth. This time he made gentle, quiet love to her, and she responded with whimpers and sighs, so quietly that the night, with all its ears, could not hear them.

Nineteen

Annette awoke in the pitch dark to the sound of her name – Annie. Only her mother had ever called her Annie. She lay awake, listening, but she heard only the wind. She had slept soundly and peacefully in Ethan's arms. Not once had she moved. Nor had she dreamed. There was just this voice calling her.

She rose and pulled on her jeans. Ethan awoke.

'What time is it?' he asked. He stroked the side of her arm while she put on her boots.

'I don't know. I can't see my watch.'

'Is something wrong?'

'I don't know. I'm just worried. If Eliana should wake up and find me gone ...'

Ethan sat up. 'Can you drive okay? You want me to follow you into town?'

'I'll be fine.' She turned and kissed him. 'When will I see you?'

'I'll come by around lunchtime,' he said. 'I want you to come over to see the house.'

Ethan lay awake and worried about her after she had gone. He told himself he'd have the phone connected the next day. He'd come early in the evening and make a fire in the fireplace, and he'd bring some sheets and blankets. It struck him that he had never bothered with this kind of thing before. Not ever. Not for any woman.

Ethan went back to Katie Anne's place later that morning. She was standing in the kitchen boiling water as he walked in, and she turned her back to him and cinched up her bathrobe. Ethan sat down at the table.

'We're going to have to talk,' he said finally.

'No. Correction. Excuse me. *You're* gonna talk.'

She poured some boiling water into a mug and turned to face him.

'I can't do this,' he said.

'Can't do what? What is it exactly that you can't do?'

'I can't marry you.'

She dipped a tea bag in and out of the water. Up and down. Again and again. Emotions washed across her face, but she said nothing. Finally, she turned and went back into the bedroom and closed the door.

Ethan took his shower, shaved, and dressed. When he came out of the bathroom she was standing at his desk looking over the blueprints of his new house.

'Where are you sleeping?' she asked. The question

confused him momentarily. It was the blueprints.

'I've got a place. Temporarily.'

Her shoulders relaxed a little.

'Let's just put it off. Let's wait.' She walked up to him and laid her hand on his chest. 'It's not too late. I mean, it'll be a nightmare. After all the plans Mom and Dad have made. But we can still do it.'

She wrapped her arms around him. 'I know how scared you get.' She was naked underneath the short terry robe. 'Come back home. Please.'

She felt so familiar to him. So known. He stroked her back and closed his eyes, wishing himself away from this moment. Deftly, she began to unbuckle his belt.

'Don't,' he urged, but she ignored him and slid down to her knees. He looked down at her rumpled hair, at the pink nails, one of them chipped, as they fumbled with the buttons on his pants. He tried to take her face in his hands. 'I've hurt you enough. Don't make it worse. Please, baby. Don't make it worse.'

'I love you so much, you bastard,' she said. Her voice was choked with tears and she pushed his hand away when he tried to stop her. Finally, he pulled her to her feet.

'Don't,' he said again, more firmly, and suddenly all her pain burst forth, exploding from her chest in long, strangled sobs. He let go of her and turned away.

'Look at me, damn you, you bastard! Can't you even

look at me?' she wailed, and when he looked around she slapped him hard on the face. Her eyes were swollen and red, and tears streamed down her cheeks. Never had he seen her so enraged.

'I never cry, 'cause you can't stand it!' she screamed. 'So I never cried in front of you but boy if you only knew!' She pulled her robe close around her, as though to shield herself. 'If you only knew how much I hid from you! How much I'm still hiding from you! Because I know it'd just scare you away! Well, take a look at me now! And, goddamn you, you remember what it looks like! When you're lookin' into her eyes, you remember mine!'

She ran out of the room, back into her bedroom, and slammed the door. Ethan stood in stunned silence, listening to her cry. Then he picked up the blueprints, gathered up all the papers on his desk, and walked out of the house. He was numb but cleansed. Purged. Her anger had done it for him. He was deeply grateful to her for that.

 Ethan pulled up in front of the old house a little after noon and Annette ran out and hopped into the truck. She was breathless and exuberant. So very different from the woman who had been waiting to greet him in his office six months before.

He made a quick turn around the yard and headed back to the road. 'I was worried about you this morning.'

'I'm fine.' She turned a smile on him, and the joy on her face swept away all his guilt and pain.

'And Eliana?'

'She woke up just after I got home. She was having a nightmare. She doesn't have nightmares very often.'

Ethan reached behind the seat, pulled out a brown paper bag and set it on her lap. 'Have you had lunch?'

'What's this?' she asked, opening the bag.

'Jack's chilli dogs. Better than Sonic's.'

'You're Christmas!' she laughed, and she rolled back the aluminum paper and bit into the dog. 'I was starved,' she mumbled, brushing a crumb of bread from the corner of her mouth.

It was a clear, cold day. Winter had returned and the sky was a seamless pale blue against the dry, brown winter hills.

'It's beautiful.'

'What?'

'All this.' She waved her napkin at the immense land that stretched around her, at the hills, at the wide expanse of sky filled with armies of clouds hanging so low Annette felt she could reach up and touch them.

'You think you could handle it?' he asked.

'Yes,' she nodded. 'I could. I know I could.'

'It's a different life. You won't get bored?'

'With you?' she laughed and finished off the chilli dog with one last big bite. 'I love you desperately,' she mumbled. She felt tears sting her eyes as she said it and she tried to brush them away.

'Move over here next to me,' he said softly.

She wadded up the foil and wiped her hands on the napkin and stuffed it back in the bag. Then she slid over next to him and laid her head on his shoulder.

'Have you told her?' she asked quietly.

'Yeah.'

'How did she take it?'

'Not well.'

'That was to be expected.'

'I didn't handle it too well. I'm not very good at that kind of thing. I don't like hurting people.'

'I'm afraid for you, Ethan. I'm afraid of what they'll all do to you.'

'What do you mean?'

'Jer told me Tom Mackey's one of your biggest clients.'

'Jer told you that?'

'Yes.'

'Now why would Jer be talking to you about Tom Mackey?'

'I don't think he was implying anything.'

'Like hell he wasn't.'

'It just came up in conversation.'

'When was this?'

'Oh, I don't know. After one of Eliana's lessons.'

'Well, Tom Mackey's a big client, but he's not my only client. I have clients all throughout the state. People who don't even know Tom Mackey.'

'What do you think he'll do?'

'Honey, Tom Mackey doesn't have a shotgun pointed at my head.'

'I'm afraid you'll regret it.'

'And what about you?'

'Will I regret it?'

'Yes.'

'I'll be terribly homesick, I suppose. And I'll never really fit in.'

'I don't think I'd ever want you to.'

Ethan came to the crest of a hill and the house came into view. He slowed and turned off the pavement onto a narrow dirt road.

'What about your career?' he asked.

She reflected for a moment. 'Maybe I could still tour. A little.'

'You bet you could. It's not big time like you're used to, but there are plenty of good orchestras in the region.'

'I don't care about big time. I just want to perform again.'

'Well, I want you to think about it. Think about it all before it's too late.'

'When is too late?'

'When you marry me.'

She grew quiet.

'You will marry me, won't you?' he said.

She looked up at him. 'Do you really mean that?'

'If you only knew ...'

'When?'

He put his arm around her and whispered, 'This week.'

'This week?!'

'Tomorrow.'

'Ethan!'

'I'm afraid I'll lose you.'

'You're not going to lose me. I'm not going anywhere.'

Ethan pulled up and stopped in front of the house. It was built on the back of the hill, with the top floor facing south and the two lower floors looking north. The view was spectacular.

'It's almost finished.' He turned to look at her. 'You think you'll like it?'

She grinned up at him. 'Do you know how many times I've driven out here?'

'You told me you'd never been out here.'

'What I said was I'd sneaked a look from time to time.'

'I had no idea.'

'I was always afraid I'd run into you.' She tugged on his sleeve. 'Now, show me the kitchen.'

   When Ethan got back to the office there was a note on his desk from Katie Anne. Bonnie said she had come over to deliver it herself. Ethan opened a beer and sat down to read it.

Dearest Ethan,

   I know I should have talked about this to you this morning, but I just couldn't. I couldn't stand to see your face when I told you. I've known for a long time that something was wrong. We've gone through a lot of ups and downs over the last three years, and I think I know you pretty well. I could tell something was wrong. You were just different somehow. I was just hoping you'd get over it.

   Ethan, I'm going to have a baby. Please believe me when I say I didn't do this on purpose. You know I'm not ready to have kids. You know I'm not even really crazy about kids. And I wanted you all to myself. For a while at least.

   Nobody's going to force you to marry me. I haven't told Daddy yet. I haven't told anybody yet.

But I want you to know I'm going to keep it. I couldn't possibly do anything else. If it was somebody else's baby I might think different. But if this is all I'll have of you, then I'm going to have to love him twice as much, to make up for not being able to love you.

Katie Anne

Ethan's phone was ringing, but he didn't answer it. His stomach felt as if it had caved in, and he found it difficult to swallow. The entire room seemed to press in upon him. After a dozen rings, Bonnie came up the stairs and looked in.

'It's Mrs McNeil. Can you take it?' she asked.

Ethan shook his head and motioned her away.

'Ethan, are you okay?'

He turned his back to her. 'Take messages for me. I need to go out.' His voice sounded odd – high and strained.

'You sure you're okay?'

He grabbed his hat and coat and stuffed the letter into his coat pocket.

'I'm fine, Bonnie,' he muttered as he brushed by her.

* * *

The damp frigid air bit into his nostrils as he stood at the pump gassing up the truck. The skies had changed abruptly, and now low, gray clouds stretched like a lid from horizon to horizon. It would snow soon. He headed east along dirt roads through the hills until he ran into the interstate and took it to Beto Junction. It was snowing heavily when he pulled into the truck stop. For a long time he sat in the parking lot with the snow spinning around him, drawing itself over him in layers like the veils of a playful, flirtatious spirit, but his attention was drawn inward to other landscapes. The clouds obscured the sun and the night came upon him so gently he barely noticed it. Time was marked by the gravel crunching under the wide tires of the pickups and semis as they came and went, the beams from their headlamps capturing the snow caught unaware in its lunacy.

The thoughts that danced into his mind that evening reeled with the same chaotic confusion as the snow. Rational thought had abandoned him the moment he had stuffed the letter in his pocket. He was, instead, overwhelmed with feeling. He was aware of a stifling sense of weight, a heaviness that seemed to cut his breath short and hobble every movement. His spirit lay inert.

He sat until he was stiff and cold. Finally he drove

across the road to a little convenience store and got himself a cup of hot coffee. He had skipped dinner, something he hadn't done since his father died. He looked over the sandwiches in the store and finally bought a packaged ham-and-cheese and took it out to his truck, but he had no appetite for it, and it sat on the seat beside him as he drank the coffee. He started the engine and headed back into the storm. He knew Annette would be waiting for him by now.

His decision that night was made, quite literally, at the fork of a road. Afterward he made himself believe that there was some hand of fate at work here, but he knew this was not true. What lurked deep and nameless inside him was the ugly face of cowardice, and Ethan was too proud to recognize it. And so he continued straight, down the old county road that he had traveled countless times and would travel until the end of his life. He drove on in the night, the miles between them increasing with each minute, and the more he tried to imagine his life without Annette, the stronger her image burned into his mind, like a bright star of high magnitude burning hot in a cold night sky, its warmth dissipated by a distance of years, yet its beauty outshining all others. Countless times he stopped the car and started to go back, but each time the ugliness seemed to loom up around him, and his heart would start pounding in his chest. So he drove on, cautiously, for the road was barely visible through the blinding snow, and there was nothing to mark the distance he had traveled except the onward motion of his truck. Outside his windows, all looked the same. After a while, the darkness and the dancing snow before him dulled his senses, and gradually a veil descended upon his heart, and it grew distant and cold, retreating deep into the cavernous recesses of his soul. He willed it so.

When he finally reached the house, it was nearly two in the morning. Katie Anne was in bed, asleep. He undressed in the dark and crawled in next to her. She awoke and rolled over and put her arms around him, snuggling up against his back, wrapping her legs around his.

'You're cold,' she whispered.

'Yes,' he replied, and Annette burst out of his heart, flooding him with her presence the way fireworks explode in a summer sky and children, gasping in awe, stretch their necks upward and try to memorize for ever the fleeting colors and beauty before they dissipate into gray smoke and float away on the night breeze. 'Yes,' he repeated, 'I'm cold,' and with his back to her he curled up like a little boy protecting a secret treasure buried deep in his chest.

Katie Anne drew her fingers down his back, but when she saw he was not responding she quietly rolled over to her own side of the bed. It was good that she did so.

Twenty

After the night of his return, Katie Anne handled Ethan with deft skill. She knew exactly where she could lead him and where he would drink, and she never tried to tempt him down a path where she might encounter resistance. She gave him nothing to worry about and nothing to dispute. He worked at his office every day, including Sundays, for he showed no more interest in mass. She ate alone each evening, without so much as a sigh of complaint, for he returned late at night and ate his evening meals before coming home. Patti said one evening he had come into Hannah's for dinner but that French woman was in there with her father and daughter, and Ethan turned around and walked out again. After that Ethan went all the way to Beto Junction every night for dinner.

There was no more intimacy between them. Ethan slept in the guest room and was often gone before she awoke in the morning. He called her from the office, always perfectly agreeable. She told him she preferred not to tell her parents, or anyone else, about her pregnancy until after the wedding. Ethan agreed, and nothing else was ever said about the subject.

Despite his cooperativeness, Katie Anne feared she still might lose him at any moment. She counted the days until the wedding. She took to leaving Ethan little notes about wedding arrangements in order to avoid speaking to him. Ethan refused the traditional bachelor party that Jer wanted to throw at the South Forty, but he graciously handled all the arrangements for the groom's dinner following the rehearsal. If Katie Anne was wary, Tom and Betty Sue seemed placated. Ethan was polite and respectful as always, although not once was he able to find time in his schedule to come over for dinner in those last four weeks before the wedding. Even Jer saw very little of him. Ethan called him a week before the wedding and asked him for help moving all his furniture into his new house from the storage where he had kept it while he had been living with Katie Anne. Then there was the stable to finish, and his clients to service.

His mother and sister arrived in town the afternoon before the wedding, and he put them up at his new house. Ethan spent the night there with them. He said it was to keep them company, and also out of what he confessed was a twisted sense of propriety. It vexed Katie Anne, but she never breathed a word of displeasure to Ethan. His mother's presence was a balm to him. They played rummy until after midnight, and then, while Ethan was reading, she worked on the *Washington Post* crossword puzzles that Ethan had clipped and saved for her. At one in the morning, she finally laid down her newspaper and said, 'Go to bed, son. The night will go by quickly enough.' She kissed him on top of his head and went off to her bedroom. For a brief moment Ethan allowed himself to imagine an encounter between the two of them, Annette and his mother. He saw her standing there at the top of the stairs, all deference and respect, listening to his mother with that quiet, intense way she had to let others know she was all there, all theirs. Then the vision departed, and he turned off the light and went upstairs to bed.

At six o'clock the next morning his mother found him in the new stable laying down fresh straw for his horses. Mary made him put down the pitchfork and shower and shave, then they all went over to Hannah's for breakfast. At ten o'clock, Ethan, dressed in his tux, deposited his mother and sister at the Mackey ranch, where the eleven o'clock ceremony was to take place, with the understanding that he would pick up Jer and be back by ten-thirty. By ten-fifty, when Ethan had not yet shown up, Jer was dispatched to find him. Only by chance did Jer catch a glimpse of Ethan's truck sitting in the parking lot of the South Forty.

The South Forty was an ugly place at ten-thirty in the morning, and it looked particularly ugly to Ethan after his fifth beer. He had removed his tuxedo jacket and laid it on the stool next to him, and his starched white shirt glared back at him from the mirror behind the bar. On the countertop in a puddle of spilled beer lay his bow tie. Marty was running a vacuum somewhere behind him so that Ethan didn't hear Jer when he came in.

'Come on, buddy,' said Jer. 'Let's go.'

The sight of Jer in a tux brought a glimmer of amusement into Ethan's eyes.

'Finally got you into that penguin suit, didn't she?'

'I'm doin' it for you, pal,' said Jer.

'Well, if you're doin' it for me, who am I doin' it for?'

He had a crooked smile on his face as he started on his sixth beer.

'Let's go, Ethan. Everybody's waitin'.'

'I'm comin',' he mumbled, and slowly brought the bottle to his mouth.

'You're gonna make a fool out of yourself. And Katie Anne too.'

'I've already done that.'

Jer couldn't get Marty's attention over the roar of the vacuum so he went behind the counter and found two mugs and filled them with hot coffee. He slid one over to Ethan, took his beer, and dumped it into the sink.

'Is she there?' Ethan asked, staring down at the chipped mug.

'She's there. Waitin'. Got a little ticked off when you disappeared, but she's coverin' pretty well.'

'I mean Annette.'

'No.' Jer blew on his coffee. 'You didn't expect her, did you?'

'Katie Anne sent her an invitation.'

'Yeah, well, that's Katie Anne for ya.'

Ethan sipped the coffee. 'Thanks for comin', Jer.'

'I was worried, buddy. I've never seen you like this before.'

'I've never been like this before.'

Jer glanced at his watch.

'What time is it?'

'We've got three minutes. Then you gotta walk down the aisle.'

Ethan nodded and took a long gulp of the coffee.

'You gonna make it?'

'Yeah, I'll be okay.'

Ethan gave him a level gaze. He suddenly looked very sober. 'When's she leaving?'

'End of the week, Friday,' answered Jer.

Ethan nodded. 'She got her ticket changed.'

'Not as soon as she wanted.'

'Yeah.'

'Things'll be better when she's gone.'

'Yeah.' Ethan sighed. 'Yeah, you're right.'

At that moment, Ethan was on the verge of telling Jer all that had happened: how he had lifted the phone countless times to call her, even dialed the number; how he had driven by her house, early in the morning and late at night, lurking like a lovesick kid in the dark, hoping to see a glimpse of her in the lighted window. But he knew what he would find, what he would see in her eyes and hear in her voice, those awful things that would demand recognition, things he was so loath to confront. As time went on it seemed so much easier to withdraw behind a wall of silence and let the others wrestle with truth and pain.

Ethan picked up his bow tie from the counter. It was damp from the beer. He snapped it on and picked up his jacket.

'Let's go, buddy,' he said to Jer.

From that moment on, Ethan was swept along by the events. At the altar he stared solemnly at the clerical collar of the Presbyterian minister Katie Anne had chosen to marry them, a soft jowled man with an earnest smile, an old friend of the Mackey family whom Ethan had never met. To his relief, Katie Anne had opted for traditional vows; at one time she had wanted them to write their own, but Ethan was not at all interested. She had also thought about using some of his favorite poetry in the ceremony, but he was so uncooperative she soon abandoned that idea, too. Consequently, Ethan found no surprises awaiting him that morning. He pledged to love and honor her in sickness and in health, and to forsake all others. When he said the last part, it seemed to him her smile quivered just slightly, or maybe it was just a movement of her veil from her breath.

Ethan had expected the ceremony to make a difference. But to his surprise he awoke Sunday morning still longing for Annette. He wondered how that was possible, given the eroticism of the night before. Katie Anne had videotaped herself dancing naked and gave the tape to him that night as a wedding present. Ethan had succumbed, losing himself in the sheer pleasure of lusty, uninhibited sex, but in the morning, while he was pounding nails into the tack room wall, he finally admitted to himself that his love for Katie Anne had died. He thought that one day he might be able to tolerate her again, even enjoy her, but never love her. In a way this realization was a relief to him, and with an open face he sat down to the lunch she had prepared, and was more congenial than he had been in the past four weeks. Katie Anne noticed the change in him but she thought it was because of their wedding night. She knew he'd come around. With time.

The weather had finally cooperated. At long last they had their rain. And the winds were just right. It was one hell of a way to spend a honeymoon, as more than one friend or neighbor had commented, but Ethan was too engrossed in strategy to pay much attention to local gossip. There were the backfires to plan, the cattle to move to safer ground, the neighbors and authorities to notify, the heavy equipment to commandeer, and troops to enlist. For years Ethan had helped his neighbors with their spring burn. He'd driven trucks mounted with water tanks, pulled huge sprayers behind his tractor, or wielded fire sticks alongside other ranchers. They worked in parallel lines stringing fire across the prairie, men and women on foot, on the backs of feed trucks, on four-wheelers, igniting the brown winter grass with friendly napalm dripping from ten-foot pipes. He'd worked the mop-up crew, beating out little fingers of unruly fire with paddles and rakes. When they were done he always looked out at the blackened hills, black like the color of death, and marveled at the potency of fire and the phoenix-like regenerative power of nature, at how life and death were so mysteriously one. For in less than a week the new bluestem would appear under-neath the blackened crust, tiny green sprouts bursting with nutrients. Then they'd turn the cattle loose again, and the beasts would nudge aside the charred earth with their soft, broad lips and nibble on the green, juicy blades that tasted better than anything else in the world. The bluestem would grow quickly now, and so would the cattle. So would the pockets of the ranchers who owned them.

Now it was Ethan's turn to burn. With Tom's help he had carefully assessed the weather and the wind and planned the burn with military precision. This was his land. He had sacrificed his personal happiness in order to remain on it. Its conservation was his salvation.

Ethan stood on the bed of his truck and surveyed the burning hills. It was a spectacular sight with the red flames outlining the hills against the night sky. The burn had gone well, and the county firefighting crew that had been in a state of readiness throughout the day was now preparing to move on. His attention was torn away from the hills by the blue-and-red strobing light of the Sheriff's patrol car as it bounced down the dirt road toward them. The patrol car stopped next to Ethan's truck and the fire chief got out of the passenger side and came up to Ethan.

'How're we doing?' asked Ethan as he jumped down.

'Looks good. Fire's out by the tree line up north. It was

touch 'n' go there for a while. Sure felt like that wind was changin' on us.'

'We're about finished with the mop-up down here.'

'We're leavin' one truck over there next to the fire-break, where you've still got some flames. We're sendin' the other units back to the station.'

'Good enough.'

    When Ethan stepped under the shower that night and felt the cool water stream over his face and through his hair, he realized he had not thought of Annette all day. It was the work that did it. The physical labor. It had drained his body and mind. For the first time in months it felt as though chaos no longer threatened the orderliness of his world.

Twenty-one

It was dark in the kitchen. Dawn had not yet tinted the eastern sky. Annette sat at the small yellow Formica table, the very same one at which she had eaten as a girl, and she remembered the times she had stared out another window, not unlike this one, at the flat wheat fields of western Kansas buzzing with crickets in the hot summer sun and wished herself away. But this morning the only sound was the wind. Usually the winds calmed before dawn, but not today. It was her send-off. Her farewell. How she hated these winds. Her enemy came to bid her good-bye.

She glanced at her watch. It was not yet five o'clock. The coffee maker spurted its last few drops into the glass carafe and she rose, poured herself a cup of coffee, then opened the window. A sudden blast of warm air blew the curtains into her face. It would be a warm day. But she would be gone before the end of it. Everything was ready. For two days she had been ready. Their suitcases were packed, tickets and passports on top of her dresser next to her handbag. For over a week she had not been able to sleep or eat, so anxious was she that something might prevent her from going. Her father had been surprisingly agreeable about her early departure, for at Christmas they had decided to let Eliana finish out the school year and depart in June. But of course that was all changed now. She wondered how much her father knew. How much everyone knew. She had no way of knowing, and no one to ask. Only Jer. And Jer had revealed nothing. He was like a rock.

She had waited that night until the snow covered her old Buick in a wispy white blanket, and then she had written a note to Ethan, extinguished the fire in the fireplace, and gone back home. She had called the next morning and left a message with Bonnie, but her call was never returned. For many days she waited for him. She sped away each morning from Eliana's school, her heart racing in her chest with the anticipation of seeing him, hoping she would find a note from him or get a call. She rehearsed there in the old house each morning, for hours on end, keeping the swelling spring at bay with the sad melodies of Mahler and Gorecki, her sadness resounding through the hills each morning, carried on the waves of warm spring air, until even the beasts and the birds paused in their jubilant heraldry of the new season and listened to her.

Finally, she broke down and called him again. This time Bonnie was cool and evasive. She left another message; this, too, went unanswered. After that she quit going to the old house. The bed Ethan had purchased still sat in the living room, its twenty-year warranty blazoned on a satin banner across the corner. He never came to get it and she could not bear to look at it.

Every Friday when she left Matthew Winegarner's home she walked quickly to her car with her eyes straight ahead, determined not to look up and perhaps find his face framed in the window or, worse, not find it there at all. And every Thursday, when she drove out to Jer's to pick up Eliana after her riding lesson, a terrible sensation invaded her stomach, and her knees and arms grew weak, for fear that she might find him there or, even worse, not find him there at all. Jer looked at her differently now. There was an element of reticence in his already quiet demeanor that Annette found troubling. He seemed to want to avoid conversation with her, so Annette quit coming early to watch as she used to, and the last few weeks she took to waiting in her car.

When the wedding invitation came in the mail, she sat down and started a letter to him.

Ethan,

I just received your wedding invitation. I can't imagine it was intended in good faith. But I thank you for it, nonetheless. At least it has made things clear. Which you did not.

You flee. You run. You hide. What cowardice. I had always suspected this in you. From that first afternoon in the Sonic Drive-In when you told me about your son. If I were your son, I would hate you, too.

How, in God's precious name, can you love those poets and all those men of letters who mint their misery when misery is so distasteful to you! Conflict was their gold, and their pens flew to heaven on wings of despair.

Ethan, the Flint Hills are not everyone's Band-Aid. Yes, you love it here. But do you really think a summer out on the open range will cure Jeremy's adolescent depression? Did you expect a pleasant morning bass fishing in your little pond would cure Katie Anne's broken heart?

You told me how you had worried about your mother after your father's death. That she seemed 'down', you said. 'She didn't go so far as to break down and cry, but I was afraid she might.' Those were your words. When I expressed my astonishment at your attitude, you replied, 'I just want her *to be happy.' For God's sake, Ethan, she'd just lost the man who'd shared her life for fifty-three years. And you expect her to be happy? If she were happy, then you should worry! And what if she had broken down in tears? Would that have been truly unbearable to you? Oh, Ethan, how wrong you've got it. It used to be that women wore black for years after the death of their husbands. They wore their misery, their tears, their depression for everyone to see and acknowledge. Death is to be mourned. Lost love is to be grieved. Not shaken off. Not ignored.*

You have devastated me, Ethan. You have torn my heart from my breast. You have sheared my soul to its pinions. I was already defacing my dreams with images of your own. And you escaped like a coward so that you wouldn't have to look at my wounds.

Annette put the unfinished letter and the invitation in her pocket and got into her father's car and drove to the little church in Council Grove. She cried as she drove, and by the time she reached the church she was drained of all emotion. She knelt in a back pew and remained there for a long time, her mind free of thought, focused on a great white void that hummed with a soothing presence, until she felt a hand stroke her head and a voice whisper, 'Annie.' She looked up to see Father Liddy standing in the aisle. The compassion on his face, the recognition of her pain – although he knew not what caused it or how it came about – gave him the look of a saint, and it struck Annette that perhaps sainthood was not the absence of sin in a man but rather a profound, bondless compassion, a fearlessness of human suffering, a willingness to take it on and make it one's own.

'Will you hear my confession, Father?' she asked him.

He looked at her in his quiet manner. Annette was embarrassed when she felt a tear suddenly slip down her face. She looked down. Father Liddy sat down on the pew in front of her and laid his hand on her folded hands.

'You have nothing to confess. But I will lend you what little strength I have,' he answered. Annette reached into her pocket and pulled out the invitation and her letter. They were crumpled together. She straightened out the papers and gave them to him. He glanced at the invitation, then he read the letter. He read it several times.

'Keep it, please,' she said. 'So I won't send it.'

Father Liddy nodded and slipped it into his pocket.

Annette took a deep breath. 'I must leave here now. As soon as I can. We'll go back home. To Paris.'

He nodded. 'I understand. But I will miss you, Annette.'

'I'll miss you, too, Father.'

'I envy you,' he said very quietly. 'To be going home.'

Those words infused light into Annette's saddened heart, and the strength he had promised her began to grow from that moment on. Only once did it waver, on the evening she was out to dinner with Eliana and her father, and Ethan had come into the cafe. She had put him so far from her thoughts that his presence startled her like a ghost. It was unfortunate that she looked up just as his eyes found her, because she read on his face an emotion quite different from any she imagined him to feel. Not guilt, and not fear. Nor embarrassment. Rather, in that brief moment, his eyes communicated to her that he was floundering in a depth of agony that exceeded even her own. That his heart had taken him somewhere far away from his beloved hills, and his soul was stranded there, and he did not know how to bring it back. He held her gaze, and then Patti came up and spoke to him. He tipped his hat to her without a reply, and turned and walked out.

It was that look that held her there until after the wedding, nursing a thin hope that he would not go through with it. She could have gone earlier, but she found enough reasons to stay. She planned a recital for her students, and scheduled it for Sunday afternoon, the day after Ethan's wedding. To her astonishment, all her students and their parents attended. Matthew Winegarner performed in his wheelchair to a hushed audience, and Mrs Winegarner, who had volunteered her large home for the event, prepared cookies and punch for a brief reception. It was a surprisingly pleasant occasion, and when everyone had gone and Annette was washing the punch bowl, Mrs Winegarner broke down in tears. The two women sat together at the kitchen table and cried while Eliana pushed Matthew around the back yard in his wheelchair.

This last thing remained to be done. Annette had put it off until now because she could not bear to return to the old house. There were moments when she convinced herself it need not be done at all. Surely, if there was anything of value left in the attic her mother would have said so. It would have been in the will, or she would have written Annette about it in a letter. Ethan had said they were things she had intended for a garage sale. But perhaps there was something overlooked, forgotten. A photograph, an old dress, a treasure, a window into her mother's past.

She finished her coffee and wrote a note telling her

father and daughter where she was going, and that she would be back shortly. Even perhaps before they awoke. Then she took the keys to the old Buick and left.

The eastern horizon had lightened to a deep purple when she drove out of the driveway, and by the time she was out in the country it had washed to a pale blue. To the north she saw giant pillars of smoke rising from the fields. She had been alarmed last night driving back from Cottonwood Falls, when she had seen long ribbons of fire consuming the prairie. But her father explained how they did it every year, how it was planned. A planned burn, he called it.

As she pulled into the driveway of the old house her stomach turned over. She sat in the car with the engine idling for a long time, watching the columns of smoke move across the horizon with the wind. Finally, she regained her senses. She would not allow memories of Ethan to interfere. It was a kind of rite she had to perform for her mother's sake, and it had nothing to do with him. It would not take her long to sift through the boxes. And then she would abandon the old house and this place for ever.

The bed was still there. Everything was as she had left it. She averted her eyes and dragged her heavy legs up the stairs to the attic.

Twenty-two

The call came at four in the morning. Ethan had been asleep only a few hours and he heard the phone ringing in his dreams long before he awoke. It was the county sheriff. The worst possible scenario had been realized. The wind had come up, unexpectedly, and carried embers from smoldering cow chips into dry, brown winter pasture that had not been burned. The fire line was moving east, away from the town, into the hills, but livestock was threatened, and they couldn't be sure the wind wouldn't change on them again.

When Ethan got off the phone and went in to wake up Katie Anne, he found her sitting on the side of the bed, pulling on heavy socks.

'I heard,' she mumbled groggily. 'What's the wind speed?'

'Around twenty-two,' he said.

She shook her head in despair. 'And the sun's not even up yet.'

When Ethan had dressed, he found her in the kitchen filling a Thermos full of hot coffee.

'Your dad's going to take the Cessna up as soon as day breaks,' he said. 'We're gonna need a firebreak somewhere up north of here. He wants you to pick up the disc tractor from the Obermuellers and bring it up the road. Stay on the radio. He'll tell you where to plow.'

Ethan could smell it as he sat on the porch pulling on his boots. The woodsy, autumnlike smell of burning leaves. It grew stronger as he drove up the road in his truck with the window down. Pungent. Hard on his nostrils. The air was cluttered with flying ashes. He passed the road to the old Reilly house and had a sudden urge to turn onto it. He had not returned since the night he had spent there with Annette. A brief memory of that night exploded in his brain and he squeezed his eyes shut and shook his head to dispel the images that rose in his mind, the feel of the woman's skin next to his, her warmth, the taste of her tongue in his mouth, stirring him in a way no woman had ever done before. Profoundly. Beyond his senses. He accelerated and sped quickly north toward the fire. Let it burn, he thought. Let it burn to the ground.

Like whimsical strokes with a deadly brush, the wind painted the earth with fire. It moved with rapacious speed, a roaring dragon of ferocious heat and fury fueled by the dry winter grass. An alert was sent out to all the neighboring counties. Sirens wailed. Ranchers were awakened from their sleep. Trucks and tractors were recruited to carry water from the ponds and set backfires. But the backfires turned on their masters with a vengeance, goaded by the renegade wind. Men drove alongside the fire, spraying it with water from the tanks mounted on their trucks. But then the wind would suddenly shift, and the fire would come at them. The fire outran the fire trucks that chased it across the prairie. It trapped cattle and foxes and deer in rings of fire. It dwarfed the men and their red and green machines with its towering columns of smoke that rose like tornadoes into the pale morning sky. It swallowed up their spinning red and blue lights with its leviathan tongue. And each time, as the wind shifted, the fire turned, separated, and a new fire line was born.

Katie Anne had Jacob's Mound in her sight. A few more miles and the firebreak would be finished. Ethan's land would be protected. For the past hour she had listened to her father's voice on the two-way radio as he spoke to Clay Cochran, the fire chief, deciding strategy and plans of attack, using methods he had learned from his father and grandfather, men who had known fire as an implacable enemy. In a few minutes he would be taking up his plane, and they would have a better assessment of the scope of the fire. But they all knew one thing: it was moving fast. Too fast.

Only once had Katie Anne spoken to Ethan over the radio, and then he was out of reach. He had taken a crew west of the fire line to start up a backfire. She turned around to look at the mark she had made on the earth. The disc had torn up a fifteen-foot-wide stretch of prairie, plowing under the dried winter grass, bringing to the surface cool, moist earth that defied fire. When she reached Jacob's Mound she would turn around and come back right alongside this line, widening the break another fifteen feet, making it impossible for the fire, even with its grotesque gymnastics, to breach their land. She could see the fire now in the north, a thin line of orange flame with a smoking tail, sweeping over the hills. The air was cluttered with flying ashes, and the sun, which had risen only moments earlier, was a huge muted orange orb, barely visible through the smoky haze. It suddenly occurred to her that the old Reilly house that Ethan had bought was right in the path of the fire. The old Reilly place. Where Ethan had betrayed her. Let it burn.

She looked up and her heart seemed to freeze in her chest. There was a patch of fire on top of Jacob's Mound only a few hundred feet in front of her. She watched its movements. Within a few seconds it was down the slope of the mound and moving toward her. She threw the switch to lift the disk. Once the lumbering machine was free of the earth, she turned it southward and gave it full throttle. The heavy tractor, its mammoth engine whining, rumbled across the prairie, and behind the curtain of dust and dirt the fire rushed steadily forward. The wind, grown impatient with the fire's slow progress, blew the smoke forward, ahead of the fire line. Katie Anne saw the blue sky in front of her grow dim, and then the prairie disappeared into a dark cloud of smoke.

Annette had been sitting in the cool, dark attic with her flashlight, oblivious to the passing time and the delicate arrival of dawn. She was totally perplexed by what she had found. Perhaps this was why her mother had told everyone there was nothing of value up here. Because she had no other way to hide them from her husband. But she had kept these letters – ones she had received, and others she had written that had later been returned to her. For whom were these old letters intended? Who did she expect would read them? Why had she not destroyed them herself?

How close her mother had come to fleeing. Taking her

baby, Annie, and running away. She had written all these things to a friend Annette had never heard mentioned before. A friend she had gone to school with here in Cottonwood Falls and who had moved to Los Angeles to study painting. Beth was her name. From her little studio in a guest house in the Hollywood Hills, Beth had written her letter after letter, pleading with Emma Reilly to leave her husband. And Emma Reilly had been so tempted. From the very first months of her marriage she had recognized her folly. Charles Fergusen's persuasive charm had soured to a frighteningly oppressive severity. His demands that she adhere to his rigid authority were enforced with cold cruelty. Once she left the house to visit a neighbor without telling him – he was preparing a sermon in his study and she did not care disturb him. When he found her in the neighbor's kitchen with the door closed (the neighbor had been sweeping as they chatted and had shut the kitchen door to sweep behind it) he exploded in a violent outburst, accusing his wife of gossiping about him to the neighbors. He stormed away, driving off with their car, and did not return for two days. After Annette was born he became even more demanding. He ridiculed his wife's attempts to breast-feed the baby, insisting she would pervert the child. When Annette was only two months old he contracted pneumonia and was in bed for three weeks. Whenever the baby cried to be fed, or changed, or simply held, he would ring the bell he kept at his bedside table to summon his wife and demand some broth, or new reading material, or fresh water. And Emma Reilly Fergusen would put down her little girl in her crib, and she would run to her husband with a smile and wait on him, and the baby's cries would go unheeded. Her heart, like her breasts, swelled, ached, and then grew dry. From that time on she learned how to love her daughter silently, without passion.

Annette cried as she read the letters. The pungent smell of smoke did not penetrate the attic, and the sirens remained at a distance, always at a distance. The fire alighted upon the house quickly, consuming the old wood with hungry tongues, and Annette, her mind alive with images of the past, did not hear the crackling sound of flames.

Annie.

She jumped, her hand flew to her heart, and she turned to see a pale light disappearing down the attic stairs. Then she smelled the smoke.

She rushed to the window and drew back the curtains. The prairie was gone, obscured by a tidal wave of smoke trailing behind a thin red line of fire that was eating its way toward the house, licking up the brown grasses like an insatiable dragon. Annette scrambled down the narrow attic stairs. She lost her shoe near the bottom, stumbled, and fell against the door. It flew open and she landed on her knees on the second-floor landing. She pulled herself up and looked over the railing. Her legs froze as she saw the flames through the windows in the dining room. Pale gray smoke was creeping stealthily along the floor and up the stairs toward her. *Think clearly!*

Annie.

She felt as though a weight had settled on her lungs. Her eyes darted helplessly around, catching on muddled images of tiny blue cornflowers peeling from the walls. She rushed to the second-floor bathroom and looked for a towel. A rag. But there was nothing. She stripped off her sweater, jammed it underneath the faucet and turned on the water. The pipes whined and shuddered but only a trickle of water came forth. She cried and cursed and stamped her feet at the old house, and the smoke swirled soundlessly around her legs. Covering her face with the sweater, she hobbled on one shoe to the stairs. As her left foot hit the second step, her stocking slipped on the old wood. There was a sharp crack and wrenching pain as her ankle bent underneath her, and for that single second as she flew downward through the air to the bottom of the stairs, her body rushed to her defense with a kaleidoscope of reflexes that gave to that one last second of her life a deliriously unreal sense of eternity.

* * *

Annette Zeldin lay in a crumpled, lifeless shape at the foot of the steps, her neck bent at an odd angle, away from her body, and her legs twisted beneath her. One foot was caught in the railing at the bottom of the steps, the ankle turned awkwardly inward, her slender foot dangling in a graceful point. The flames ate their way toward her. They found her hair first, and it ignited quickly, and then was gone. Then they turned to her clothes. Greedily, they devoured her.

Twenty-three

Annette stared down at her body with calm curiosity. She knew it was her own but she felt no keen attachment to it, a little fondness, perhaps, but nothing more. She recognized herself as if she were another. The vanity and insecurities she had felt about it seemed suddenly so pointless. She watched it burn as she watched the wooden stairs burn, and the prairie, and the deer and the cattle. The fire no longer seemed to be her enemy, but something ravishingly beautiful that belonged to the earth and had its place there. And there was, in this place of mortal fear and terror, a tremendous energy, and she recognized this energy as a multitude of spirits released by the fire. Her mother was there with her. The voice behind that persistent *Annie*, no longer buried under layers of consciousness, was now clearly revealed. Annette's spirit ascended above the old house and she saw all things at once. She saw the prairie, and the fire, and the people struggling to contain it. She saw the huge lumbering tractor throwing up dirt in its race across the field as it tried to escape the flames, and she saw the smoke overcome it. She saw the pretty young woman jump from the towering machine and run down a narrow corridor of grass with walls of fire on each side, and she saw her stumble and fall to her knees, then crawl, until the smoke and heat overwhelmed her. She saw the airplane emerge from the gray smoke and set down, and the father, masked and coated in yellow armor, race through the narrowing corridor to the pit and throw himself upon the burning body of his beloved daughter. She saw him carry his blackened child in his arms, pressed tightly to his bulky body, and she saw him stride through the flames like a god. She saw the airplane take off and disappear into the sky.

Mama, stay close to me.

I'm taking you home, Annie.

How beautiful you are, Mama.

It's my love you see, Annie. There's nothing to restrain it now. Nothing to tie it down. No need to hide it.

What is this, Mama? This darkness? I can touch it.

We're on our way home.

I know this place.

We've been here before. There. Can you see the light? Can you feel the light?

Oh, yes. It feels like your arms around me when I was little.

It's much greater than that, Annie.

Slow down, Mama. Don't go so fast.

Annie ...

Mama!

As she called out she felt an ache throb through her, and she marveled that her spirit could feel such torment, such anguish. She felt her mother move toward the light, faster, faster, and yet she herself slowed and seemed to be slipping backward, away from the light. The serenity she had felt was shattered, and she did not know if her anguish was from losing the light or from leaving the earth. It was both, and she recognized suddenly with a memory that was a vestige of her bodily knowledge that this anguish was choice.

Her mother's presence was gone, and within the instant of a thought, she found herself in her daughter's bedroom. Eliana was asleep, her glorious mane of hair swept over her pillow in artless beauty. Her perfect hands, the little fingers relaxed, were gracefully splayed over the whiskers and yellow glass eye of Cozette, the stuffed toy mountain lion her mother had given her for Christmas. She breathed. She breathed. Annette looked upon her daughter's peaceful face, and the ache that had troubled her earlier now consumed her soul. Words from her catechism leapt through her mind; she should love God more than her father and mother, more than her husband, her child. No, not her child. Precious. Where was the serenity her mother had revealed to her? Where was the light? She had transcended this world. She could not return to it. Her body lay there on the floor of her mother's house, burning. And her daughter lay there asleep on an old daybed in a run-down clapboard house in a little prairie town in Kansas. Alone.

I will not leave you. Not for all the beauty of heaven. I cannot leave you. I cannot leave this earth. I love you too much.

Then a dull peace settled over her. It had none of the beauty she had known earlier, but the anguish had gone. She looked around her, at her sleeping child, at her mother's room, those possessions that had once meant so much, and although her spirit was free, she knew she was now earthbound. She would never again see the light. But as she looked upon her daughter's face, her lonely spirit rejoiced.

It was late in the afternoon by the time Ethan got to the hospital. He had been setting backfires with a few brave hands up north of the main fire, and one of his men had been overcome by smoke and had to be taken to the local hospital. On the way into town he was waylaid by a local sheriff who had been sent to track him down.

Ethan was overcome with guilt. As he sped down the interstate he muttered inarticulate prayers, and his eyes, already inflamed and dried from the smoke and heat and wind, burned with tears that never fell. Katie Anne's vanity and selfishness now seemed to him like small blemishes on a character that was ultimately sound and good. He tried to prepare himself for the worst. But nothing could have prepared him for the looks on the faces of Betty Sue and Tom Mackey when they turned toward him as he came rushing down the corridor. Their eyes were flooded with the kind of pain he had spent a lifetime avoiding, and he would have given anything to turn and run. He could have borne the pain alone, but this look in the eyes of parents when their only child is being taken from them, this made the breath catch in his chest, and he took Betty Sue in his arms so that he would not have to look into her eyes. She shuddered and he felt her wither up in his arms, a small, slight force unequal to the burden. Tom stood beside him, looking down at the ground, his dirty nails biting into the soft felt rim of his hat that he kneaded the way a kitten kneads its mother's breast. His soot-darkened face was streaked with tears.

'How is she?' Ethan whispered.

Neither of them answered for a moment. It was Betty Sue who finally spoke. 'She's not . . . it's not the burns. She was burned pretty badly. Her face ...' She broke down sobbing and Tom, finally winning out against the tears, finished.

'It's the smoke. She inhaled so much smoke.'

After a moment, Ethan guided Betty Sue to a chair.

'Where is she?'

'Down there. The second room,' answered Tom.

'Ethan ...'

'It's okay.'

'She looks ...'

'It's okay.'

Ethan stood in the doorway. There was little he could see. She had an oxygen tube down her throat and an IV in each arm, and her face seemed to be wearing a mask of some sort. He could tell that most of her hair was gone.

'Mr Brown?'

Ethan turned.

'I'm Dr Eagleton.'

He gasped for breath. The woman speaking bore a striking resemblance to Annette.

'We still haven't got her stabilized, but I think we'll be able to pull her through.'

'She's pregnant,' Ethan blurted out. 'About eight weeks, I think.'

'We'll do an ultrasound right away.'

'I'm the only one who knows about this.'

'I understand.'

Ethan waited in the hallway while they wheeled in the equipment. For the first time since the news of the accident, he allowed himself to think about Annette. She would be gone now. Her plane would have already departed.

'Mr Brown, can you come in here please?'

As Ethan entered the room he forced himself to look closely at Katie Anne. One side of her face was black and crusty from third-degree burns. The other side was puffy and blistered. Her eyes were swollen shut. Her arms and chest were wrapped in bandages. They had lifted her hospital gown and smeared a clear jell on her stomach. Her stomach, Ethan noticed, was still lovely, smooth and pale and unblemished. It rose faintly with her shallow breath.

'Mr Brown, I want you to see this.'

The doctor guided Ethan's attention to the monitor while she passed a detector over Katie Anne's stomach.

'Your wife's not pregnant.'

Ethan stared at the black-and-white image of Katie Anne's womb.

'You mean she's lost it?'

'If she did, it wasn't recently. There's no sign of a fetus.'

'Are you sure?'

'I'll be glad to get another doctor in here if you want.'

Ethan stared at the snowy black-and-white image on the screen.

'I don't understand.'

'Did she have positive test results?' She spoke quietly, soothingly, and her voice too reminded him of Annette.

'I don't know. I don't know what kind of tests she had done.'

'Were you married recently?'

'Just last week.'

'It's possible she missed a period or two. That's a very stressful time for young women.' Dr Eagleton placed a gentle hand on his arm. 'We're going to do everything we can to pull her out of this.'

Ethan slipped out of the room and down the corridor in the opposite direction from the alcove where Betty Sue and Tom waited. He couldn't face them just now, so he went into the stairwell and sat on the steps. It had been such an elaborate lie. The morning sickness, the loss of appetite, the secrecy. But there were other things, things he had shut away in the back of his mind until now. Once he came home while Katie Anne was putting away groceries, and he set about helping. He was reaching into a bag to pull out a bottle of shampoo when she had grabbed the bag away from him and told him he needn't help. He had noticed a large box of tampons in the bottom of the bag with the shampoo, but it didn't strike him at the moment as anything unusual. And her eating was another thing. She claimed she was never hungry even as she cooked and baked; though Ethan rarely came home to eat, the food still disappeared. As he remembered all these things, the extent of her ruse became clear to him. For a long time he sat there on the narrow steps with his back against the cold white wall, staring at the wide gold wedding band on his finger.

Eliana crept quietly out of bed and felt her way along the dark hallway to the kitchen. She closed the kitchen door behind her and groped along the wall until she found the light. The kitchen was spotless, as her mother had left it early the night before. Only her mug sat on the kitchen table where she had sat that morning when she was still alive. Eliana's eyes flooded instantly with tears at the sight of the mug and she went to it and sat down and cradled the thing in her hands. No one ever used it but her mother. It was rather small and delicate, painted with an artless picture of sheep grazing in a green pasture and a deep dark blue sky and white clouds. The porcelain inside had black cracks like veins, and Eliana stared down it like a deep, dark well. She sipped the coffee, which was cold and stale, and although the taste disgusted her she forced herself to drink it.

'Take me with you, Maman,' she mumbled, wishing the coffee to be a painless elixir that might put her to sleep and wake her up in another world where her mother still lived. A hot tear rolled down her cheek and she angrily wiped it away. Those tears did no good, and she was tired of crying.

That morning Eliana had stood in the doorway and heard the sheriff tell her grandfather that her mother had been killed in the fire, and she had seen the sheriff's embarrassed, pained look when he saw her standing there. After his visit, Charlie Fergusen had locked the front door and taken his telephone off the hook, and then he had closed himself in his bedroom. For a long time Eliana had lain in her bed, and then she had dressed and gone into the backyard where Bubba stood waiting at the fence. She sat there most of the morning, clutching his black fur through the chain link fence, holding her face up for him to lick away her salty tears, which seemed never-ending. She kept waiting for her grand-father to come out and holler at her to come inside, but he never did. The sky was very dark that morning, and the wind blew black ash over her and over all the town, and all the prairie. It was her mother's ashes, mixed with ashes of the trees, the grasses, the animals. It was all mixed together now. Everything was one again.

When Bubba ran off, she made a bed for herself in the dirt behind the bushes, and she pretended she was a baby foal and her mother had been sold to a wealthy sheik and taken far away. She laid there and whimpered and neighed and scratched the earth with her little nails.

Sometime in the early afternoon she went inside. She pretended that her mother was out giving a lesson and would be home any minute, and she ran off to the shower and washed her hair and cleaned her nails. When she came out of the shower the house was still silent. She knocked on her grandfather's bedroom door but there was no answer, so she went off to her bedroom, closed the door, lay down on her bed, and prayed for God to let her die. She did not die but finally she fell asleep.

She was very hungry now; she had eaten nothing all day, and her grandfather had still not come out of his room. She set the table for three, with place mats and napkins folded carefully on the left as her mother had taught her, and she poured herself the last of the milk and sat down and ate some graham crackers. She was still hungry, however, so she climbed up on the counter and opened the cabinet. She saw some cans on the top shelf, but she couldn't quite read the labels, so she tried to stand, pulling herself up by the shelf. The shelf was held by only two pegs at opposite corners (for seven years Emma had reminded Charlie to pick up some pegs at the hardware store but he always forgot), and as Eliana lodged her weight against it, the shelf tilted toward her, sending the entire contents sliding onto her head. Heavy tins of peaches in syrup, green beans, chicken noodle soup, tomatoes, corn, peas, and even a glass jar of artichoke hearts in olive oil that Emma had been saving for

Annette's next visit crashed down to the floor in a terrible clatter, denting the linoleum and breaking the porcelain in the sink. Eliana screamed and covered her head with her hands, and when the terrible noise had finally stopped she looked up to see her grandfather standing in the doorway.

'What are you doing in here!' he bellowed, and his voice seemed even more terrible to her than the crashing tins and glass. He stepped forward and looked around the kitchen. Cans still rolled across the floor and the artichokes lay in thick pools of oil and broken glass. 'Clean it up! Clean it all up!' he commanded, shaking his gnarly finger at the artichokes as though condemning them to hell.

'Yes, Grandpa,' whispered Eliana. Her heart pounded in her little chest as she scurried down from the counter and crawled underneath the kitchen table. She hid there, watching his feet, and when he went out and closed the door she crept out and quickly began picking up the tins. Her little shoulders shook with silent grief and her delicate features were distorted into a mask of sadness and pain. As she methodically picked up the tins, one at a time, she began to grow in resolve. She didn't know where to find a broom so she pulled the dish towel from its hook and cleaned up the artichokes the best she could, then she turned off the kitchen light and tiptoed back to her mother's room. Their suitcases lay open on the bed, neatly packed as her mother had left them, and Eliana pulled out her jeans and cowboy boots and slipped them on. She put on her white cowboy hat and her coat and stuffed an extra T-shirt and underwear in the pockets, then she picked up her mother's violin and turned out the light. She could hear the television in the living room, so she sneaked back into the sewing room, closed the door behind her, and sat down on the bed. Her heart was pounding and she was terribly thirsty but was afraid to make a sound. Finally she rose from the bed and tried the window. To her relief it opened easily. She gathered up her belongings, crawled outside, and within minutes she was racing down the road as though ghosts were at her feet.

Traveler lay on the porch of Ethan's new home, waiting for his master to return. He had not been fed since the evening before, and his instincts, which were keen, told him to wait in this place. From time to time his ears pricked up and turned like radar as they detected a truck in the road, but it was late now and no vehicles had been by for a long time. He whimpered quietly. His instincts also told him something was amiss, and his animal intelligence was searching for clues in the cold night air. What he found, however, was something quite unlike anything he had known before. It came to him in the form of a light and a presence, but it was strange to him because it had no bodily odor and made no sound, nothing he could recognize as human. Yet he was unafraid. In this light was a great power. It was no human master, but master it was. He rose as though commanded, and set off at a trot down the long drive to the main road.

By now Eliana was far out of town. She was terrified, but she would not go back home. She clutched the violin and her Cozette to her chest, and between her whimpers and sobs she practiced her growls, for she was now a mother mountain lion herself, ready to defend and protect her baby. The dark was absolute – clouds full of ash blocked the stars and the moon, lying all around her like a nightmare, concealing awful monsters and witches and wolves. She cried for her dead mother and prayed to her guardian angel, but the monsters would not go away. She was growing very tired, and the violin and Cozette seemed like rocks in her hands. She had been running or walking for more than an hour, and her little legs, already weakened by fear and grief, would carry her no longer. But whenever she stopped to rest, she heard the monsters approaching through the fields in the dark, and she felt their hot breath on her back and sensed their claws were only inches away. Suddenly a noise caught her attention. At first it was masked by the wind, but then it grew more distinct. It was coming at her through the field. She began to run as fast as she could, but she went only a few hundred feet and then collapsed at the side of the road, bursting into tears. The tears flooded her face and filled her mouth, and when she opened it to call her mother's name, it seemed to her that she was drowning. She curled up in a ball and prayed the monster would not see her in the dark. Suddenly, she felt a cool nose at her ear. She looked up and there was Traveler, panting heavily, his dark eyes glowing in the night like guiding stars. The child threw her arms around his neck and clutched him tightly. Traveler, who was more accustomed to cattle than children, did not particularly care for this kind of fondling, but this new master, whose presence he still felt although the light had gone, told him to sit and not stir, so he tolerated the kisses and the little fingers kneading his fur, and the warm human breath in his ear. After a while, when his master commanded it, he rose and led the little girl into the night.

Twenty-four

Normally, Jer didn't notice pictures hanging on walls, but this one caught his attention. It was a scene all too familiar to him: a rustic farmhouse bedroom, an open window, a dog curled up asleep on the bed with his head on the pillow. The room was simple and unadorned: only a small oval braided rug on the floor and a drab, colorless chenille bedspread like the kind he had on his bed as a kid. He wanted to crawl in there with the dog and hide. He turned away from the picture, which hung at the entrance to the hospital cafeteria, and looked for Ethan.

He found him in a booth at the back, concealed by an artificial ficus. He had a cup of coffee in front of him and a piece of apple pie with a few bites taken out of it pushed to the side. The coffee looked cold. Jer slid into the booth across from him.

'How's she doin'?' he asked.

'Hangin' in there.'

'How about Tom and Betty Sue?'

'They've checked into a hotel across the street. Betty Sue was nauseous. From the shock. They gave her some medication and it knocked her out. I told Tom I'd call him if ... if there was any change.'

An awkward silence stretched between them. Jer reached for a discarded sports section of the morning paper that lay folded at the edge of the table and glanced at the front-page story.

'Cardinals look good this year,' he said.

'I don't follow them much.'

'Yeah, I know.' Jer laid down the paper.

'Get yourself a cup of coffee,' said Ethan. 'They're still open.'

'Naw, thanks. I can't stay long. We're still moppin' up. Gonna be a long night.'

'How's it going?'

'We got it licked. Finally.'

'Anybody else get hurt?'

Jer took a deep breath. 'Yeah,' he replied. 'One of the volunteers from Strong City. Smoke inhalation.'

'Bad?'

Jer shook his head. 'No. They released him.'

'How about property?'

'Your house is safe.' Jer tried to swallow and it felt as if his throat were paralyzed. 'But the old Fergusen house ...'

'Did it go?'

'Yeah.' Jer could hardly hear his own voice.

'Just as well,' mumbled Ethan. There was a long silence. Ethan stood up. 'I'm gonna get a hot refill. Sure you don't want something?'

'No thanks.' Jer caught him by the sleeve. 'Ethan?'

'Yeah?'

Jer's mouth felt as if it was full of cotton. 'Annette was in the house.'

The coffee cup that dangled from Ethan's finger slipped to the floor and shattered, but Ethan never felt it leave his hand, nor did he hear the crash. He slowly turned to look at his friend.

'What?' His voice was but a whisper.

'She was in the house when it burned. I guess she'd gone back there for something. Charlie Fergusen said she went off early that morning when everyone was still asleep. She planned on being back before they woke up. They found her ...' Jer's voice broke suddenly, and a strange artificial sound, like a high whine, burst from his chest. It was the first time Ethan had ever heard him cry.

Ethan walked quickly through the hospital corridors, looking for a way out. *Damn sonovabitch,* he screamed to himself. His eyes bore into the walls; he looked high, above the gazes of the nurses, the occasional visitor. He had to avoid their eyes. Their friendly, guileless eyes. If they saw into his eyes it would shatter him. If he could just hold it in until he got outside. *Where's the damned outside?* He found himself in radiology and had to turn around. He came to an elevator and pushed the button, but he didn't wait. He moved on, around the corner, his long legs eating up the miles of white corridors. He stopped a nurse and muttered at her angrily, wanting to know the way out, but he didn't wait for her reply. He felt it beginning to rise in his chest, and he hurried away before she had finished. She called after him, that he was going the wrong way, but he ignored her. He tried to control his breathing, but he could no longer stop the tears. They flooded down his face, soundlessly, without reproof. Furtively he wiped them away, with the back of his hand or his sleeve, but they were too much for him. They would not stop.

He walked for a long time, through the great white bowels of the hospital, down long endless corridors of sickness and health. He cried until his face was soft and tender, like a child's, and when at last he saw a rest room, he went in and shut the door. As he blew his nose on some toilet paper, he caught sight of his face in the mirror, bloated, streaked with pink, his nose red, and it shocked him. It looked just like Katie Anne's had looked the night he had left her. It looked the way Annette's must have when she waited and he never returned. He sat down on the toilet and laid his flushed face on the cool enamel sink. His great chest shuddered with each breath. Eventually calm settled over him.

It was a long time before he could return to Katie Anne's room. He stopped at the door and looked in on her. The woman on the bed now seemed to him like someone else's wife. It was a tragic accident, but not his own. He turned and caught a glimpse of Dr Eagleton at the end of the corridor just as the door was closing behind her. He had a sudden urge to speak to her and he hurried down the corridor after her. She had gone out through the emergency exit, and Ethan followed her. He opened the door and looked up and down the stairwell, but there was no sound of a door closing or of feet on the stairs above or below him. He stood there, disappointed, for he felt a strong need for another presence just then. As he turned, his hand on the door, ready to open it, he paused. He had heard no sound, but he knew he was not alone. A chill ran through him, and he turned to see Annette standing on the landing below him. The first thing he noticed was her beauty, although afterward he could recall nothing about the way she dressed, or how she looked. All he knew was that she was there. For what seemed a long time he stared at her, and although she never touched him or drew near to him, he felt her love pouring through him like heat from the sun. In the dim light of the cold stairwell he experienced a radiance he had never felt before. It was as though an aura, like a net, arose from her and descended upon him, drawing them together, as though they were one, breathing with the same lungs, feeling with the same hands, looking with the same eyes, thinking with the same mind. She spoke to him. She told him that he must take charge of Eliana. Be the child's guardian. That there was no one for the child to turn to, that she had run away from her grandfather's house and should not be forced to return. She told him that for all the beauty of heaven, she could not leave this earth. That she loved him.

Ethan heard a shout in the hallway, then the sound of running feet. He glanced away, toward the door, and when he looked back Annette was gone. He called her name, and then he ran down the stairs after her, three flights, all the way to the bottom and out the door, but the halls were empty. His heart pounded as he walked back up the stairs; he tried to rationalize what he had seen. Perhaps it had been his overwrought imagination, his distress. No. No one would ever be able to convince him of that. He was an intelligent and rational man, but he knew she had appeared to him. She was still with him.

As he neared the third floor he could hear the shouting in the hallway above, and what sounded like equipment being rolled down the hall. He opened the door and looked down the corridor; the commotion was outside Katie Anne's room. He rushed down the hall, and there was such bedlam, with shouts and orders coming from all directions, that no one seemed to notice when he slipped into the room and stood in the corner. The room was filled with nurses and technicians, and Dr Eagleton was bending over Katie Anne. He realized then it had not been her he had seen going out the exit. She looked nothing at all like Annette.

'Take her off the ventilator! Use the ambu bag!'

'We're not getting a heartbeat.'

Dr Eagleton was pumping Katie Anne's chest while a nurse pumped the air bag, forcing air into her lungs. Another nurse watched the monitor. Ethan could see it over her shoulder; it was flat. Lifeless.

'Still nothing.'

'Okay, repeat the atropine.'

The nurse slapped a needle into the doctor's hand and she injected the atropine.

'That's the third?'

'Yes.'

The others stood in silent watch as Dr Eagleton continued pumping her chest and the nurse pumped the air bag. They worked together, in perfect cadence, but the cadence slowed, gradually, and finally they stopped.

* * *

Annette saw all of this. She saw Ethan in the corner, and the valiant doctor, and all the dedicated people. *It's too late. Her spirit left her long ago. She's gone.* Suddenly Annette felt a presence with her. It was not her mother; her mother was freed. But here was another presence, a strong, powerful friend, and as she looked upon the blackened, lifeless shell, the body that would inspire no love, the face that people would turn away from, the anguish of choice overwhelmed her again. It came upon her all at once, and she had a vision of her life far into the future, what would be her struggle, her suffering, her glory. She also knew in that timeless moment that all this knowledge that she now had would be taken away from her, and she would be cast into darkness. She felt this knowledge come to her from her friend, and she understood then, with godlike compassion, the frailty and limitations of man. She had one fragile glimpse into eternity, and then she plunged into darkness.

Dr Eagleton jumped with fright when the lifeless body beneath her suddenly shuddered as though jolted by a powerful electric shock. The patient's chest moved as breath poured in and out of her lungs.

'Get her back on the ventilator!'

The room, which had been subdued by the pallor of death, now burst into activity. The monitor was plugged back in, the ventilator reconnected. As they worked, they hid their awe, and their tears, behind masks of professionalism, but each of them knew he had just witnessed a miracle. Then Katie Anne opened her swollen eyes and a sound came from deep within her ruined body.

'Eth ...'

'She's conscious!'

Ethan pushed his way through them and bent over the bed. Her eyes were only slits in her swollen face. Her whisper, barely audible, was little more than a breath passing through her black lips.

'Eth ... Ethan.'

'I'm here. I'm here.'

'Eli ...' She fell back into sleep.

Twenty-five

When Jer opened the stable door in the cold light of dawn, he was met with a growl. He stopped in his tracks and looked around, trying to place the sound. His own dogs were in the house eating, and they had given him no warning of any danger around the place. All the horses were quiet. He took down a rifle from a rack above the feed buckets, picked up a flashlight, and slowly made his way the length of the stalls. As Jer approached Big Mike, the horse turned his head to look at him.

'You okay, fella?'

Jer reached out to stroke the horse's nose, and he heard the growl again – low and persistent, a gentle warning. It seemed to come from one of the stalls.

Cautiously, Jer continued down the corridor until he came to an empty stall. The gate stood open, and in the corner, on a low pile of hay, he could make out a dark form. He shined the light on it.

'Traveler! What the hell're you doin' here, boy?' said Jer with a sigh of relief. 'You give up on your master? That it?' As he approached, the dog's tail began to wag, but the animal didn't budge. 'Who you got there with you, boy?' Jer knelt down beside the dog and pulled back the horse blanket. When he saw the long, pale hair full of straw, the white cowboy hat, and the violin case, his heart lurched; he gently gathered the sleeping child in his arms.

'You did good, Traveler. You did good, boy,' he kept repeating as he walked toward his house with the little girl in his arms and the dog at his heels.

'Does her grandfather even know she's gone?' asked Ethan. He was watching Jer whip up batter for pancakes, his strong, callused hand flying in even strokes around the big metal bowl. Jer had always amazed him with his unheralded talents, like cooking. The cowboy had more cooking paraphernalia than Ethan had ever seen in any woman's kitchen, even his own mother's. Jer had never set foot in a gourmet restaurant, but his food was some of the best Ethan had ever tasted.

260

'Sure he does. Sheriff went around to tell him.' Jer lifted the skillet and tilted it to spread the hot oil evenly over the surface. 'He didn't even call. He knows she's here. He just doesn't give a damn.' He poured the thick batter into the skillet, then took some eggs from a carton on the counter and began breaking them into a bowl. 'You eatin' with us?'

'I'm not hungry.'

'Well, maybe not, but you stay and eat with us.' He broke two more eggs into the bowl. 'You send her back home and she'll just run away again. Hell, the kid never knew her daddy, and now her ma ...' Jer's voice broke suddenly. He beat the eggs with a fury, trying to hold his tears in check. Ethan rose to leave.

'I'd better be gettin' on home.'

Jer pointed the steel wire whip at him. 'You stay where you are!'

Ethan stared at him in amazement.

'You're one sorry bastard, Ethan Brown,' he went on. 'You could've had her, you know.'

'What the hell are you talking about? You're the one who told me I'd never be able to live here ... that I wouldn't have a friend in all of Chase County ...'

'Yeah, well, maybe I did, but that was my head talkin', not my heart.'

Jer looked up all of a sudden, and Ethan turned around to see Eliana standing in the doorway rubbing her eyes. Ethan saw the look on her face and it cut through years of memory, back to the time when Jeremy was that age. She looked confused and afraid.

'Where's my mama?' she asked in a clear voice.

The two men only stared back at her.

'She isn't really dead, is she?'

They didn't answer her, and so she knew this horrible nightmare was real, and her mother wasn't ever coming back. Her pretty little face, worn and tired, suddenly dissolved in tears. Ethan stood frozen in front of her; he had never felt grief so real and pain so utterly tangible as he did at that moment. He could not turn away, and it shook him to his core. An instantaneous fury leapt from his heart and flew at God, for all the children whose hearts had been ripped apart like this through the vagaries of fate. Damn this fire. This wind. Damn God.

Jer rushed over and swept her up in his arms.

'Hey! How 'bout goin' out and sayin' hello to Big Mike before we eat? He's waitin' for you to feed him some oats. You wanna do that? Okay?'

Eliana nodded and clung to him, burying her wet face in his big neck as he carried her out the back door. Ethan watched them from the window. Jer had forgotten the pancakes, and Ethan had the good sense to pick up the spatula and flip them.

* * *

The legal aspects of Eliana's guardianship were relatively simple for Ethan. When, after five days, Charlie Fergusen had made no attempt to contact his granddaughter, Ethan paid him a visit. In his most courteous and civil manner, Ethan presented him with his options.

'Charlie,' he began, removing his hat and wiping his boots on the mat as Charlie opened the door, 'I'll be brief.' He stepped inside. 'I have here in my hand a complaint against you filed by the State of Kansas in which you, the defendant, are accused of neglect and abandonment of your granddaughter, Eliana Zeldin. And here, in my other hand, I have legal papers all drawn up and ready to sign, wherein you assign sole legal custody of the child to me. Now, tell me, sir, which one would you like to have?'

Ethan had expected a battle. He had expected to be cursed and abused. Instead, Charlie Fergusen, without a word, turned and disappeared into the kitchen. Ethan found him going through all the drawers, rummaging through the contents with trembling hands. He looked up as Ethan appeared in the doorway.

'Can't find a pen. Looked for one yesterday. Nell came by and said she'd go to the store for me if I'd make her out a list, and I tried to find a pen then. I'll need a pen for the funeral. It's tomorrow.'

A sudden wave of pity swept through Ethan, and he walked up and laid his hand on the old man's shoulder. It was very thin underneath his sweater, and for the first time Ethan took note of the changes grief had wrought on Charlie Fergusen this year. It was all there, in the downward slant of his shoulders, his gnarled, trembling hands, his thin, white hair, his lifeless eyes.

'Charlie,' he said, 'there's not going to be a funeral. She was buried yesterday. Remember?'

Charlie paused in his search and looked up at Ethan with confused eyes. After a moment they cleared.

'Oh, yeah. I forgot.'

Ethan pulled out a chair. 'Here, Charlie. Sit down. I have a pen.' The house was dreadfully still. It was such an ugly, repellent stillness, thought Ethan, thick with loneliness and misery. Charlie turned through the document and with arduously precise strokes of the pen signed his name where Ethan indicated. Ethan took the signed document and left quickly. His own loneliness was all he could bear. He had no stomach for Charlie's.

There was, in Cottonwood Falls, that type of person who saw God's wrath in every hailstone and every lightning bolt. But no one, except Ethan Brown himself, faulted Ethan Brown. So when he walked into the county coroner's office and requested they turn over to him the charred remains of Annette Zeldin, they did so with respectful deference. And when he took her remains in the back of his truck to have them cremated, no one questioned his authority. And despite the fact that the plot next to Emma Reilly Fergusen was destined for her husband, Charles, no one dared contradict him when he gave instructions for a small grave to be dug, just large enough to accommodate the urn with her last remains. He did it all alone, without anyone's help or anyone's company. Word gets around, however, in a town like Cottonwood Falls, and that morning while Ethan stood next to the chain-link fence that surrounded the little cemetery, watching them dig her grave and recalling how he had first seen her standing here less than a year before, other people arrived. The first was Father Liddy. He stood at a distance, just inside the fence. A little later Jer showed up with Nell and Eliana. But no one approached Ethan, and he acknowledged them only with a nod and a gentlemanly touch of his hat. The five of them watched while the two men dug a grave in the rocky soil.

The fertile topsoil of the Flint Hills hides a layer of hard rock from which the hills derive their name, and even a small grave for a small urn took most of the morning to dig. After a while Jer took Nell and Eliana back, and only Father Liddy remained. Father Liddy sat down on a limestone bench and stared off into the hills. He held what looked like a letter in his hands, but he shared it with no one. Later in the morning, Mrs Winegarner arrived with her husband and Matthew. Matthew's father carried him to the bench where Father Liddy sat, and they talked for a few moments. Then Mrs Winegarner took Matthew's violin out of the car. Ethan watched as the little boy reverently opened the case and lifted the instrument he so cherished. He took only a moment to tune the strings and rosin his bow, and then played 'Amazing Grace,' followed by an Irish lullaby. The little boy's playing was remarkably clear and melodious, and what he lacked in precision he made up for in passion. When he had finished, he put his violin away, and his father carried him back to the car and they drove away. When the grave was dug, Ethan climbed down into it and Father Liddy passed him the urn. Father Liddy left after throwing a handful of earth into the grave, but Ethan stayed until the hole was filled. Over the next few days, several arrangements of flowers appeared on the grave, sent by Annette's students. Father Liddy, too, took out some flowers, as did Nell. But at the end of the week a high windstorm passed through northern and eastern Kansas, blowing over semis and knocking down power lines. Two people were killed in the storm, with record winds of up to sixty mph, and Annette Zeldin's grave was swept clean of every trace of human remembrance.

Twenty-six

Dr Eagleton personally believed Katie Anne's progress was as miraculous as her return to life, but to Ethan she gave a subdued report tempered with professionalism. From the time she had told him about the false pregnancy, she sensed there was something broken between the couple, and although she knew better, she nonetheless carried a personal burden for it. Her patient had taken to confiding in her, and although Dr Eagleton tried to maintain a professional distance, she had developed a sincere fondness for the young woman. She had worked with many burn patients, and she got so she could read the pain in their eyes, in the way they gripped with their hands, in a turn of the head. But this young woman was unusual. Through the pain there was a continuous struggle to be free of it all, as though she had some innate knowledge that this torture, this crucified, lost flesh, all would be past; as though she were able to live in the future and distance herself from the gruesome and tedious task of healing her body. And this future, for her, seemed to be full of hope, although her husband gave her little of that.

'Ethan was in love with her,' said Katie Anne as Dr Eagleton, her hair tucked under a cap and her mouth covered with a mask, carefully removed the top layer of bandages from her patient's back.

'With whom?'

'With the little girl's mother.'

With deft, precise movements, Dr Eagleton lifted the gauze squares and dropped them into a metal basin. She felt the young woman flinch as she pulled back the bottom layer, revealing the moist, raw flesh underneath.

'It's looking good. I don't see any infection.' She continued peeling off the bottom layer of gauze. 'And now she's coming to live with you?'

'Yes.'

Katie Anne winced when a patch of gauze stuck to her skin.

'Sorry about that. You sure you don't want anything for the pain?'

'I'm sure.' Katie Anne took a deep breath. 'It won't last long.'

'So, about the little girl ...'

'Eliana.'

'That's a pretty name.'

Katie Anne was silent as Dr Eagleton began applying fresh sterile bandages. 'I think you'll be able to start some therapy in a few days.'

'When can I go home?'

'When you've got new skin.'

'I wasn't really pregnant, you know.'

'I thought that might have been the case.'

'I did it to keep him.' She paused. 'It was a pretty awful thing to do.'

'Katie Anne ...' Dr Eagleton looked down at the young woman, studying her inquisitively. The redness on one side of her face had gone a shade purple, and there were still bandages on the other side where she had third-degree burns. Her hair had been cut short all over, but there were still patches where there was only stubble. She had lost her left ear altogether.

'What?'

'You don't believe this was a punishment, do you?'

Katie Anne stared back into the cool blue eyes with her own deep dark ones. 'I don't know. But I think this little girl is my savior.'

*   *   *

Katie Anne remembered when Ethan had come to ask her about it. He had tried to be helpful in those first weeks of her recovery. He drove an hour and a half to visit her every evening, and then drove an hour and a half back to the ranch. There was never a visit when he didn't bring her something, a card from a friend, a new magazine, her favorite CDs from the house, a little sprig of spring flowers. But he smiled only with his mouth, not his eyes, and his care was bolstered with platitudes, not love.

On this visit he came with a small bouquet of daffodils.

'Ethan, you don't have to bring me something every day, you know.'

'These are from your mother,' he called from the bathroom, where he was filling up the vase with water.

'Just the same.'

He set the flowers down on the windowsill.

'You look tired,' she said. 'You've been working hard.'

'We took in another shipment of cattle today.'

'How's the land look?'

'Good. Real good. Those little fellas are gonna get real big this summer.'

She knew something was troubling him, but he went

on talking about the ranch and the work. After a while, he became quiet.

'What's on your mind, Ethan?'

His hands were sweating, and he wiped his palms on his jeans. 'I've decided to take in Eliana Zeldin. I don't know if you know about her mother ...'

'I know. Patti told me.'

There was a long silence between them. Ethan kept his eyes down, fixed on the backs of his hands.

'She didn't leave a will, and her father, Annette's father ...' Ethan stopped. He had never spoken her name aloud in front of Katie Anne.

'Poor old guy,' she said after a moment.

'He's an asshole.'

'He's lost everything, Ethan.'

'He hasn't lost his granddaughter.'

'Some people can't relate to children.'

'Then they better not have them.'

His words hung like a heavy sword in the air, cutting off their breath. They had flown out of him, words he had carefully caged in the back of his consciousness, walled up behind temperance and civility. Katie Anne saw this was just the beginning. All the pain from her body was nothing compared to the tribulations she would endure from now on. Ethan was not a vengeful man, but he would not forget.

'What were you saying? About Eliana?' she asked.

Her voice was gentle and steady.

'I've been named her legal guardian.'

'Did her grandfather agree?'

'Yes.'

'That must have been hard for him.'

Ethan looked at her. There was so little about her that was recognizable. Even her voice had an unfamiliar, raspy quality. 'I didn't ask you about it,' he said. 'I thought it was a decision I had to make on my own.'

She nodded. There was no way he could tell what she was thinking. Unless he moved very close and looked into her eyes.

'Besides, I don't imagine it'll be for too long. The court's trying to locate the next of kin. They have some family out in western Kansas.'

'Do you think that's a good idea?'

'I don't think she should keep living with us.'

'Why not?'

Ethan leaned forward and looked at her curiously. 'That's a strange thing for you to say.'

'Ethan, I don't have anything against this little girl. My God, she's all alone.' She stopped then, and she felt as though something had passed through her mind. A thought, but it was so fleeting, so shapeless, and she couldn't catch it or see it or even feel it. She sighed. Somehow, she sensed it was important.

'What's wrong? Are you okay?' he asked.

'I'm fine.'

'I'd better go.'

She looked up at him as he stood and put on his jacket. His visits were always like this. Regular, steady, but short. And they never connected. There was nothing but this coarse exchange of information, about work on the ranch and messages from home.

'Where's her mother buried?'

He shot her an odd look. 'Out at the Old Cemetery. Next to her own mother. Why?'

'I just wondered.'

He leaned over and kissed her on top of her bald head.

' 'Bye.'

' 'Bye, Ethan.'

That night, Katie Anne had a dream about a beautiful woman with pure white hair. The woman sang to her a song that seemed very familiar, yet the words were strange and foreign sounding. And in the dream the woman called her *Annie*. When she awoke in the night, she felt as if the dream were not a dream at all, but rather another life lived at some point in the far distant past or future. No one in her family and none of her friends had ever called her Annie. She lay there in bed on her side, feeling the pain in her body and fondling this name in her thoughts. It sounded so pleasant and familiar that she decided, in her half-conscious state, that this would be her new name. It was only suitable that she have a new name. She would have a new face and a new family. And as the weeks went by, she began to sense, with more and more affirmation, that she was a new being. Her flesh had burned, and she was regenerated, and with this transformation, from the flames, phoenix-like, rose this sense of newness.

Twenty-seven

Eliana didn't like the idea of going to live with Ethan Brown for two reasons: he had broken her mother's heart, and she would have to leave Big Mike. The first of these reasons she kept to herself, but the second she shared with Jer one evening as they played cards at the kitchen table.

'So, you'll take Big Mike with you,' said Jer as he rearranged his cards. 'You got any Sammy Sharks?' he asked.

'Really?' breathed Eliana, her eyes widening like moons.

'Of course. Come on. Play. Sammy Shark. You got any?'

'No. Go fish.'

Jer drew a card from the deck. 'Ethan has his brand-new stables finished, and I've already talked to him about it. To tell you the truth, it was his idea.'

'It was?' she said quietly.

'Hey, he knows you and that horse are linked at the hip. Your turn.'

Eliana's cards were all askew, and Jer took them from her and fanned them out neatly, then gave them back to her. She clutched them tightly, her little fingers turning white at the knuckles. 'You have any Wilbur Whales?'

Jer scowled. 'Drat it,' and he slid two across the table to her. She grinned.

'Will you come visit us?' she asked as she stuck the cards into her hand.

'About every day, I'd say. Ethan's not much of a cook, so I got the job of head cook at the ranch for a while.'

'So you'll live over there, too?' Her eyes lit up just a little.

'Well, almost. I've got a lot to take care of here at my place. Can't go off and leave all these animals to fend for themselves.'

'I can come over here and help.'

'Well, maybe in the summer, when school's out. You'll have time then.'

Eliana went very quiet. 'Am I ever going back to France?'

'Do you want to?'

'I don't know.' She laid her cards on the table, and Jer saw the sadness drop down over her eyes like a veil. 'I don't want to play anymore. I'm tired now. I want to go to bed.'

꩜ Jer drove the child and her two suitcases, one of which was filled with her mother's things, over to Ethan's ranch that spring evening when the windstorm was blowing through the state. Ethan stood waiting for them on the front porch as they drove up, escorted by Traveler, who greeted them with a first-rate performance, racing alongside the truck, barking at the wheels and leaping at Eliana's hand as she reached for him through the open window. It was, in appearance, an enthusiastic and joyous arrival, but in appearance only. The little girl trembled inside and the man on the porch smiled too much. They avoided looking at each other, and as Ethan showed her around the house and her room, he kept glancing at her for signs of approval, but there was none. He noticed then how different the child was, as if the light had been torn from her eyes. They brought her bags up, and the violin, and a small box of toys and some things they had brought over from Charlie's house, and they left her alone in her room.

After the master bedroom, the room was the nicest one in the house, and it was on the same side as the stables, so she had a clear view of the pasture from the window. In the back of his mind, Ethan had always thought of this as Jeremy's room, anticipating the day when his son would come to visit again, and so he had put up a poster of Joe Montana in his crimson jersey, and set out on the dresser a photo of himself and his son when the boy was five, the year Paula had taken him and gone away. He had left the room as it was, telling himself Joe Montana was better than a blank wall, but he was honest enough to admit it was due more to a streak of stubbornness. On his way down the stairs he felt suddenly ashamed of himself and asked Jer if he'd take Eliana shopping over the weekend to find some posters she might like, and maybe a new bedspread.

'You take her shoppin',' was Jer's reply.

ॐ It was not the masculine tone of the room that displeased Eliana as she sat on the bed and looked around after the men had left: it was the room's dullness. Although she could in no way articulate it, the entire house lacked the vibrancy that had surrounded her growing up. She was only seven, but she had a keen sense of aesthetics, and she knew what was beautiful and what was ugly. This house was not ugly, but it was anemic. Everything was either too new, or too contrived, or too artificial. In her mind she pictured her home back in

Paris, filled with exotic and unusual objects her mother had brought back from her tours when she was younger, and the bright red geraniums at every window that always guided them home like beacons as they returned from their shopping on winter afternoons when the fog lay dense upon the city. She remembered the serape rug that lay on the dining-room floor; its woven designs and muted, multifarious colors had often entertained her infant eyes, and her little fingers had often traced the mysterious patterns along the floor as she crawled through the maze of chair and table legs. She saw the paintings on the wall, some of them original works by friends of her mother, and particularly a print of a woman and her two daughters, which had been her mother's favorite; she remembered the look on the woman's face as she clutched her two daughters to her sides, a look that had always frightened Eliana, although she did not know why. Her mother had always seemed to make everything so beautiful, even when they had little money. At Christmas they had searched through the woods in the Bois de Boulogne looking for low-hanging mistletoe, and they had put bright red bows around the necks of every inert creature in the house. The house had always been awash in color and music and things that smelled good. Out here everything seemed to be dulled, as if the people and the place and all their things were tempered with the color of dust. A terrible wave of homesickness came over her, and she curled up on the bed with Cozette and stared at the beige wall that still smelled of new paint.

A strange thing happened to Katie Anne while she was in the hospital. Patti, whose company she had always found so entertaining, began to get on her nerves. Patti seemed to feel it was her responsibility to monitor Ethan's movements and make regular reports to Katie Anne. The fact that he had taken over legal guardianship of Eliana set her all atwitter.

'Geez, how can you let him do that! After all you've been through and he brings her kid in to live with you.'

'No, to live with him. I'm not there.'

'Well, all the same. You will be, when you get out of here.'

'He didn't really give me a choice.'

'Jerk.'

'Ethan's not a jerk.'

Patti lowered her voice to a conspiratorial whisper. 'Everybody's talkin' about it.'

'I'm not surprised.'

'Everybody think's it's really strange that the two of you are gonna take in this kid.'

'Her name's Eliana.'

'It's a weird name.'

Katie Anne felt herself bristle inside, and suddenly she wanted to reach out and strike Patti, slap her across the face for all her stupidity and mean-mouthed ignorance. 'I think it's a pretty name,' she answered with a strained voice.

'Every time he looks at the child he's gonna think of her mother.'

'Maybe. But I think Eliana's needs are a little more important right now.'

'Wow! Have you ever changed your tune! I remember you used to tell me there was only one thing you wanted in life, and that was to be Ethan Brown's wife, and you'd do anything it took to get him to the altar.'

'Did I say that?'

'Course you did.'

'Well, I got him. So what's the fuss?'

'Now you gotta keep him.'

Katie Anne was quiet for a moment, then she said, 'I know what I look like.'

'Honey, you think you had to fight to win him, well I tell you something, that was nothin' compared to what you're gonna have to do to keep him. And the first thing you need to do is get that kid out of there. Send her back to Paris to her dad. Where is her dad, anyway? Does she even *have* a father? Doesn't anybody know where he is?'

'Patti, I don't feel like listening to this.'

'Okay,' she said, and abruptly stood up. She was offended now, and she picked up her purse and grabbed her jeans jacket from the back of the chair. Her jaw was set in a grim, hard expression that made her look blunt and coarse. It struck Katie Anne that Patti was not a very intelligent girl, and she wondered why it had never bothered her before today.

'Thanks for comin',' said Katie Anne, but Patti was already gone, out the door.

Katie Anne let a few days go by, and then she wrote Patti a very polite note asking her not to come back to the hospital for a while. She didn't tell any of this to Ethan, and during those long weeks in the hospital she held much to herself. She felt like retreating into this newness inside her, which was as fragile and delicate as new skin, and create, out of this quietude, her new person. It was as if she were looking at everything through new eyes, and she had to form opinions and attitudes, as if nothing were given, and everything had to be questioned again. She wore her thoughts tentatively, as though trying on clothing before a long mirror, and she had to look closely at herself to decide if this was really her, if it felt right, if it fitted, if it was long enough, if the color was right for her skin. She found she was abandoning old attitudes, and old friends, and with this realization came a frightening sense of nakedness. The nakedness made her seem very alone. Her parents had never given her a religious education, and now she missed having a concept of God that she could turn to, in rage or in thanks, for despite the turmoil in her heart, she was profoundly aware of having been given a twelfth-hour gift of life.

The thought that hovered in her mind more persistently than any other, more worrisome than thoughts about Ethan, more distressing than thoughts about her body, were thoughts about Eliana. As the weeks went by, she began to query Ethan.

'Have you fixed up that room yet?'

'Well, not yet. I had to move cattle last weekend.'

'Where was Eliana?'

'I took her over to Nell's.'

'Is that dumb Joe Montana poster still hanging up?'

'I haven't had time . . .'

'How much time does it take to take down a poster?'

'More time than I've got!' he snapped.

'Well, then, take the time. I've told you, you don't have to come out here every day. What are you trying to prove? That you're a good and faithful husband? Come on. Be honest with me.'

Ethan went very quiet. 'You don't want me to be honest with you. I don't think honesty is really a good idea right now.'

She paused for only a beat, then she was back again. 'If you come see me a couple of times a week, that's fine with me. And take down that damn poster and go buy a pretty pink bedspread. No, not pink. She probably doesn't like pink.'

'She doesn't. She already told me as much.'

'Well, take her with you. Bring her into Kansas City and take her to a department store. Or a mall. And don't be stingy, Ethan.'

He smiled at her. A real smile. With his eyes. Katie Anne saw it and it warmed her deep inside.

'Are you getting her to school on time?'

'Yep.'

'Where does she go for lunch?'

'She walks over to Nell's. Nell fixes her lunch everyday.'

'Why don't you take her out sometime? Go pick her up and take her out to lunch. She'd like that.'

Ethan sighed. 'I don't know about that. She doesn't feel real comfortable around me.'

'That's to be expected.'

'I don't think she likes me very much.'

'Well, you broke her mother's heart.'

There was no malice in her voice. They were silent for a while, and for the first time since the fire he felt at ease with her.

Twenty-eight

꙳ Ethan Brown was a stubborn man, and once his mind was set in a particular matter, there was little that could be done to change it. And Ethan was convinced, absolutely, of Katie Anne's cunning and deviousness. He and Jer had spent many evenings arguing the matter, but nothing could be said, no proof, no testimony could be presented at which Ethan did not scoff. His cynicism had penetrated his being so thoroughly that it now took its place in his moral life as somewhat of a worldview. Jer, however, continued to hold out that Katie Anne's experience had brought about a radical change of attitude; his belief was also shared by Katie Anne's parents, who sensed that, although Katie Anne never once treated them with disrespect or unkindness, a vague distance seemed to have established itself between parents and child.

She had always confided openly to them, particularly her father, but now she kept to herself. They knew very little of the workings of her mind and heart, and it troubled them.

They had been so worried that they sent a psychiatrist to speak to her. He concluded she was suffering from depression, and he gave her a long list of questions designed to get at the root of those vague psychic malfunctionings. At first she made a real effort to answer candidly. But the whole thing backfired. When she saw that some of the questions were repeated at intervals, worded slightly differently, to test for consistency of responses, or to detect dissembling, she saw the test as a kind of lie detector, and she was furious. She lost faith in the whole process, the test, the psychiatrist, even her parents. She wrote a scathing letter back to the psychiatrist and told him she had just come through a nightmarish experience that brought her perilously close to death, that she had lost some of her facial features, much of the skin and flesh on her right shoulder and back, and had gone through weeks of excruciating pain. It was normal that she might be depressed. Call it whatever you wish, she was simply taking pain and loss at face value. Struggling through the long black tunnel, blindly, groping for light with the tips of her fingers. That she did not want to share any of this with anyone seemed a normal thing. She told him his test was stupid. That anyone who wasn't depressed in her condition would be a little insane. And she sent it back to him with only the first few pages answered. What she didn't tell him, however, was that something about the test had deeply unsettled her. There were questions that asked how she felt about things, about people. And she realized, as she pondered each question, that there were a lot of things she wasn't really sure about. It all confused her. It was this newness thing. This torching of her heart.

Katie Anne was two months in the hospital, and this allowed Ethan enough time to formulate a possible solution to his messy life. As the day of her release grew nearer, he clung to his idea like an invisible buoy that kept him bobbing along the surface of events. Tom and Betty Sue had wanted her to stay with them upon her return home, knowing that Ethan would be gone all day and she would be home with Eliana to care for. But Katie Anne wanted to go home, and home was Ethan. She would manage fine.

She was quiet in the truck that day as Ethan drove her back from Kansas City. Ethan was doing his word thing, throwing them out by the hundreds to confuse the situation and baffle his opponent, like a kind of emotional smoke screen, a technique he used when he was uncomfortable, and after a while she simply said, 'Ethan, let's just have a bit of quiet, can we?' Then she turned to the window and gazed silently at the hills.

Everything looked very fresh and new to her. Indeed, all the outdoors struck her with a marvelous clarity, as though everything were vibrating with an inner light. Ethan sensed something unusual about her that afternoon, a certain serenity that was apparent in the way her hands lay quietly in her lap, the way her head turned slowly in response to his questions. Before today he had thought it was the pain that made her move like this, but now he thought otherwise.

When they arrived, she didn't want to go in the house.

'Let me just sit on the steps out here for a little while,' she said as he helped her out of the truck. She walked with a cane, and she lowered herself gently onto the top step while Traveler looked on.

'I look funny, don't I, boy? Come here. Smell me. I haven't changed.'

Ethan watched as the dog approached her and lay down next to her. She scratched him behind the ears and under his chin, and Ethan remembered the only other moment he had ever seen her pet the dog: the night when he left her.

'Where's Eliana?' she asked, looking up at him. Her face had healed well; there was still a discoloration of the skin on one side, and her hair was growing back unevenly. She wore a black scarf around her head to cover her missing ear. Ethan noticed with a sudden pang of pity that she was wearing just a touch of makeup, a light dash of color on her lips and cheeks, and he remembered how she always used to labor so tediously over her make-up, agonizing over the color of her lipstick or eyeshadow.

She turned away, suddenly self-conscious under his gaze. She had been able to cope well in the hospital, surrounded by nurses and doctors who had only known her like this, but her heart sank whenever Ethan looked at her.

'Why are you staring at me?' she said to him. 'Do I look so different out here?'

'No,' he lied. 'It's Traveler. You never liked him much before.'

'Yeah, well that was my loss, wasn't it, fella,' she said to the dog. She dug through his fur and found a burr, then patiently worked it out, spreading the matted clump of fur apart with her fingers, strand by strand.

'Where's Eliana?' she asked again as she tossed the burr into the yard.

'I don't know where they are. Jer's truck's here. Maybe in the stables.'

'I'll go find her.' She pulled herself up with the porch railing, and picked up her cane.

She met Jer coming from the stables. A big grin broke out on his face when he saw her. He stopped in front of her and opened his arms wide. 'Can I hug you?' he asked.

'You bet,' she said, smiling.

He put his arms gently around her and she laid her head on his chest. 'Oh, Jer, you feel so good,' she sighed as she slipped her arms around him. Ethan had not shown her this much affection, and with a sudden clarity that chilled her like a cold wind, she knew it would be a long time before he would touch her again. They stood there for a long while. 'Jer, do I look too awfully scary?' she asked.

'No,' he whispered, still holding her. 'You look great. Real smart with that scarf on your head.'

'Where is she?'

'Eliana?'

'Yeah.'

'She's out there brushin' down Big Mike. We just came in from a ride.'

'Did she know I was coming home today?'

'Yeah.'

'What'd she say?'

'Nothin'. The kid's not much of a talker. At least not anymore.'

At the entrance to the stables, Katie Anne closed her eyes and breathed in the sharp odor of animal, straw, and leather. It was late June now, and the warm late-day sun laid a gentle hand on her back. She walked through the stables, talking to her horses, one by one, stroking their silky noses and velvet muzzles. Big Mike was tied up at the end of the corridor, and she found Eliana mucking out his stall. She had never seen the child before this moment.

'That's no fun, is it?' she said.

'I like it,' replied Eliana without looking up.

'Then you're a good horsewoman.'

Eliana worked on without looking up, scooping up the manure and dropping it into a big gray bucket.

'I'm Annie,' said Katie Anne.

There was something about the way she said it that made Eliana pause and look up. In the dim light of the stables, with the black scarf on her head, she did not look hideous the way Eliana imagined she would look. She was leaning on a cane, and although her voice was soft and young, she seemed somehow very old.

'I know,' replied Eliana.

'I'm glad you're all right. I was worried about you,' she said, and she lowered herself down onto an upturned bucket and leaned her head back against the stall. Eliana found it a little odd that this strange woman should be worried about her, but she said nothing, only went back to mucking out the stall. She carried the bucket of manure to the big wheelbarrow outdoors, then spread fresh straw down on the ground, and when the stall was neat and clean she brought in the horse and took off his halter.

'You really love that big guy, don't you?' said Katie Anne as she watched Eliana remove his halter.

'Yes. I love him more than anyone in the world. Him and Traveler.'

'Two very worthy creatures.'

Eliana carried the halter to the front of the barn and hung it up with the rest of the tack, and she called back to Katie Anne from the door.

'I'm going inside now.'

'You go on. I'm gonna sit out here for a while,' Katie Anne replied from the stall.

Eliana stood quietly at the entrance for a moment.

'You sure?' she called.

'Yeah. Ethan's grilling some steaks tonight.'

'Oh.'

'That's all he knows how to do.'

'Yeah, I know.'

'But Jer's a good cook. He's been feedin' you well, hasn't he?'

'Oh, yeah.'

Eliana didn't know what else to say, so she turned and walked back to the house. To her surprise, she had felt at ease in the woman's presence, and her face was not all that frightening. What Eliana particularly liked was the fact that the woman had not tried to make friends with her or ask her a lot of boring questions. She just seemed to want to sit there and have her company. Eliana thought that was okay, and she broke out into a run, and then skipped all the way back to the house.

༄ Ethan and Katie Anne slept together in the same bed that first night, and Katie Anne lay awake much of the night, hoping for him to move next to her, to reach out for her, to touch her. The memories of their love-making surged into her thoughts; she saw their bodies together, naked and beautiful, she saw the way he had looked, the way he had felt, the way she had gripped him, stroked him, rubbed herself against him, their ferocious-ness, their exquisite tenderness, their deep moans and whimpers and cries, and finally their laughter. For the first time since the fire, she became aroused, and in the night, thinking he was asleep, she nestled up behind him. He had come up very late and, without turning on the light, had crawled into bed and turned his back to her. Only now did she dare move close to him. She slid her arm around him, and as soon as she touched him she felt him grow tense. His shoulder was hard to her, like a wall. She slid her hand around to his waist, and as she moved it lower, he stopped her.

'Katie Anne ...'

'Are you ever going to touch me again?' she whispered.

He sighed deeply, and he gently took her hand and moved it away.

'Katie Anne, I've filed for an annulment.'

She drew back her hand as though he were fire.

For a long while she lay there in the bed, her heart beating wildly. She still had the memory of his skin on her hand, and it seemed to throb. In the darkness, everything whirled around her. It was like a nightmare she had frequently experienced as a little girl, and it sometimes came back to haunt her while she was awake. Sensations, something deep and voluminous pressing down onto her and making it so she couldn't breathe, and still everything spun around her.

'I'm sorry.' His voice was flat.

'I'm sorry for what I did, Ethan.' She rolled away from him and the tears flowed quietly down her face, drowning her eyes, emptying her heart. He made no reply, and she wrapped herself in a blanket of thoughts, trying to imagine she was not abandoned, flung out on this terrifying open prairie in the darkness, alone. She saw herself in a place of warmth and confinement, with high close walls, thick with centuries. She saw in her mind places she had never seen with her eyes, and these places soothed her and calmed her terrified heart.

Then she said something that struck him as very

unusual. She said, 'That's okay, Ethan. I really don't think I belong here anymore.' Her voice caught in her throat, and she spoke the next words through a strangled sob. 'But I love you. I love you more than I ever did before, if that's possible. Not only more. But different somehow. I'll never get over you.'

He wanted to say, 'Yes, you will,' or, 'You'll find someone else,' or any such meaningless platitude, but the words never rose from his throat. He lay there, blocking out his feelings with a stern and bitter mind. He said, 'I want you to know, it doesn't have anything to do with ... with what's happened to you. With the way you look. It's not that. I'm not that callous.' But what he thought was this: If you were Annette, he thought, you could be deformed, hideous, and I'd take you in my arms and love you until the sun quit shining.

The remainder of his night was plagued by dreams, as it often was. Sad dreams. Catastrophic dreams. Dreams of big heavy structures caving in all around him, lumber alive with flames, ceilings crashing down, raining fire. Bodies underneath his feet. He kept turning them over, looking for someone he knew, but they were all strangers. Sometimes he was looking for his father, sometimes Annette, sometimes Katie Anne. They were all there in that wreckage but he could never seem to find them, and it seemed as if he were forever searching.

The next morning, Ethan found Katie Anne in the kitchen making pancakes. She turned to him and said brightly, 'I told you Jer didn't need to stay over. I can manage fine. Let the guy go home.' And when Eliana appeared on the steps in her nightgown, Katie Anne ushered her off to the bathroom and saw to it she washed her hair, and while the little girl was in the shower she stalked through the child's room, picking up the trail of underwear and socks that had been scattered there over the past week. When Ethan left for work he heard laughter coming from the bathroom, and he wondered what on earth they could be laughing about. Jer was sitting on the front porch when he went out, drinking his first cup of coffee of the day and smoking a cigarette.

'So, you told her yet?' he asked.

'Yeah.'

'Didn't waste any time, did you?' Jer shook his head. 'You're a real shit.'

'I suppose I am.'

Jer didn't expect such easy acquiescence. He looked up at his friend. Suddenly, he saw how much Ethan had changed over the past year. The boyish bonhomie that had so endeared him to men and women alike seemed to have faded. There was a cynical turn to his mouth now.

'I think you need to give the girl some credit, Ethan.

I'll be the first one to admit, I never thought Katie Anne had it in her to pull out of something like this the way she's done. She used to whine about a chipped nail, and now she's hobblin' up and down the stairs with a face that any kid would die for on Halloween, and I never hear her complain. And she seems to really take a liking to having Eliana around ...'

'That's all put on,' interrupted Ethan.

'I don't think so.'

'Sure it is. She's manipulating the whole situation. Katie Anne can play a role up to the hilt. Underneath that generous soul is a spoiled, selfish little brat who's fightin' tooth and nail ...' He didn't finish his sentence. Jer was staring at him.

'You used to love her.'

'I guess I thought I did.'

'You can't do this.'

'I remember you said those same words to me once before, friend.'

Jer noticed a tone of voice Ethan had never used with him before. There was animosity behind his words.

'I just told you what I thought was right.'

'Okay, then let me tell you what I think is right. I'm going to try to find some of Annette's relatives and see if one of them'll take Eliana. And I'm going to get my marriage annulled.'

'On what grounds?'

'I have good reason.'

'You want to tell me why?'

'Nope.'

'Okay. And then you're gonna live out here all alone with your horses and your cattle and your land.'

'That's right,' he said, and he got into his truck and drove off to work.

When Katie Anne had dried the child's hair, she offered to braid it for her. Eliana was delighted.

'I used to practice on my Barbie dolls,' Katie Anne confessed. 'I had dolls with all kinds of hair. Long, short, frizzy, everything. Once I cut the hair on one of them, and I cried for days afterward because I couldn't braid it.'

When the braid was finished, Eliana looked at it in the mirror and smiled. 'This is the way my mama used to do it.'

'You look very much like your mother right now,' said Katie Anne softly. The little girl turned around to face her; she wore a very solemn face, and Katie Anne thought she'd never seen such a grave child.

'I thought you'd hate me,' Eliana said quietly.

'Why would ...' she began, and then she caught herself. She took a deep breath. 'I don't hate you at all. On the contrary, I ...' She paused. She sat down on the bed and stared at the brush. It was a strange kind of brush, and she wondered if it was French. 'Eliana, you should know this. Ethan doesn't want to be married to me anymore. He's getting the marriage annulled.'

'What does that mean?'

'It means ... it just means we won't be married any-more.'

'You mean divorced?'

'Well, sort of. But it's ... different. It's like it never happened. It sort of says the marriage never really took place. It never happened.'

'But how can you say something didn't happen when it did?'

'Ethan loved your mommy. That's who he wanted to marry.'

'Really?'

'You didn't know that?'

'No,' she answered quietly, shaking her head. 'My mommy cried a lot the month before she died. She was very sad.'

Katie Anne studied the bristles on the hairbrush. She could not bear to see all the heartache in the child's eyes.

'I don't think he's ever going to forget your mommy. That's how much he loved her.'

'Do you still love him?'

Katie Anne took a deep breath and looked up at the unicorn poster that now hung over the child's bed. 'I can't remember when I didn't love him.' She got up and placed the brush on the dresser. 'I'm glad Joe Montana's gone.'

'So am I.'

'This room is so bare.'

'All my toys and things are still in Paris.'

'I'll talk to Ethan about that.'

Eliana and Jer helped move Katie Anne's things to the downstairs bedroom. They did it together, but no one asked any questions. When they were done, Katie Anne lay down and rested, and Jer took Eliana out to check on his herd. She was real proud of her braid, Jer told Katie Anne later in the day. You could tell by the way she held up her head.

Nothing else was said about the annulment. That Katie Anne had taken the initiative and moved herself downstairs seemed to be a concession of sorts, but she made no pretense of moving out of the house, and Ethan thought it was best not to press the matter until the legal work was finished and the annulment was final. He had no stomach for confrontations, and despite his bitterness, he was not a cruel man. If Katie Anne Mackey and Ethan Brown had ever once connected along certain conduits of sympathy, those channels were now down. Crumbled, smashed debris swept away in an ocean of freak and yet not so extraordinary events. The kind of events that happen every day across the world to some people, that others read about in their evening standard and forget the instant they lay down their paper and rise from their chair. The fortunate and the unfortunate. Thus is divided the world. Ethan Brown refused himself such meditations; Katie Anne did not. And so they lived in a certain kind of harmony for the first weeks after Katie Anne's return – Ethan shutting his eyes to misery, Katie Anne taking in everything with eyes open wide.

Twenty-nine

Ethan was not blind, however, to certain peculiar changes in Katie Anne, changes that caused others to admire her but only served to harden his heart. Ethan tossed them off as cosmetic ploys she designed and carried out to present to him a new facade. But what puzzled him was her modesty. Indeed, sometimes it occurred to Ethan that even she herself was not aware of how different she had become.

Several nights after her return, after Eliana was in bed, Ethan knocked on her door.

'Come in,' she answered.

He opened the door. She was sitting up in bed reading. She laid down the book as he came in.

'You need anything?' he asked.

'No. Nothing. Thanks.'

He stood awkwardly in the middle of the

room. His eyes were drawn to the book.

'What are you reading?'

She held it up to show him. 'I can't pronounce it.' She smiled, a little self-consciously. It was a copy of Victor Hugo's *Les Misérables*, an immense, densely worded 1,300-page volume. 'Dr Eagleton gave it to me. It was kind of a joke, really. The title, you know. But it's really good.'

Ethan had never known Katie Anne to read a book. Her mother had occasionally passed along a new James Michener or Danielle Steel that she thought her daughter might enjoy, but even those seemed to lie around the house, swept from one table to another, until her mother finally took them back, unread.

'You sure you don't want me to bring the television down from my bedroom? I don't need it.'

'No. I won't watch it at night.'

'You used to. You used to be glued to that screen.'

'I know.' She laid the book down and passed her finger along the spine. 'Maybe because I watched so much of it in the hospital when I couldn't move very much. There was nothing else to do. After a while it just all seemed so ... so pointless. Then Dr Eagleton started bringing me some books ...'

'I could have brought you some.'

'I know.' She fingered the pages. 'It's really good,' she said, and Ethan detected a note of shyness in her voice.

'Once I got into it, it was sort of hard to put down. I'm sure you've read it.'

'No.'

'You haven't?'

'No.'

'Oh.' She seemed a little disappointed. Ethan sensed she wanted to talk about the book, but didn't know how.

'Are you sleeping okay down here?' he asked finally.

'Yes, fine,' she replied, and she went back to her book, shutting him out of her world. There it was. She had dismissed him from her thoughts and, without saying as much, from her room. He left, mumbling a quiet 'Good night.'

Then one afternoon he came home and found her in the kitchen listening to her Walkman. She was washing lettuce in the sink and the water was running, and she didn't hear him come in. She turned and jumped and let out a squeal that cut through to his heart, so much it reminded him of her laughter when they had first met, that joyful, playful time when they had done such outrageous things, like making love in the back of his truck in the middle of the afternoon in the parking lot behind the South Forty, things that had so appealed to Ethan's withered soul.

'Sorry,' he said, grinning. 'Didn't mean to come up on you like that.'

He noticed right off how nervous she was. She rushed to dry her hands and turn off the music, but not before strains of violin had reached Ethan's ears from the head-phones dangling around her neck.

'I thought I'd try something different tonight. I got some salmon steaks and I thought we could grill them. I made up this marinade ...' she blurted out.

Ethan hated fish, and Katie Anne knew it, but he was too distracted by her nervousness to comment on it.

'What are you listening to?'

'Oh, just something I ...' She grew even more flustered. She plunged her hands into the sink of icy water and drew out some large leaves of romaine.

'Look at this great lettuce I found today. We always eat that iceberg stuff. I thought we'd try this for a change.'

Ethan shrugged. 'Whatever you want.' As he left the room he noticed the cassette case on the kitchen counter. He picked it up and looked at it. It was Annette's recording of Sibelius's violin concerto, and there, on the front, a picture of Annette and David Zeldin.

'Where'd you get this?' he asked, and the still, cold emptiness of his voice made her heart stop. She looked up to see him holding the cassette, staring at her with eyes that made her shiver.

'Where'd you get this?' he asked again. His tone was shrill and harsh. In all the years she had known Ethan, Katie Anne had never heard him speak to anyone like this.

'I bought it ...'

'You *bought* it? Why?' His body was tense with rage.

'I ... I bought it with Eliana.'

'*Why?*'

'Ethan, you don't need to talk to me like th –'

'*Why are you listening to her music? Why'd you go out and buy this?*' He was shaking the box at her now, and she was afraid he might throw it at her.

'I bought it for Eliana!' she yelled at him, and the tears welled up in her eyes. 'I bought it for her! We were looking at music, and she saw it, and she wanted it so I bought it for her! Damn it, Ethan, she doesn't have anything left! You haven't done anything about her stuff, her toys, the things her mother owned; anything that was hers is still sitting there in Paris! You're the trustee! You should have taken care of those things! You should have had them shipped to her! Why didn't you?'

'Because she's not staying here! That's why! I've been in contact with her relatives, some cousins I located, and they're gonna take custody of her. They're coming to get her at the end of July.'

She felt as though he had just struck her and knocked the breath out of her.

'You can't do that,' she whispered.

'I'm her guardian. I can do whatever I think is best for her.'

'That's not best for her.'

'I don't know why you're so concerned.'

She pulled out a chair from the kitchen table and sat down. Her chest felt tight, as though stones were pressing down on her. 'Please. Don't do this,' she whispered.

'Why?'

She took a moment to answer. 'I don't know. I honestly don't. I just don't want her to go.'

'If you think it's going to make a difference, about us ...'

'That's not it.'

He didn't believe her for a second. 'Well, it won't. I'm still pursuing the annulment. Regardless of what happens with Eliana.'

'I know you are. I know ...' She broke into tears then, and Ethan left the room.

Several nights after that, Katie Anne was awakened in the middle of the night by a cry. She sat up and listened.

'Maman!'

The sound carried clearly through the silent house, straight to her ears. She fumbled for the light next to her bed.

'Maman!' came the child's cry again. A primordial response surged from deep within her. She sprang up, and her arm swept the lamp to the floor. Groping through the darkness for the door, feeling the broken glass underneath her bare feet, she hobbled toward the cries, her dulled mind struggling to make sense of these sounds and cries in the night.

'I'm coming!' The stairs seemed to take for ever. 'I'm coming! I'm coming, precious!' She muttered it over and over, like a litany to fight off the evil spirits. 'I'm coming!'

She found Eliana sitting up in bed, wide-eyed and terrified.

'It's okay, it's okay, honey.' Katie Anne rushed to the bed and took the child in her arms. 'It's just a nightmare. It's okay, I'm here.' Katie Anne could feel the child's sobs as her little chest rose and fell with each breath, and her own heart beat frantically, drowning out the timid beat of the child's. She held her as tightly as she could, and slowly, with the child in her arms, her heart began to calm. 'It's okay. It's okay,' she repeated, over and over. She wondered what had made her panic like this, run from her room in the middle of the night to rescue a child from her nightmare. What child is this, she thought, that moves me with her sorrow? That heals me with her love?

'It's over now,' she whispered, rocking the little girl in her arms, back and forth, back and forth. 'It's over, it's gone.' As she spoke, Eliana's arms fixed themselves around her waist, and the child nestled her head deep into her breasts. Katie Anne kissed her head, brushing her lips over the wondrously silky hair. 'It's okay, precious,' she whispered. She felt as if she could hold her like this for ever.

She looked around to see Ethan standing in the doorway. He had hastily thrown on his robe and was still drawing the sash around his waist. 'She okay?'

'Yeah. She just had a bad dream.'

'She used to have a lot of them.'

'You go on back to bed. I'll take care of her.'

'You sure?'

She nodded. 'I'm sure. Go to bed.'

For a long time she sat there, holding the child. She tried to remember some nursery rhymes, but all she could remember were some lyrics from country-and-western songs. She finally thought of an old Janie Fricke tune, and she hummed that as she rocked the little girl in her arms. After the child had gone back to sleep, Katie Anne lay down on the bed next to her. She was struck by the softness of her skin, and with her scarred hand she reached out and stroked the child's cheek. Then she leaned close and brushed her lips against the silky hair, inhaling the child's sweet smell. She knew the smell of spring on the prairie, the smell of blood on a newborn calf; she knew the smell of certain diseases, too, and infections. And she knew the smell of fire. But this was new. She lay there for a long time and finally fell asleep. She awoke several hours later and got up and groped her way back downstairs to her own room. In the morning, she awoke to find Eliana standing in her room, watching her.

'Did you come into my room last night?'

'You were having a nightmare.'

'I know.'

'I have them, too.'

'You do?'

'Yeah.'

Katie Anne rolled over and tossed back the sheets. Eliana crawled into bed and lay down next to her.

'I dreamed I was looking for my mother and I couldn't find her,' said the child. 'It was sad. That's all I remember. Being very sad.'

They lay there next to each other. Katie Anne noticed how lovely the little girl's hands were.

'The worst ones are when I find her and I'm happy. Then when I wake up it's worse.'

Katie Anne took the child's hand.

'Do I look too scary to you?'

'Not anymore. I'm sort of getting used to you.'

'If you ever wake up and get scared again, and if I don't hear you, you come crawl into bed with me.'

'You sure you won't mind?'

'Not at all.'

Thirty

Katie Anne became a virtual recluse after the fire. Ethan urged her to invite her friends to the house, and Patti and Whitey still called from time to time, but she discouraged their visits, and she inevitably cut short telephone conversations with them. When she ventured to Cottonwood Falls or Strong City for groceries or other needs, she always took Eliana with her, and the little girl was always the focus of her attention. They seemed to form an island in a sea of curious faces; they turned their eyes toward each other and saw only each other, shutting out the cruel world around them. Between the two of them they chose rice over pasta, pork chops over steak, the Looney Tunes sleeping bag over the Mickey Mouse. They seemed to need no one.

Then one hot Friday morning in early July,

only an hour after he had left for work, Ethan came back home. Katie Anne heard his truck and went out on the front porch to meet him.

'Where's Eliana?' he asked as he walked toward her.

'She's out back. Why? What's wrong?'

Ethan removed his hat and wiped the sweat from his forehead.

'Charlie Fergusen's dead. He committed suicide.'

Katie Anne stared at him blankly.

'Suicide?' Her voice was a whisper.

'He hanged himself. Clay said it looks like he didn't die right away. He said it looked like he was trying to get free.'

Katie Anne sat down on the porch swing. She looked away from Ethan, out toward the hills.

'I thought I'd better let you know. We'll have to tell Eliana. But I don't think she should know it was suicide.'

Katie Anne didn't turn around.

'Katie Anne?'

He sat down beside her.

'Are you okay?'

'It's my fault,' she whispered.

'Don't be silly.'

'I should have gone to see him. I should have taken Eliana and gone to see him. She hasn't been to see him since she ran away.'

'And he hasn't been to see her.'

314

'It was wrong.'

He gently laid a hand on her shoulder. She was crying.

'Why? You didn't have any obligation to him.'

She turned toward him, and it looked as if she wanted to contradict him, but her lips moved only slightly, and she didn't speak. She got up and went inside the house.

Ethan didn't follow her inside, and she was glad. She had a desperate urge to kneel. She walked around the house looking for a place, and finally she went into her bedroom and kneeled at the side of her bed. Her mind was blank, but she saw images of Charlie Fergusen, hanging from the end of his belt in some unfamiliar place. She saw him squirm and kick and struggle to get loose. She saw his hands clawing at his neck, tearing his own flesh to loosen the leather noose. She saw his eyes grow wide, and his face lose its color, and she saw him dance in the air a slow, graceful ballet, waltzing, waltzing, slower and slower, tiring, until the music stopped and his feet were still. Katie Anne ran into the bathroom and vomited, and then lay down on her bed and cried until she fell asleep.

She had a violent argument with Ethan that evening; she didn't want Eliana to know her grandfather was dead. Ethan had never seen her so virulently opposed to him. When he finally conceded, she went off to bed, and the following morning she took Eliana off to Kansas City on a shopping trip. She called him that evening and told him they had decided to stay overnight, and would be back Sunday evening after the funeral.

Katie Anne had never been fond of the city, but now it loomed in her imagination like a refuge. She could hide beneath her wide-brimmed straw hat and her sunglasses, and if she said or did anything unexpected, no one would be amazed, or surprised, or confused. They were always saying that about her, sometimes with pride, sometimes with regret, how different she was. She was tired of hearing it. She yearned for a place where she could freely grope her way into a new life, where she could become the new creature growing within her. Once she was on the road with Eliana, she was swept into a great joyous mood of anticipation. As the Jeep sped along the highway, for the first time since her accident she believed in her future.

'Hey, I've got an idea. How about, to start with, if we go to that museum up there. I think it's called the Nelson.'

'I've been there,' answered Eliana.

Katie Anne glanced at her. 'Doesn't excite you too much, does it?'

'My mother used to take me there,' she said quietly.

'Oh. Okay. Let's forget it, then.'

'No. I want to go.'

'You sure?'

'Yeah. It's okay.'

Katie Anne reached over and stoked the child's cheek.

'You tell me if ever I do anything to make you hurt inside.'

Eliana turned a wide-eyed face to her. 'You don't ever hurt me,' she said solemnly.

'Good.' She patted her leg. 'Have I ever shown you how a horse eats corn?'

Eliana grinned. 'Show me.'

Katie Anne gripped her little thigh and squeezed, throwing the child into spasms of laughter.

Katie Anne had never set foot in a museum, and she knew nothing about what she saw on the walls of the Nelson, but she found it utterly exhilarating, as if her starved senses had found food, and her hobbled spirit had finally found music to make it dance. They spent a good deal of time in the twentieth-century gallery, and they talked about the paintings. Katie Anne was amazed at the child's imagination, at the things she saw, and how well she expressed what the pictures made her feel. They took their time; they sat on benches and browsed through the bookshop, and they had tea in the courtyard. Katie Anne bought a poster for each of them: Eliana's was a reproduction of a Michelangelo sketch of a horse; her own was a print by a famous Austrian artist who had died young, from influenza, when he was in his late twenties. According to the clerk, the artist had lived in Vienna at the turn of the century, and the blatant sexuality of his paintings had branded him an outcast in the restrictive Catholic community where he lived. What Katie Anne found so intriguing were the warped lines and disjointed angles he gave to the human body, the haggard faces of his women, and above all the translucent quality of their skin, as though one were looking straight through them into their bruised and blackened souls. The print she bought was a self-portrait of the artist and his model, and although the woman looked nothing like her at all, she saw herself there, instantly and assuredly. It was as though this stranger, decades dead, had painted her as she was now, as no one else knew her, as if he had captured something invisible and laid it out for her to see. She quickly had the clerk roll it up, with Eliana's poster, and slip it into a tube. As they left the museum that afternoon, Katie Anne felt she had found something very precious.

They made some sensible purchases that afternoon, some socks and underwear for Eliana, and then they turned their energies to more frivolous things. They bought a miniature stable replete with miniature tack and a toy horse for Eliana. They also bought a huge stuffed lion, a mate for Cozette, a big plush thing that lay on its stomach and took up the entire back seat of the Jeep.

Late in the afternoon they checked into a hotel on the Plaza, and Eliana went swimming in the rooftop pool while Katie Anne, wearing her hat and sunglasses, her body covered with a long Oriental-looking robe she had purchased at a boutique in the hotel, sat at a table at the side of the pool. That night they ordered room service and ate in bed while they watched *I Love Lucy*. They laughed a lot, and after Eliana had fallen asleep, Katie Anne sat in the dark and listened to music on her Walkman, a symphony by Mahler she had purchased that afternoon with Eliana's encouragement. The Mahler had been sitting there at the check-out counter, a new release, and she had picked it up on impulse. Now she sat in the dark and listened, enraptured, and felt a fullness inside. She looked down at Eliana snuggled close to her, asleep.

'Oh, God,' she murmured quietly in the dark. 'Don't let him take her away.'

They changed their minds and stayed Sunday night, too. Ethan did not see them until he came home from work Monday afternoon. He was surprised to find that he had missed them, and when he returned (he was home unusually early) he found them setting up the stable in Eliana's room, unwrapping all the tiny paraphernalia and arranging it around the stable, the bale of hay, the buckets and sack of feed, the blanket rack. There was even a dog that looked surprisingly like Traveler. Ethan found them on the floor, playing like two children, and when Katie Anne looked up at him, he was struck by something unusual about her. She looked somehow different, but he couldn't quite figure out what it was about her that had changed.

For the next several days he was exceptionally gentle to her, and Katie Anne felt herself open up to him again. Her eyes softened whenever he walked into the room, and when she was near him, she felt desire swell inside her. For the first time since the accident she hoped he might be having a change of heart.

Then, one evening later in the week, Katie Anne found Ethan out on the porch, sitting alone. It was one of those rare summer evenings when only a mild breeze stirred the grasses, and with the rising of the moon came a front of mild air that felt like spring. The parched land seemed to sigh, as if a cool hand had been laid upon its feverish brow, and even the crickets and the cicadas ceased their raucous summery rhythms and retreated into silent reverie.

Katie Anne sat down next to him on the porch.

'Can I join you?'

'You bet,' he said congenially. It was hard to read him without looking into his eyes. He was always so pleasant and so congenial. *Even when he's breaking your heart, he's so damn nice.*

She sat there next to him, without speaking, basking in his presence, imagining that somewhere in his heart there still lurked some love for her. He had said nothing more about the annulment since their argument, and she was hoping he had changed his mind. For days now, seeing his gentleness all over again, she had longed to ask him, but was afraid.

'I wish everything could stay like this,' she whispered. 'Just like this.'

His breathing changed, and she thought perhaps he was going to say something. She waited.

'I died, didn't I?' she blurted out. The thought had come to her all of a sudden. Ethan turned to her in the darkness.

'Yes. You did. You were ... technically, you were dead.'

'How long?'

He shook his head. 'I don't know. I'm not sure. Several minutes maybe. It seemed long.'

'What brought me back?'

'I don't know. They'd taken you off all the life support.'

'I think I remember heaven. I remember something so terribly beautiful. But for all the beauty of heaven, I could not leave this earth.' She turned and looked at him in the darkness. 'I love you too much.'

She sat there, willing him with every nerve, every fiber in her body to reach out and take her in his arms, to soothe back her hair the way he used to do, to kiss away the tears in her eyes, to cradle her deep within his manly strength and love her again. When he made no move toward her, she reached out and laid her hand on his knee. She left her hand there for a long time, without moving it, waiting for his touch that never came.

'Ethan,' she whispered, 'until you learn to forgive me, you'll never see how much I've changed.'

'I know you've changed,' he replied. 'I know how hard you're trying.' He suddenly got to his feet and walked down the steps. The night was aglitter with stars, and there stood Ethan, surrounded by earth and the firmament, so desolate and alone. 'But that's the trouble,' he went on. His voice grew to a high pitch as he spoke, strained. 'You think if you act like her, you think I'll love you. You think if you read a book or try to sound intellectual, you think it'll change things. But I'll never ...'

She rose to her feet and cut him off. 'That's not true, Ethan!'

'... be able to love you like I loved her.'

'I'm not trying to act like anybody, damn it!'

'The hell you aren't. I can see right through you. You're fake. You're full of lies.'

She stared at his back in the darkness. She wanted to take up a clump of earth and throw it at him. How he trivialized what she had gone through, the murky, vague feelings, the emptiness, the confusion, the sense of having lost something, and then the miracle of having found it again.

'You have no idea what I'm feeling inside,' she said. Her voice was low and threatening, like distant thunder.

He wanted to tell her he didn't care.

She stood behind him on the steps, and he could hear her breath as she tried to calm her tears.

'Ethan,' she whispered finally, 'don't drive us away. You've already made one mistake you'll regret for the rest of your life. Don't make another one.'

Then she turned and walked into the house.

Ethan walked down to the stables, and as he walked he thought about what she had said. She had taken him by surprise. She had not flailed her arms at him, or pounded on his chest, or screamed or yelled at him. Instead, she had cut through his defenses with razorlike insight. It bled him, and as he walked through the grass he felt as if he were drowning in emotions. Suddenly, there heaved from his throat a mournful cry, and as he walked across the prairie in the warm night air, he bellowed out all his rage, his pain, his losses, his loves. He roared and roared at the placid night, his mouth gaping like a wound, blasting the air with his sorrow. Once he had thrown himself on the powerful tide of woe, he found he could not stop. He came upon a hedgerow, and he fell to his knees at the foot of a tree. Like a little boy, he cried. His great shoulders shook mightily, and he cried. It was a sound so wrenching that it silenced the creatures that roamed the plains.

When he could cry no more, he lay there in the dark and let his mind rest. For a while he drifted into sleep, but he was aware of his surroundings, of the prickly grass underneath his face, and the thorns at his back. He was quiet now, and into this quietude, into this emptiness came an infinitesimal truth, a flicker so fine and faint that, had he not been perfectly still, perfectly empty, he would never have seen it.

But for all the beauty of heaven, I could not leave this earth.

He heard it again. *But for all the beauty of heaven, I could not leave this earth. I love you too much.*

He tried to recognize the voices. Katie Anne's he could recall, but the other, the other hung so faint in his memory, and it had been the voice of a spirit, and how does one recall the voice of a spirit?

His mind summoned memories, and he began to see something that frightened him, that thrilled him, something he could almost believe, almost, but not quite. He got up and began to walk back toward the ranch. He had come miles in the darkness, and he had been gone for hours. As he walked, he tried to recall the odd incident, the words, the actions, the gestures, those subtle changes he had so firmly discredited which had taken place over the months. As great as his disbelief was, nothing else made sense except this. He needed some time now, time to observe her and watch her, to listen. To test her. As he grew closer to the house, he saw the lights were on in Eliana's bedroom upstairs. He broke into a run.

They were gone. Suitcases had been dragged out and packed, hurriedly. The toy stable was still standing in the middle of the floor in Eliana's room, and all the toys lay around it. The new big lion – Aslan she had named him – sat at the foot of her bed. And the book Katie Anne had been reading, *Jane Eyre*, lay open on the coffee table in the living room. But they were gone. Ethan got in his truck and drove off to look for them, but the roads in the Flint Hills are long and dark on a summer's night. He finally went back home and waited for daylight, and then he called Tom and Betty Sue.

They were polite, but they would not tell him where she was.

'She called us, Ethan, and told us she was leaving, but she didn't say where. She said they were gonna take a little trip. A vacation. She said not to worry. She'll keep in touch.'

Two days later, Tom Mackey called and said he had heard from her.

They were in Paris.

Thirty-one

Ethan rode his horses hard that summer, and he drove his cattle all over the Flint Hills as if he were a fugitive looking for somewhere to hide out in the endless waves of prairie. Word gets around, of course, in a town like Cottonwood Falls, and everyone knew that Katie Anne had walked out on him and taken Eliana, but Ethan wouldn't talk about it to anyone. He never showed his face around the South Forty anymore, and unless he had some business in town, he stayed away from his office. He gave Bonnie a month's paid vacation and took his legal files out to the ranch and worked from his home office. But people liked Ethan Brown, and his absence was felt in Cottonwood Falls. His bright-eyed charm and his deep laughter were conspicuously missing from all those places that he had frequented: Hannah's Cafe, the

South Forty, the gas station opposite the courthouse where his truck was often found up on the rack. He bought himself a new truck that month, but he was such a frugal man, even that didn't seem to lift his spirits.

Ethan had over 10,000 head of cattle to care for that summer, and he worked himself and his cowhands summer hours from dawn to dusk, mending fences, carrying out vet checks, vaccinating, rounding up strays, and generally watching over the huge brutish babies like a mother while they doubled their weight and ate their way to a healthy profit. He was content as long as he was working, but the evenings spent alone at his ranch were unbearable. He took to sleeping out on the range with the wind and the rattlesnakes; sometimes Jer or one of the cowhands stayed out with him, and once Tom Mackey drove out at dusk to join them. On those nights Ethan could pretend the world was a solid place, fortified by staunch male defenses. They talked cattle, and cursed the politicians in Washington, and ate pan-fried steak and fried potatoes cooked over a Coleman stove, then they stretched out in their sleeping bags and gazed at the stars until they fell asleep. But even this ploy worked only temporarily; after a while the earth became hard under his back and the night sky unbearably bright, and one night, at around midnight, when he was out there alone, he packed up his equipment and drove back to his ranch.

His beloved hills had turned dark and sour on him.

The jagged rocks just below their smiling green surface seemed to puncture his old joy, deflating him. They stretched before him in the starlit night like the pouting curves on the cheeks of a sullen child. They appeared to him now in the dark light in which so many others had seen them. Impenetrable, they gave up so little of themselves. He recalled Willa Cather's words: *Between that earth and that sky I felt erased, blotted out.* His beloved hills. For the first time in his life they afforded him no peace.

For weeks he waited for a word from Katie Anne, but none came. He would find reasons to call Tom and Betty Sue, and he would work into the conversation a question or two about her, but they were vague. Yes, she was fine. She had called them just yesterday. They were in Paris. They were in Geneva. Katie Anne was having some cosmetic surgery done at a clinic in Switzerland; Eliana was planning a week at a summer camp in the mountains with some friends from her old school. Ethan didn't ask when she was coming home.

He finally sat down and wrote her a letter. It was the kind of letter one would expect of him, articulate and intelligent, full of wit and artful turns of phrases. But there was nothing to betray the terrifying loneliness he was living, nothing to betray the mortal dread that gripped his throat when he thought he might be losing her for ever. Despite his intellectualism, Ethan had always been a rather simple man. In his scholarly days he had flirted with certain dramatic postures; he had gone through his existential period, his romantic period. But they were brief and very fanciful. Ethan was his father's son, a straightforward man of straightforward morals. He firmly believed that happiness was a state of mind, and it ranked up there in the pantheon of values alongside hard work and honesty. Happiness was his stalwart; it was his David that could bring down any Goliath. There was no tragedy so devastating that he could not overcome it with a certain state of mind. And so, when he wrote Katie Anne, he belied, with every word, the anguish he was feeling. He looked at the letter and prided himself on how it sounded, how happy, solid, unperturbed it sounded. *Attitude,* he said to himself. *Yes, attitude. If I just keep a good attitude about it all, the world won't come crashing in on me.* But his world had crashed in on him. He walked over the rubble every morning when he came into the kitchen to make his coffee; he kicked aside the debris every night when he sat down on his porch with a beer in his hand and looked out upon his beloved land. His house stood strong and tall around him, and yet his life was splintered timber. Still, he forced a smile in the letters to Katie Anne. He believed he could will her to come back with his happiness.

His letters went unanswered. He questioned Tom and Betty Sue. How long did the mail take to Europe? Could it

be possible that she didn't receive it? Had she moved
again? The fear that she might never return began to
grow as the days passed and he had not heard from her.
His cynicism faded. This was no ploy, no elaborate
scheme to win his heart back. Ethan knew that now.
Betty Sue had shared one of her letters with him; she had
stopped by one evening, when Tom was gone, and brought
it for him to read. She did this against her husband's
wishes, for although Tom loved Ethan Brown like a son,
he loved his daughter much more, and he felt that his
child must have been deeply wounded to run so far away,
to a place she had never aspired to, with a little girl that
was not even her own.

Dearest Mom and Dad,

   *I know I just called, but I find I actually enjoy
writing to you. Maybe because I feel I have things
that need to be said with paper and pen.*

   *I'm learning a little French, but my pronuncia-
tion is dreadful. I'm afraid I have no aptitude for
languages. Of course, Eliana does much of the talking for us. I have long since given up trying to
explain who I am. So now she just introduces me as
her mother, which I don't mind.*

   *It's dreadfully expensive over here. Our stay in
Switzerland was of course not at our expense, but I*

am trying to come up with a solution for our
lodging here in Paris. I have enrolled Eliana in her
old school for the fall. I don't know how long she
will attend, but I don't want her to fall behind.

I was glad to locate her friends. She was growing
very bored with me, although her affection for me
(if I'm not mistaken) seems to grow stronger. She is
very protective of me. When people stop and stare
at me in the street, she presses my hand more
tightly. The French are very rude, I find. It's
amazing how long they can stare. I tried it once, on
the bus with Eliana, to hold the gaze of a stranger.
A girl. She was only about eighteen. But she stared
me down. Just this straight, impassive stare. Of
course, even though the plastic surgery has done
wonders, I still feel like a walking curio, one of
those knickknacks you find in the antique stores
here that invite long, studious examination. But it
doesn't bother me so much anymore. Not like it
did back home. I don't know why, but I feel
immensely protected. I know that sounds absurd.
Here I am, so far away from all I cherish, but I feel
safe. Walls rise up around me, and I feel safe. Can
you imagine that? I have always hated the city. But
this city is different. It's nothing like anything I
have ever known or imagined. It has made an overwhelming impression on me with its grandness

and its misery. There are holes gouged out of the huge stone blocks, from machine-gun fire during the last war. The city seems to weep with joy. I think I could find anything here.

Betty Sue waited quietly while Ethan finished the letter. He handed it back to her. He had grown very solemn.

'I never knew she could write like that.'

'Oh, I did,' said Betty Sue as she very carefully folded the letter and put it back into the envelope. 'When she was in high school, she used to write the most beautiful poetry. At least I thought it was beautiful. It wasn't really poetry, I guess, it was ... sort of like this. She showed it to us. It sort of surprised us, that she wanted us to read it. That isn't what teenagers are like.' She slipped the envelope into her purse. 'But I guess it was just a phase. When she got out of school she lost interest in it.' She hesitated for a moment. 'Ethan, we've spoken to her since this letter. She's ... she's found a place. I think she intends to stay for a while.' She shook her head. 'It breaks my heart to have her so far away, when she's ...' Her voice began to tremble and she broke off. She stood up and went to the door. 'But she seems so much happier than she did here. I was really worried about her. I'm not so worried now.' She smiled brightly. 'Besides, Tom and I are going to visit her in October. I'm excited about it. I've never been to Paris.'

Several days later, in the middle of the night, Ethan got up, took a piece of his business stationery with 'Wordsworth' at the top, and wrote:

Dear Katie Anne,
    I'm a mess. Please come home.
    Love,
    Ethan

He sealed it, put five stamps on it, and wrote AIR MAIL in large print on the envelope, and in the middle of the night, with Traveler sitting next to him on the front seat of his truck, he drove into Cottonwood Falls and dropped it into the mailbox at the post office. Then he went back home and went to sleep. For the next few days, he was happy. He called Jer and they went out for a beer, and he told him things were going to be okay. But when two weeks had gone by and he still hadn't received an answer, he called Betty Sue and asked for Katie Anne's telephone number.

'She got your letter, Ethan.'

'She did?'

'Yes. She got it last week.'

He was silent.

'Ethan, she asked us not to give you her number. She doesn't want to talk to you.'

⁓ The next week, Ethan received the notice that the annulment was final. It was a shock to him. He had completely forgotten about it. But it had been plodding along the paper trail, working its way from desk to desk, waiting for the thudding stamp or the scraping pen before it was decree. Now it sat on his desk, reminding him of what he had done.

⁓ The night before Tom and Betty Sue left for Paris, Ethan stopped by. These days he knocked instead of walking in. Tom came to the door.

'Evenin', Tom.'

'Ethan. Come on in.'

Ethan stepped inside, but he stood self-consciously at the entrance and refused Tom's invitation to dinner.

'I just wanted to drop this by. It's something for Katie Anne. A book I thought she might like to have. Please make sure she gets it right away. As soon as you get there.' Then he turned and walked back to his truck. Tom

Mackey watched him go. He had never seen Ethan Brown walk like that.

'What is it?' asked Betty Sue as she walked up behind him.

'Something Ethan brought by. It's for Katie Anne.'

He gave it over to his wife and looked out at the dust trail left by Ethan's truck.

'God bless his soul,' sighed Tom, and he shut the door.

Thirty-two

From the window of the Continental Airlines jet Ethan could see Kansas City sprawled below him like a cancerous growth on the face of the earth, but then the city passed from view, and below him stretched a bank of green treetops, as ethereal as clouds. His own land was barren now, the color of rust, deep coppery red against the bluest of skies, the color it took on every autumn. Just a little darker than desert sands, he thought. He had never been to the desert, but this was how he imagined it: shaded curves of copper that fell away into darkness where the hills dipped away from the sun; a landscape of black and gold rippling below, dream-like in its endless repetition and modulation; so immense it slowed your body, your thoughts. It was pointless to rush somewhere else. There was nowhere else. Ethan fell asleep, lulled by the undulating waves of prairie in his mind.

He changed planes in Chicago. He noted how different the people looked, even here, still in America. The incredible scope of human imagination stunned him. He was an observant man. He had learned, on the prairie, how to search for variety in the microcosm. Each square foot of land was infinitely different. He had dislodged spearheads chiseled in the days when the Romans were invading Britain and Christ had not yet been born, and he had cradled in his hands the fossils of tiny sea creatures that had swum in the prairie when it was the Permian Sea, although there were no humans to name it then. Yet as he sat at the bar in the airport drinking his beer, he was stunned by the extraordinary diversity of the human race, something he never saw back in Cottonwood Falls. He felt terribly uncomfortable, the way he used to feel at the state fair as a kid, surrounded by things irreverent and grotesque, and he longed to go back home. He drank three Buds before his flight was called.

The price he was willing to pay for his ticket was sufficient testimony to his ardor; the only seats available on the last leg of the flight were first class. The advantage of first class, however, was that the drinks flowed freely. Ethan had never developed a taste for hard liquor, and wine still bore the stigma of pretension, for his prejudices were far reaching, and his beef and his beer were sacred to him. But the gin had looked nice in the hand of the woman next to him, glimmering underneath the tiny spot of light that framed her red nails and her diamond ring, and so he had ordered one of his own. To his surprise it tasted good.

The cabin was dark as they took off – the pilot had wanted them to see the city lights below, but Ethan sat next to the aisle and he was glad. The darkness hugged him with its arms, and his own gin-and-tonic swam around tinkling ice that fell soft on his ears. The panic he had felt in the airport slowly receded and the alcohol finally numbed his mind.

He was served dinner on a linen-covered tray and wiped his mouth on a white starched-linen napkin. He cut his meat, which was, he confessed, tastefully seasoned, with a silver knife, and ate colorful vegetables with a silver fork. Coffee, served in a china cup, was taken with his apple tarte (good, but not like his mother's, which undoubtedly benefited from the name 'pie'). He fell asleep partway into an English film about a mad English king, and awoke when the stewardess was setting up his breakfast tray and daylight was creeping in around the drawn shades of the portholes.

He lugged his suitcase off the revolving belt and set it down at his feet. Standing there in a sea of

Europeans, his new chocolate brown alligator boots all of a sudden seemed very wrong. A wave of self-consciousness washed over him. He picked up his suitcase and followed the crowd of passengers marching toward customs. He was vaguely aware of the way things looked and smelled, new and unidentifiable, the smell of humans who had different habits from his. Take them individually and they don't seem all that different, but throw them together and the distinction is swift and piercing. He searched the crowd to see if there were other people who looked like him.

He tried to calm his stomach. He shouldn't have eaten breakfast; he hadn't been hungry. It was the middle of the night to him, and he could feel it. Every nerve in his body pleaded for darkness and repose. He felt better in the taxi. He could hide in the back and stare out of the window. Hide his pointed toes under the seat in front of him. But the train station was a nightmare. He kept reminding himself it could be worse, this could be France, and he wouldn't understand anything. He got lost of course, several times. He was not used to train stations. He was used to prairies. He knew where everything was on the prairie.

When he finally got his ticket and found his train, he was sweating. Beads of perspiration hung on his brow and lip and his armpits swam underneath his coat. At least they were friendly to him. They helped him find his seat, and he settled into it like a hare in a burrow. He caught his breath and then struggled out of his coat. There he sat, his briefcase on his wrinkled khakis, hugging the smooth worn leather that carried, among other precious things, his AA guidebook of Europe. He had tried reading the section on England the day before he left but it had made him nervous. Now he was too embarrassed to get it out.

He slept again, the swaying metal hips of the train lulling him to sleep as it curved northward through town and country. Several passengers sat next to him that afternoon, but he wasn't aware of them. He could feel the sway and hear the rumble as he slept but nothing else. It was a soothing sound.

Ethan awoke with a start and looked out the window. He was stunned to see his hills. Rockier perhaps, and rising higher to mountains in the distance, and too green for this time of year, but his hills nonetheless. Anxiously he looked around. The wagon was full, and people were standing in the aisles, lifting down their luggage from overhead racks. Ethan caught the eye of another passenger and asked where they were.

'Windermere,' he answered. 'End of the line.'

Ethan had only glimpses of the town from the station. What he saw mostly was tourists. This was not what he had expected. This crush of people and cameras. Many wore hiking shoes and shorts, and carried packs of equipment. He waited patiently in front of the station and watched them. Occasionally he would glance up at the hills. Fells they were called in this part of the world. Finally, he saw his name on a sign waving in the air above the crowd. Ethan picked up his bag and worked his way toward the sign. It was being held aloft, rather absentmindedly, by a young man leaning against the door of roadster convertible, chatting to a girl who had stopped to admire his car. Ethan approached him.

'I'm Ethan Brown.'

The young man's face whipped toward Ethan and stared at him curiously. The girl was suddenly forgotten. This stranger from America made an impression on him. A muscular man, the way he like to imagine Americans. He noticed the cowboy boots right away and grinned.

'I say, I thought that might be you. I'm from the Drunken Duck. Here, let me take your bag.'

The young man upended the suitcase in the narrow back seat of the roadster and Ethan slid into the front next to him.

Once out of Windermere, the road, bordered by a low stone wall on each side, curved steeply up into the mountains. Here Ethan noticed a stark change. It was getting close to evening and the sky was a bank of pale gray. Gray mist lingered on the land, and the fellsides, clothed in a mosaic of pasture and woodlands, breathed a green breath that swam in his nostrils. Never had he smelled such green before. It smelled as it looked, a heavy blue-green, thick with moisture and black soil. Sheep grazed the land.

Ethan had wanted accommodations in Grasmere, a village a few miles down the road from Windermere and the home of his beloved poet, Wordsworth, but there was nothing available on such short notice, and so he was booked into the Drunken Duck. Over the roar of the roadster, the young man told Ethan the story behind the old coaching inn. It had been built in the seventeenth century to accommodate travelers going through the long and steep Kirkstone Pass on their way to the northern boundaries of England and on to Scotland. The inn sat nestled into a curve of the landscape surrounded for as far as the eye could see by nothing but the gently rolling fells ridged by meandering low stone walls. Pike How and Middle Dodd, Rydal Fell, Caudale Moor, Caiston Beck, and Hagg Gill, this was the vernacular of the inn's whitewashed stone-and-gray-slate roof.

It had come by its name when Victoria was on the throne, when its landlady had opened her door one Christmas morning and found three ducks lying dead on her doorstep. She thought it provident, and awoke her young daughters to help her pluck the ducks for a grand

Christmas dinner. The creatures were almost plucked bare when one of the ducks lifted its head and, in a swift retaliatory blow, bit the younger daughter on the wrist. Terrified, the little girl flung the duck into the air, and it came down, featherless and infuriated, into the arms of her mother. It seems the ducks had wandered into a pool of beer leaked from a broken barrel, and they had paddled and drunk their way to near death. Once she got over her disappointment at not having roast duck for Christmas, the landlady, distressed at the sight of the naked ducks, set about knitting sweaters for them until their plumage grew back. The ducks enjoyed immunity after the incident, and died of old age.

The inn was miles away from the train station at Windermere. It was miles away from everything. But from the moment he set foot inside, he was overcome by a sense of civilization. Within these walls sat artifacts from centuries of human endeavor. Within was another world, fortified and softened by civilization against the windblown rain and snows without. Here, man had lived and man had thrived. He had carved, etched, painted, spun, and hammered his way into history. History hung thick on the walls.

Immediately upon entering, Ethan found himself succumbing to the grandeur and charm of the old inn. Despite its isolation, the inn was not wanting for patrons. At the entrance stood a boot rack full of muddied rubber walking and hiking boots, just recently removed, and above it hung an assortment of hats, old straw fishing hats, felt hats, tweed caps, hats for all tastes and all occasions. The clutter was more like that of home than hostel, and Ethan sensed that the people who came through these doors came here not by chance. To the right was the pub, and through its open door Ethan glimpsed a roaring fire in a high stone fireplace, wood beams in a ceiling darkened by wood smoke, and the high gleam of bright wood endlessly polished by tweeds and wools. The light was reflected in rows upon rows of beautiful glass bottles massed together like a shimmering army against the backdrop of a huge mirror. A pleasant chatter came from the pub. Drinking hours were well under way, for it was a Saturday night, and the light was fading from the sky.

For most of the evening he was able to forget the purpose of his journey, caught up as he was in the activity of the Drunken Duck. It was a highly sociable place, due in part to its very nature and the nature of the English, but also due to its situation high on the windswept fells. Ethan drank his beer, a very good lager the bartender recommended because it resembled American beer, cold and highly carbonated, and he ate his beef and potatoes in the dining room, and had his first taste of English trifle. He had not eaten all day and the food and drink soothed him and returned him somewhat to his normal state of mellow ease. He then returned to the bar and sat there, talking to the barman, who listened quite intently to Ethan's stories about cattle ranching in the Flint Hills, for in the bartending trade, stories are to be minted: they are lucre, they are gold.

Ethan stayed until the pub closed and then went to his room. There were books, and Ethan plunged into them with curiosity, for the inn had been bought and renovated in the twenties by a retired colonel who had spent his entire career in India, and the books were a taste of a place worlds apart from Ethan's world. He read until almost three in the morning, and then went to bed. The maid had shown him how to close the shutters so that the morning light would not disturb him, and before he shut them, he pulled back the curtains and gazed out at the blackness of the hills. The sky had cleared slightly, and a new moon cast faint light across this corner of England.

What happened to Ethan that night, late when all were sleeping, was a coalescence of light, and meditation, and memory, a moment when thought reaches deep into the soul and body, sweeping through veins, lighting along invisible paths strung together like webs, when neurons and blood and the energy of human life are trying to deliver up a message to us, and we can read it only if we are truly alive, and if we can imagine. Ethan, who had never been a man of imagination, imagined that night, and what he found was a connection to English soil, a sense of belonging to this, a land far away, not his, strange, foreign, unknown. But he was connected to it nonetheless. He knew then that when he returned home, were he never to travel again, he would never be the same. He suddenly felt sweep through him an incredible nostalgia for this land, for England, and he saw it as if he were already cut apart from it, as if he had already left it, and he felt adrift, homeless, an exile.

He lay in the wide, strange bed that night with his eyes wide open, staring at the dark, and he fell asleep lulled by the swaying motion of a train.

Thirty-three

Ethan was driven back into Windermere the next day after lunch, and he waited at the station all afternoon, greeting all the trains arriving from London, but Katie Anne was not on any of them. Between trains he sat at the pub across from the station and read some brochures he had been given about Wordsworth's home in Grasmere. He determined he would get up early the next day and go into Grasmere before the trains from London began arriving, and pay homage to the bard who had so inspired him with his crafting of words, but the next morning he could not rouse himself and, like the previous morning, kept falling back into a drugged sleep until the maid woke him at eleven-thirty.

On the second day he became restless, and between trains he wandered the streets of

Windermere. It was Monday and the weekenders had gone, and he was beginning to feel at ease in the town. He discovered another pub, the White Hart, an establishment fashionable with walkers, sporting on its walls an astounding collection of stuffed animals that glared down at the boisterous customers with frozen stares. Later, after the third train had come and gone and Katie Anne had not arrived, he ventured back to a bookstore and bought himself a handsomely bound edition of Wordsworth's poetry, along with a complete collection of Coleridge's works. That afternoon, fortified by his lager at the White Hart and determined to shake off the despondency that was growing in his chest like a hard lump as the second day passed and Katie Anne still had not arrived, he followed a walking trail that led back to the Drunken Duck, but his boots were made to gouge the ribs of a horse, not for walking, and he ended by hitching a ride up the road with a delivery truck headed for the inn.

On his third morning, rested from an early evening brought about by his hike up the fell, he was able to get up at dawn and catch a ride into town. He was directed to a good shop that specialized in walking boots and shoes, and Ethan gently folded his cowboy boots into a plastic bag and walked down to the White Hart for lunch in his new walking boots. This established a rhythm to his life for the next few days, and despite his growing disappointment at Katie Anne's silence, he looked forward to his trips into Windermere each day. He broke down and bought himself a walking stick, and found what a mighty tool it was when, early one morning, he ventured out along the Pennine Way, passing scores of walkers who were making their way from coast to coast along part of the trail.

It was that evening, his fifth, after he had returned to the inn from his walk and taken his seat at the bar, that he made the decision to leave. She had not responded to his plea. He had hoped that the book he had asked Tom to deliver might kindle something in her – a memory, long forgotten. He allowed himself to think back to the night she had left, and he tried to recall the way she had looked when she had spoken to him.

Don't drive us away. You've already made one mistake that you'll regret for the rest of your life....

He tried that evening to recall other words, too.

For all the beauty of heaven, I could not leave this earth....

The words he recalled perfectly, but what was fading from his memory was where and when he had heard them. Visions that had once blinded him with truth now seemed like faint shadows in his mind. She had been dead only six months, but he could no longer conjure the whole of her face. Just her lips, that was all he could see now in his memory, her mouth when she held it just a certain way, when he had made love to her and he had opened his eyes and seen her mouth, moist and warm, with her warm breath flooding out over his face. It seemed he could recall just this about her, only this. Everything else was fading. He felt himself growing aroused, and tears stung his eyes.

He didn't know how long the woman had been sitting next to him, perhaps seconds, perhaps minutes. He hadn't noticed when she had slid up on the barstool. But now he felt her presence, and the emptiness that seemed like a huge cavern in his soul was suddenly flooded with warmth. That's how he knew it was her. The tears that had been stinging his eyes rolled down his cheeks, and he kept his head lowered and tried to brush them off with the back of his hand in such a way that no one would see. She didn't speak to him, nor did he speak to her. After a moment, he took her hand, removed it from where it lay on the bar, and held it gently on his lap, warming it in his large, rough hands. It nestled there, and he sighed a deep sigh that shook his chest. They sat that way for a long time. Once she withdrew her hand from him to adjust the long woolen scarf that had slipped from her shoulders, and he waited impatiently to take it back again.

'Well, is this the Mrs Brown we've been waiting for all this time?' asked the bartender with a smile as he cleared away Ethan's empty glass.

'This is she,' said Ethan quietly.

'Welcome to the Drunken Duck, madam,' he said with his best Irish smile, for he had come over from Dublin to fish in the lake one summer, and stayed for the rest of his life. 'How do you like our country?'

'It's lovely,' she said, and Ethan thrilled at the sound of her voice.

'Will ye be stayin' longer now, Mr Brown? You'll not be goin' on to Paris tomorrow?'

'No. Not now.'

'Well, I'm glad to be hearin' that. Will ye have another lager? And what would you be havin', madam?'

'The same, please.'

As the bartender moved aside, Ethan caught their reflections in the mirror behind the bar. She was staring at him. The light from the fire touched her hair with streaks of golden red, and her skin glistened milk white in the darkness. He looked at her mouth. He studied closely the way she held it, and without turning to look at her, he raised his hand to her lips and touched them lightly with his fingers.

'Do you see me now?' she whispered faintly, and he almost didn't hear. He could feel the words on his fingers as she spoke.

'Yes. I see you now. Yes.'

'Am I still so terribly ugly to you?'

His hand moved across her face, touching the skin with his fingertips.

'You're beautiful.' His hand moved down her neck. She caught it and kissed it. 'I was afraid you wouldn't come,' he said gruffly.

'I almost didn't.'

'Why did you?'

She waited for a long time before she spoke. 'Why did you send me that book?'

He looked at her face in the mirror. He could see her eyes.

Take a look at me now! And you remember what it looks like! When you're looking into her eyes, remember mine!

She had screamed those words at him. Once. Long ago. The shame of that moment, of the pain he had given her, washed over him, and he had to look away.

'I sent you that book ...' He hesitated. 'I thought it might mean something to you.'

'Should it?'

He shrugged. 'Only if you want it to.'

He shook off a sudden ugly flash of doubt. It didn't matter, really. If it meant anything to her or not. It didn't matter. What mattered was this: whoever this woman was, he loved her to the very depth of his soul.

'I'm glad you're not talking so much at me. If you start talking at me, you might drive me away.'

He nodded, and once again her hand found his under the bar, in the darkness, and they clung to each other, adrift in the convivial chatter and bell-like sounds of glass clinking glass.

'You were coming to Paris?' she said.

'Yes.'

'How were you going to find me?'

'I don't know.' He paused. 'But I wasn't going to go back home until I had.'

After a while, he rose from the stool.

'Come with me.'

She hesitated. He laid his hand on her shoulder, standing behind her, looking at her in the mirror. Her eyes tortured him.

'It's all right. Come.'

In the room, he moved a chair over to the window for her to sit. Then he turned off all the lights and opened the shutters. The cold sweet air rushed in on them. Ethan stood behind her with his hands resting gently on her shoulders.

'What do you see out there?'

She was very still, and finally, after a long silence, she

sighed. 'Oh, Ethan. What do you want from me? What is it you expect from me? I feel like ... like if I give the wrong answer, I'll lose you.'

Ethan was momentarily stilled by her blow. He felt her shiver and he leaned down and wrapped his strong arms around her fragile body, protecting her. His breath warmed her neck and his deep voice fell softly against her ear.

'Then I will ask you one last question, and whatever you answer, regardless, I will lay you down in my bed, and I will make love to you.' Her body shifted ever so slightly, and he could see her breasts rise, full and soft.

'Will you marry me?'

He kissed her then, to stop her reply, for he feared he might lose her again.

Epilogue

The English bed was high and very deep and soft, and the cool Irish linen that they lay upon that night felt quite different on their skin. And as they lay in each other's arms they could see, sparkling in the distance, the lights from Grasmere, the home of Ethan's beloved poet, William Wordsworth.

Ethan never asked her again about the book he had sent her. It was not, strangely enough, Wordsworth, but Yeats. Nor did he ever ask her what she did with the book. They lived many years together, as man and wife, although not as many as Ethan would have liked. And although he knew his wife well, he thought, knew her intimately and profoundly, the scars on her body and on her soul, he never knew the whereabouts of his book of Yeats's poetry, the book he had given to her father to deliver to her in

Paris. It was, of course, the very same book Annette
Zeldin had borrowed from him and kept, until her death,
when Ethan retrieved it from Charlie Fergusen's home.

Much to his profound regret, Ethan outlived his wife.
By the time she died his face was deeply lined from sun
and wind, and a horse had crippled him a little, but he
was still healthy and his heart was strong. Several days
after his wife's funeral, Eliana, who now lived in New
York with her husband, sent him a small package. The
enclosed note said:

Dear Daddy,

*I'm so sorry I had to leave so quickly after the
funeral. I hope you are getting along all right. At
least Adam's not far, although I know his studies
keep him too busy to spend much time with you.
All the same, we are only a phone call away.*

*Let yourself grieve. If Mama taught you any-
thing, let it be this. But do not let your grief pull
you down. You have two sons and a daughter who
need you, and we all love you dearly.*

*We will of course be back for Adam's graduation
in the spring. I'm so sorry Mama didn't live to see
him go this far. He'll make such a fine vet. And,
Lord knows, you need a new vet in Cottonwood
Falls. I envy him, you know. You remember when I*

wanted to be a vet? But other muses sang louder.

The enclosed is something Mama wanted you to have after she died. She said it was important that you not see it until after she was gone. She was very careful to keep it hidden from you all those years. Give my love to Jeremy.

Your loving daughter,

Eliana

P.S. The page that is marked is the one she marked for you. She said it would mean something to you.

Ethan carried the book outside and sat down in his chair on the porch. It was a still morning, without a trace of wind. With trembling hands he opened the book to the marked page. Although his eyes were blinded by tears, he knew the poem. He knew it by heart.

When you are old and grey and full of sleep,
And nodding by the fire, take down this book,
And slowly read, and dream of the soft look
Your eyes had once, and of their shadows deep;

How many loved your moments of glad grace,
And loved your beauty with love false or true,

But one man loved the pilgrim soul in you,
And loved the sorrows of your changing face ...

When his eyes cleared, Ethan noticed the tops of the cottonwoods in the grove down by the stream were perfectly still.